C0-ATW-023

A
HARLEQUIN
Book

SHARLIE FOR SHORT

by

DOROTHY RIVERS

HARLEQUIN BOOKS
Winnipeg • Canada   New York • New York

SHARLIE FOR SHORT

Originally published by Mills & Boon Limited,
50 Grafton Way, Fitzroy Square, London, England.

Harlequin Canadian edition published May, 1969
Harlequin U.S. edition published August, 1969

*All the characters in this book have no existence outside the
imagination of the Author, and have no relation whatsoever to
anyone bearing the same name or names. They are not even
distantly inspired by any individual known or unknown to the
Author, and all the incidents are pure invention.*

The Harlequin trade mark, consisting of the
word HARLEQUIN® and the portrayal of a
Harlequin, is registered in the United States Patent
Office and in the Canada Trade Marks Office.

Standard Book Number: 373-51304-6.

Copyright, ©, 1969, by Simon & Schuster, Inc. All rights reserved.

Printed in the U.S.A.

The Author's thanks are due to Messrs. Macmillan & Co., Ltd., for permission to quote from W. E. Henley's "Invictus."

CHAPTER ONE

MONA HANDSMERE lay back in an easy chair, hands clasped behind her head, watching Sharlie Raven packing. Mona's hair was naturally platinum blonde; it curled all over her small head in a froth of silken bubbles. Her skin was fair and petal-fine, her mouth the Cupid's bow of fiction but seldom of fact, her features small and perfect, and her eyes as blue as willow-pattern china.

Fretfully she said, "I think you're mad. Stark, staring crazy! How you can think of burying yourself in Somerset when you might get a job in London, I *can't* imagine!"

Sharlie smiled. "I know you can't." Her oval face, framed in a shining bell of light brown hair, was bent above the nightdress she was folding. Her eyes were dark blue; she had very white teeth and an expressive mouth, gentle and kind and made for laughter.

Sharlie was an orphan, her parents having died when she was barely nine, within a few months of one another. Her only living relative had been an aunt, a spinster, living in a flat in Knightsbridge, who, having no mind to let her comfortable routine be dislocated by her small niece, had packed her off without delay to the boarding school where she had first met Mona. Having no home of her own, it had been pleasant to be welcomed in Mona's, where she had several times spent her holidays. She had just completed a course at a select secretarial college when her aunt's health had broken down. Sharlie stayed with her and helped to nurse her through her last illness, and after she died Sharlie was only too glad to accept Mona's invitation to spend a few weeks at her parent's home in York before starting to look for a job.

"I suppose you mean I've no imagination," Mona said. "Well—I know I haven't, and I think I'm better off without it. Nowadays it's better to be practical. One's got to be alert, to grab every opportunity that comes along. It makes me mad to see you flinging yours away! You're twenty-three, you haven't got a family to tie you down, and you've got qualifications that would get you a good

7

job in London. You could have such *fun*! You could meet all sorts of people if only you played your cards properly!"

Sharlie said mildly, "I suppose everybody has a different idea of 'fun.' . . . I know it's hard for you to see my point of view. But then you've always had a home. Since I was nine I've always lived either with crowds of people, as at boarding school, or in a lonely London flat. That's why I don't want a job in London—I've discovered how lonely one can be, among hordes of people. I want home life, for a change, and this post of secretary-chauffeuse, living in, may give it to me.—If I get the post, that is! When Mrs. Ramswell sees me, she may take an immediate dislike to me and send me packing without even trying me out on a typewriter or a car!"

"I call it very odd of her to have you on approval."

"Oh, no—it's only natural for her to want to see me before engaging me. And as she's paying my expenses I see no objection."

Mona sighed. "I do think life is aggravating and unfair! You want home life—and I'm aching to escape from it! I'm sick and tired of it. But Mother and Father are so determined I shall stay with them. I must say I do think it's most frightfully selfish of them!"

"It's natural enough that they should want to have you with them, their only child. After all, you don't really need to earn your own living as I do," Sharlie commented.

"I'd break away if I had any money of my own. But if I did, Father would cut off my allowance. That's why I'm persevering with this cookery course. Though I'm a first-class cook I may as well have a diploma to prove it. You never know when it might come in useful."

For the hundredth time Sharlie marvelled at the astonishing fact that Mona, whose exotic prettiness looked far more suited to a film studio than a kitchen, should have what amounted to a genius for cooking. To look at her slight willowy figure and ethereal colouring one would never have suspected her of being greedy, but it was undoubtedly her love of good food that accounted for her flair for cooking. One should never, she decided, judge a person by appearances! She paused a moment in her occupation of stuffing tissue paper in the toes of shoes, to look at Mona thoughtfully.

"And what then?" she asked. "What do you really want to get from life?"

"A wealthy husband," Mona answered promptly. "I want a Rolls and pearls and a mink coat and everything that belongs with them."

"And if you could have all that without the husband?"

"M'm . . . On the whole, I'd rather have the husband, too, if he were good-looking, so that other women would envy me." It was typical of her not to ask in return, "And what do *you* want out of life?" Sharlie had long ceased to expect Mona to take any interest in her thoughts or interests.

"That's the only thing that makes me wonder if I'm being a fool to concentrate on cooking," Mona went on pensively. "At least it'll give me a chance to get away from here. But it isn't a career that'll help me to make useful contacts . . . Sometimes I wonder if I'd have done better to take a secretarial course and get a job in London."

"And wear cute little dresses with dazzling lingerie touches and have a Cinderella ending by marrying your employer?" Sharlie suggested, smiling.

"Exactly! Mightn't it be a good scheme?"

"It might, if it worked out that way. But so many employers are already happily married that if I were you I'd stick to what you are so super at. Anyone can learn to be a secretary. As a cook you're quite outstanding."

Mona sighed. "Yes . . . But I wish I were outstanding at something that would involve meeting lots of eligible men! You won't forget me, will you, if you come across a millionaire or a duke who isn't already involved with a wife?—But if it's a duke he must be rich, remember!"

"I'll remember," Sharlie promised, laughing. She never knew whether to envy Mona for her worldly minded attitude to life, or to be sorry for her, for her lack of perception that made her miss so many of the small delights of every day, the little things that added up in Sharlie's own life to so great a sum, but of which Mona was oblivious. The changing pattern of the clouds, a spider's web spangled with mist, the sound of running water, a lamplit window on a snowy night, the smell of pinewoods after rain, of autumn bonfires, of gorse warm in the sun— none of these meant anything to Mona. Still, people who

9

were imperceptive doubtless missed many a sorrow as well as many a pleasure . . . And it was hateful to be critical of someone who had given one hospitality, above all when one had nothing to offer in return. For Sharlie did not count warm sympathy, quick understanding, nor the spending of vitality as repayment for more material favours.

Mona, though generous enough with anything she did not like or would not miss, was niggardly when it came to the expenditure of effort. So, though next day she went to York with Sharlie in the car hired to take her to the station, since Mr. Handsmere took the family car during the week to drive him to and from his office, she did not go to see her off at the station, but told the driver to drop her at a cinema. Sharlie had been sorry to bid farewell to Mona's parents, a kindly, downright, Yorkshire couple, as different from their daughter as a pair of sparrows from a golden oriole. They had been good to her, and she was grateful. But her only feeling at saying good-bye to Mona was a vague remorse at feeling so little regret at parting.

Mona said, "Well, don't forget to look out for a millionaire for me!"

Sharlie said, "I'll remember!" And through the back window of the taxi watched Mona hurrying into the cinema, her mind already on the film.

Waiting in the station for the London train Sharlie looked composed and cool, a slender figure in her neat travelling outfit of bird's eye tweed, chosen as the ideal background for accessories of any colour. To-day they were of very deep blue, almost as dark as navy—cashmere pullover, felt hat, suede bag and gloves and shoes. Inwardly she was tremulous with excitement—for it *was* exciting, to be setting out upon a journey that might alter all the pattern of her life . . .

She was relieved, when the long train clattered in, to see that there were plenty of empty seats. To have to search and struggle and finally squeeze in, unwelcome, among reluctant fellow-travellers, would have dimmed the brightness of the gay adventure, spoilt the fun of travelling first class for the first time in her memory.

"Here you are, miss. A carriage with only one gentleman—if you don't mind a smoker?" said her porter.

Sharlie said she didn't mind at all, and was presently established in the corner seat by the door, facing the engine.

Opposite her, in the corner by the corridor, a man averted his appraising glance and became absorbed in his magazine as she looked in his direction. Probably he was thinking that on a long journey a chatty young woman might become tedious, and had no mind to become embroiled in conversation. Well—he would find that this particular young woman made no opening gambit, no suggestion that it would be nice to have the window shut, nor that she would like her suitcase moved. With studied indifference Sharlie laid her hat beside her on the seat, shook out her hair, took up a paper, and began to read.

Richard Heronshaw felt a trifle bored by the invasion of his solitude. Having had the carriage to himself from Edinburgh he had hoped his luck might hold good at York, as at Newcastle and Darlington; it was agreeable to be able to stretch his long legs slantwise, without necessity for considering someone else's feet.

When York was left behind he scrutinised the intruder over the pages of his magazine. She had laid her paper on her knee and now was looking at the passing country, her profile turned towards him. It was an attractive profile, with clearcut features and a small head beautifully poised on a long, slender throat. Something about it seemed to Richard vaguely familiar. Had he met the girl before, or merely seen her somewhere? Hard to tell, without seeing her full face.

To settle the matter, he took his cigarette-case from his pocket, and leaned forward, holding it out to her.

"Will you have a cigarette?"

Startled, Sharlie turned her head. Already he had noted that she had long slim legs with slender feet and ankles. He saw now that she excelled in other points that in his opinion made or marred a woman's looks; good eyes, good teeth, a fair, clear skin; and noticed with approval that she had been clever in the use of lipstick, using one that only slightly emphasised the natural deep rose of her lips.

"Oh—thank you so much, but I don't smoke."

Her voice was clear and low; a pleasant voice, he thought.

"D'you mind if I do?"

"Why, of course not!"

She turned again to the window. Nice of him, she thought, to ask her if she minded, in a smoking carriage. Having set him down at first as arrogant and aloof, she reversed her opinion. In appearance he was attractive, with broad lean shoulders, thin dark face and quick, bright hazel eyes that looked as though he had an alert mind and a sense of humour . . . Then she forgot him.

Her mind was filled with speculations as to whether she would get the post in quest of which she was travelling, what the Ramswells and their house and neighbourhood would be like, how long she'd stay with them—if stay she did; she mightn't be at all the sort of person Mrs. Ramswell wanted. She wondered what new contacts waited for her round tomorrow's corner; whether to-day's journey would be a milestone in her life or just a passing episode, quickly forgotten.

Her thoughts were interrupted by an exclamation from her companion.

"Got it!" he exclaimed triumphantly. "I've been wondering where I'd seen you. Tell me, weren't you at the York Charities Ball a few weeks ago?"

"Why, yes, I was. But I'm afraid I don't remember—?"

"Meeting me?" he finished for her. "As a matter of fact, we never actually met. But I knew Mona Handsmere when I was stationed at Catterick, and I thought I caught a glimpse of her, and you with her, among the crowd. The party I was with left early because of the crush, and I had no chance to speak to her."

"Yes, there was an awful crowd, wasn't there!" She added that it had been clever of him to recognise her, then regretted the casual remark, in case it should have seemed like fishing for a compliment; some men would have taken it as an opening for tiresome flattery. Not this man, however. He replied in matter-of-fact tones that he happened to have rather a good memory for faces.

They drifted into talk, exchanging news of Mona, discovering mutual acquaintances among Mona's friends in

York, comparing notes on hostelries in the city and its surrounding neighbourhood. He told her he had been on leave in Scotland, where he had spent ten days in a fishing inn with a party of friends, and was now on his way back to join his regiment which was now at Colchester.

"And you," he asked, "you've been taking a holiday?"

"For a month or so."

"How are you liking being a lady of leisure?"

"I enjoyed it for a month, but I'm on my way now to see about a post. Even if I could afford a life of leisure, it would bore me very quickly."

The arrival of the ticket collector interrupted them, and when the man had gone Sharlie turned again to the window. She had been enjoying talking; so, she thought, had her companion, but she wasn't going to risk it. After a moment, from the corner of her eye, she saw him take up his magazine again.

When they had emerged from the second of the long tunnels heralding King's Cross, he broke the silence.

"I wonder—"

She turned enquiringly. "Yes?"

"If by a lucky chance you're free this evening, I wonder if you'd be very kind and have a meal with me? My name, by the way, is Richard Heronshaw."

"I'm Sharlie Raven. It's very kind of you . . ." She hesitated. Knowing nobody in London, she had been prepared to spend a solitary evening, going perhaps to see a film.

"Do come!" he persuaded her. "I'm frightfully respectable! I won a prize for Punctuality and Perseverance at my dame school at the age of seven. *And* my sister's married to a man who manufactures woollen underwear. Oh, and once I had a second cousin twice removed who went to darkest Africa as a missionary—though as she hasn't been heard of for umpteen years she may have been devoured by lions or cannibals or something."

"In that case surely you should be knocking up Mr. Harrod or Mr. Selfridge and demanding a black armband, instead of contemplating an evening's revelry with a complete stranger?"

"Not at all. We Heronshaws never wear our hearts on our sleeves. We gave it up after Culloden, when one of my ancestors had his slashed to pieces by an English soldier. Since then we've kept them tucked away beneath our ribs."

Sharlie reminded him that she had been talking of an armband, not his heart, but he ignored her.

"And as we would undoubtedly have met at Mrs. Mandrake's dance if I hadn't gone up to Scotland—not forgetting that you know Margery Helliwell, who would have been my sister's bridesmaid if she hadn't had mumps instead—I hardly think we can be accurately described as strangers. Not complete ones, anyhow. Nor do I like your use of the word 'revelry' in connection with a meal eaten with dignity and discretion at a restaurant whose choice I leave to you."

"Oh, dear!" Sharlie exclaimed in mock dismay. "I've hurt your feelings!"

"Wounded them, yes. Deeply, but not irreparably. All that I ask to heal them is the sunshine of your presence in the dark hour of my bereavement. Though to be honest I must own I never actually *met* my cousin Agatha—or was her name Amelia?"

"In the circumstances," Sharlie told him gravely, "I feel it would be most uncharitable of me not to dine with you. To be alone with your own searing thoughts of one who meant so much to you would be—er—wellnigh overwhelming!"

"You must have graduated in a correspondence course in oratory!" he said admiringly. "I owe you my profoundest thanks for saving me from being—er—overwhelmed. Poor Agatha! One can but hope that in her hour of trial she felt herself a worthy follower of Jonah.—Where would you like to dine?"

"I'd rather you decided that." She had been going to add, "I don't know much about London restaurants," but instead, preferring him to believe her more sophisticated than she was, said lightly, "Places change so, don't they? And I've been in the north, and out of touch for some time."

"I'll book a table at Franchini's, then. According to my friends it's as good a spot as any at the moment, and certainly they did me very well when I dined there on my way north. Or would you rather not bother to change into

14

a long frock? They're pretty sticky there, these days, about admitting anyone not in evening dress."

Not long ago Sharlie had acquired her first long evening frock. The dance for which she had bought it had been cancelled, and she had had no opportunity for wearing it. She felt thrilled as a child bidden to her first party, but made her voice sound casual as she answered that Franchini's would be fun, and she had a dinner dress conveniently near the top of her suitcase.

It would seem strange to be going out without Mona, who had been her companion on so many parties and foursomes in York. For although Mona was so lovely that every man who saw her was enchanted by the spell of her blue eyes and flaxen hair and rose-leaf skin, so far no man who had spent an evening with her seemed to want to make a second date. She was shrewd enough to see that it would be to her advantage to become inseparable from Sharlie, who for some mysterious reason Mona could not fathom was always in demand for dances or anything else that was afoot. And Sharlie, who had no wish to go out on her own, no special escort with whom she would have liked to spend an evening unaccompanied, had been glad enough to say when someone asked her to a dance that she would like to go, but it would be more fun, wouldn't it, if he could bring a friend and Mona came along as well? And if he disagreed, she said that she was sorry, but in that case she couldn't come, having arranged to bear Mona company on that particular evening. It was one way, she felt, in which she might in some small measure return the kindness she had had from Mona's parents. But for her, Mona's outings would have been few and far between . . . poor Mona, who had yet to learn that if one would be popular one must listen as well as talk, feign interest many a time one did not feel it, and give sympathy as well as ask it.

Richard arranged to call for her at her hotel, and presently they parted on the platform at King's Cross.

Mrs. Ramswell had suggested that Sharlie should spend the night at the Combermere. It was situated in a quiet street between Park Lane and Berkeley Square, and was a sedate hotel much patronised by country families when their younger members had occasion to try on a bridesmaid's outfit, visit the dentist, or have tonsils given expert attention. Sharlie was welcomed by an elderly receptionist with a motherly manner, and wafted upstairs in a lift worked by an important small boy under the benevolent supervision of the lift attendant and the watchful eye of his nannie. A page, carrying her suitcase, led the way to a small bedroom, comfortably furnished, rather after the manner of a bedroom in a country house, with curtains, chair covers, and bed vallance of flowered chintz.

As soon as the page had gone she opened her suitcase to take out her evening dress. Anxiously she held it up to see if it were creased, but she had packed it carefully, with quantities of tissue-paper, and all was well.

Later, refreshed and glowing after a bath, and ready for the evening's outing, she inspected herself critically in a long mirror. The dress was simply cut, in misty hyacinth blue, flattering to her colouring. There was no trimming of any sort, all the effect depended on cut and line. Over it she would wear a wrap of a deeper blue. The colour emphasised the blue of her eyes. She had felt extravagant in buying the dress but was grateful now to Mona, who had egged her on: the right clothes did give one confidence and poise—qualities in which, at the moment, she felt herself lamentably lacking.

She was glad that after all she was not going to spend the evening by herself. When one was weary life took on a different colour, as though a grey film had been laid across its rosy glow; at night, the gay adventure of the morning was apt to be transformed into an alarming undertaking. The prospect of striking out all on her own had seemed good fun, but now, in these unfamiliar surroundings, it seemed suddenly frightening to be launching out to sink or swim with no one of her own behind her, no one at all who really cared what happened to her.

The ringing of the telephone beside her bed startled her from her reverie, and she was glad to hear that "A gentleman is waiting for you in the lounge, miss."

She stood a moment in the entrance to the lounge, not seeing the figure in khaki she had expected, feeling forlorn and lost. Then with an irrational lifting of her spirits she saw him. Richard had met some acquaintance and had for a moment turned away from watching for her coming;

also, he had changed into "blues," which had prevented her from immediately recognising him. Seeing him, surrounded by a crowd of strangers, Sharlie felt, absurdly, a warm sense of reassurance, as though he were a friend, someone who mattered, a part of her life's background, instead of the acquaintance of a few hours.

Turning again to see if she had appeared, he came across to her at once.

"How nice of you to be so punctual! I hope you're not too tired to feel like gadding out?"

"I'm not a bit tired, thank you!" she assured him, not quite accurately.

"Shall we be getting along, then?"

She had not realised how tall he was until they walked together to the door, her head on a level with his chin— and she was five-feet-seven. He had a taxi waiting.

When they were under way he said, "I can't say that I care about the way folks have these days of plunging into Christian names two minutes after meeting. But if you don't mind, shall we be 'Sharlie' and 'Richard' for this evening? It's embarrassing, manoeuvring with 'You'! And when two ships are passing in the night, it seems a pity not to let that night be a friendly one, I think. Don't you?"

Sharlie agreed. But she felt faintly disappointed by his mention of "ships passing in the night." It seemed to set a limit to the pleasure of the evening: an end to what might have been only a beginning.

Franchini's was crowded when they arrived there. A group of people waited uncertainly by the door, but the head waiter, seeing Richard, came at once to show them to their table. Heads turned to watch them as they wound their way among the tables. There was something about Richard, Sharlie thought, something unconsciously commanding in his carriage, some air of distinction, that must always have the effect of making people notice him. She did not know that people were not saying "What a striking man!" but "What a good-looking couple."

From several directions as they passed across the room Richard was hailed by friendly voices.

A pair of subalterns, dining with two pretty girls, grinned at him cheerfully. "Good evening, sir! Have a good leave?"

A tall man with an eyeglass on a broad black ribbon, whom Sharlie knew from photographs to be a distinguished diplomat, said as they went by his table, " 'Lo, Richard! H'are you?"

And a girl a year or two older than Sharlie, lovely and assured, diamonds winking in her ears, a sable cape tossed across her chair behind her, raised her glass towards him in a charming gesture.

"Ricky! Where've you been hiding lately?"

Sharlie had seen her in the pages of the *Tatler* a few weeks ago, photographed as she left St. Margaret's, Westminster, after her wedding to the heir to a famous earldom.

Richard gave them all a friendly saluation, but kept on his way.

They had a corner table. Watching him order dinner Sharlie knew that by some lucky trick of personality of which he probably was unaware, the corner table, the special dish of which there was not enough for everyone, the service of the most efficient waiter, would always be reserved for Richard. Or was it that one got what one expected out of life, and Richard, having a high standard of expectancy, found it fulfilled?

A man at an adjoining table smiled in greeting. Richard signalled back. Sharlie said, "You seem to know somebody at every table! I suppose, roving about the world all your adult life, you must have made stacks of friends."

"Stacks of acquaintances, anyhow," Richard agreed. "Those two lads in my regiment are Tony Felder—he won the National last year on Kandahar, you may remember—and Copper Kendall, Ravenswood's elder son. He's mad keen about yachting. I see his father's going as Ambassador to Brussels."

Sharlie felt the shadow of a gulf between them, born of her shyness and their short acquaintance, widen suddenly into a yawning chasm. She had not realised it in the train, but now with every moment it became more evident that they belonged to different worlds. The girls of Sharlie's world earned their own living, saved up for treats and holidays, took it for granted that one must manage without the luxuries one would have liked but couldn't afford. The girls of Richard's world lived in a setting of flats in Mayfair, luxury restaurants, long, low purring cars, country houses where they didn't have to help with any chores, Ascot, Eton and Harrow, hunting, point-to-points, holidays abroad . . . How could she and Richard ever speak each other's language, reach across the gulf created by their different interests and outlook?

With a faint shock of surprise she realized how much she wanted him to like her, how greatly she was tempted to act a worldliness and sophistication that were foreign to her. But she had the sense to know that even if she won his liking she could never keep it by pretending to be something she was not. Far better to be natural, to be herself, even though he thought her gauche and ignorant and dull.

Richard began telling her about his leave, spent in a tiny fishing inn in the Border country, of how much he had enjoyed the long days on the hills or by the river; encounters with keepers, shepherds, crofters, tramps; evenings by the wood fire with his friends and a variety of wayfarers.

Sharlie found herself telling him of the holiday she'd once spent in a farmhouse in the Yorkshire dales, to help the farmer with his harvest; of how weary she had been at the day's end, and yet how glowing with a sense that the day's work had been well worth while; of the farmer and his wife, their robust outlook on the world, their kindliness and hospitality; of the meals in the farm kitchen, with its flagged floor and the great hook in the ceiling where in earlier days hams and sides of bacon had been hung.

They talked of country things; of birds, and the strange ways of hares, of wild cats and foxes; argued laughingly as to the respective merits of the seasons, Sharlie preferring spring, while Richard said there was no time as good as autumn.

She told him how she had answered an advertisement in the Personal Column of *The Times* for a secretary chauffeuse, living in.

"D'you think you'll like it?" Richard asked.

"I haven't got it, yet!—I thought I would. But now I'm rather wondering. They must be frightfully rich, these people—" She hesitated.

"Yes?" he encouraged her.

"And I'm wondering whether I'll be—I don't quite know how to put it—"

"Whether you'll be a fish out of water?"

Sharlie nodded. "Yes. Whether it may be lonely, living among people who belong to such a different world from mine." She hadn't thought of it until coming to Franchini's had implanted the notion in her mind.

"M'm. That's nonsense—but I do know what you mean. I've been in the same boat myself," said Richard thoughtfully. His bright dark eyes were understanding as he looked at her over his coffee cup.

"My people never had a bean. I never did anything that cost money as a boy. My pleasures were hill climbing, swimming, watching bird life. Then my great-uncle insisted that I should follow the rest of the family into the Midlothian Hussars—said he'd leave me all his money if I did. He was a very wealthy man. And as I was going into the army anyhow, there was nothing to be said against obliging him, except that it's an expensive regiment and it didn't occur to the old boy to give me an allowance, though he'd never have missed it . . . The other subalterns could afford expensive cars, horses, all manner of things I had to do without. They had been brought up to hunt and shoot and ski. Their talk was all of things I didn't understand."

"Weren't you very lonely?"

"Very, at first. I felt inferior, too—at nineteen one hasn't outgrown snobbishness! I hadn't, anyway. Then I told myself the things I cared about and understood were just as worth while as the interests of the others. I discovered that one's world is not—or need not be—a matter of outside circumstances, but of one's thoughts and personality. *They're* the important things in life! I'm sorry, I'm afraid all this sounds frightfully priggish and pompous! Am I being a hideous bore?"

"No. On the contrary, you're being a great help!" She smiled at him. "Do please go on pouring good sound common sense into me! I need it extra badly, at the moment."

He laughed at that. "Thank you for putting it so politely! Well—you've asked for it! Keep an open mind to other people's interests, but hang on to your own as well. Don't bother about what people call The Right Thing. Make your own standards. What's right for someone else may be all wrong for you. Never be a chameleon, or you may lose yourself and end up as an inferior copy of someone else, someone not half so charming as yourself."

Sharlie nodded thoughtfully. "M'm . . . When one thinks of it, just being oneself is rather an adventure!"

"*Isn't* it! But so few people ever seem to find that out!"

"I wonder . . . One can't tell. For all we know, the most prosaic and stodgy people may be having all kinds of exciting happenings going on inside them!"

Their eyes met, lit with laughter, understanding, and appreciation. Joyfully Sharlie realised the gulf between them had been bridged. No, not bridged: had closed as though it never had been. She thought: He likes me—likes me quite a lot. Perhaps our goodnight needn't be good-bye after all, in spite of what he said about ships passing in the night . . .

While they were talking waiters had been clearing tables from the centre of the room, preparing it for dancing. Now the orchestra that had been playing softly throughout dinner at the other end of the long room swept into the rhythm of a waltz.

Richard said, "Let's dance, shall we, before the floor gets crowded?"

As he slid his arm expertly round her, she was tense and rigid in her anxiety to dance well; better than she had ever danced in all her life. After a few minutes Richard relaxed his grasp of her, holding her away from him, looking at her with one eyebrow quizzically raised.

"Lord love-a-duck! Anyone might think I was a sitting of eggs you were afraid of breaking! Let yourself go, child. Stop worrying, and leave the rest to me."

Something in the unexpected absurdity of that "Lord love-a-duck" made Sharlie break into spontaneous laughter that automatically relaxed her tension.

"*That's* better," Richard said approvingly, drawing her closer. "Don't think. Listen," he commanded her, and she obeyed, yielding herself, lissom and effortless, to his direction.

The music took possession of them. They were a single entity, floating, drifting, eddying on its tide until its wave broke in a triumphant climax and the spell was broken, too.

So they spent the remainder of the evening, dancing, exploring one another's thoughts, absorbed in mutual discovery, often breaking off in the middle of a sentence, so swiftly understanding flowed between them.

At last the band rose to its feet to play the National Anthem, and Sharlie went to get her coat. The eyes that looked back at her from the cloakroom mirror were wide and bright, her cheeks were delicately flushed; happily she saw that she was looking her best.

It had been a perfect evening. Surely it must have a perfect ending! Surely he would ask for her address, suggest a further meeting somewhere, somehow, some day! Surely two people who were, so to speak, so perfectly tuned in on the same wave-length, *couldn't* just drift apart . . .

Richard was waiting for her in the foyer. "I've got a taxi, but it's such a lovely night, and only a short way to your hotel—I wondered if you'd like to walk, to get some fresh air before you try to sleep?"

"I'd love to!"

So he paid off the taxi and they stepped out together into the fresh May night. A full moon lit the streets with brilliant silver light and cast deep ebony shadows to lend mystery and glamour to corners that by day were ordinary and uninteresting. Their two pairs of feet sounded unnaturally loud as they walked through the empty streets where only an occasional passing taxi broke the silence: Sharlie's footfalls, quick and light, measuring three to two of Richard's longer stride. She paused as they were turning a corner, lifting her face, breathing deeply.

"I'm sure I smell faint country scents trying to reach us through the petrol fumes!"

Richard sniffed the air. "Yes . . . I remember saying something of the sort walking through Grosvenor Square after a dance, and being told, half-seriously, that what I smelt was probably the scent of ghost flowers blowing through the centuries from the days when Mayfair was a place of fields and streams and country lanes."

No man, thought Sharlie, would have said that: it must have been some girl who was his companion on that bygone summer's night . . . some girl who still, for all that

22

she could tell, might play a leading role in Richard's life. Yet he was not the sort of man to make no mention, in the circumstances, of his engagement, if engaged he were . . .

Five minutes more at most, and they would be outside the Combermere. And still he'd said no word of future meetings, nor expressed a hope of seeing her again. Desperately she tried to turn his thoughts towards the future, by asking whether he was going on to Colchester to-morrow?

Richard said he was, but made no reciprocal enquiry as to her own plans. Instead, he began telling her of a Roman pavement that had recently been found while structural alterations were being carried out in the barracks where his regiment were quartered. At any other time Sharlie would have been interested, but now, while she mechanically uttered polite sounds—"Yes? Really! Oh, very interesting!" all her mind was focused on willing him to say something, anything to transform their meeting of to-day from a brief episode, soon to be forgotten on his side, into the beginning of a longer story.

Now they were standing by the Combermere's revolving door.

"Well," Sharlie said, "Good night! Thank you so very much for giving me such a lovely evening." *(Say something —say it! Ask me for my address—tell me you'll write to me when my plans are settled, on the chance that I'll be able to go out with you again—)*

"Thank you for coming. It was charming of you." He took her hand. "Sharlie—"

"Yes?" *(Say it now—oh, say it quickly, before it's too late—)*

But Richard only gave her hand a little shake, and dropped it as he said, "Good-bye. I hope you'll get that post, and like it!"

And somehow she forced herself to say "Good-bye!" gaily and casually, and to turn away into the quiet hotel where the night porter was the only living being in sight, and the empty lounge seemed peopled by the sad ghosts of those who had met here and would meet no more.

The Wiltshire fields were misted gold with buttercups, cow parsley foamed along the ditches, may-blossom, rich and sweet as clotted cream, lay thick on every hawthorn as the train bore Sharlie through the countryside to Bath, where Mrs. Ramswell had said a car would meet her. But though the scenery was far lovelier than the Midlands she had passed through yesterday, she wished with all her heart that she was travelling on yesterday's journey rather than to-day's. If only she could relive the past twenty-four hours, surely she could say something, do something to make Richard like her more than he had evidently done. She had been so certain, for a brief happy hour, his liking equalled hers. But if it had, surely their evening must have ended differently!

Everything she saw led her thoughts in his direction. A Queen Anne house by a walled garden in a park set her wondering if he liked that period; she had a preference for Georgian architecture. The book a fellow passenger was reading made her wonder whether he read a great deal, and if he liked novels, or like so many men preferred biography or travel.

Not knowing what manner of person would meet her when she arrived at Bath, she took the small case that was all the luggage she had brought, since if she stayed the rest would be sent after her, and stood waiting near the barrier until somebody should come in search of her. But when the platform was nearly empty and still no one had appeared she asked the ticket collector's advice.

"How far is it to Lacey Transome? Can I get there by bus? Somebody was to have met me, but so far they haven't come."

"There's a bus goes that way from near the Abbey, every hour—" the man was telling her, when a girl who had approached them from the far side of the barrier and, unseen, looked Sharlie up and down, asked in a deep husky voice, "Are you being met from Swanswick Hall?"

Sharlie turned. The questioner was a girl of her own height, so striking in appearance, so superbly groomed, as to be more deserving of attention than many a more beautiful woman. Her hair was dark red, deep and rich as Spanish mahogany. She wore it combed back from a centre parting, thick and straight and shining, to cluster on her neck in rich sleek curls. Her brows were thin and strongly marked above her deepset, heavy-lidded eyes: strange eyes that made Sharlie think of agates, for they were in colour dark, transparent green, curiously flecked with yellow. Her nose was delicately cut with rather a high, curved bridge; her mouth was contradictory, the thin line of the upper lip seeming to indicate austerity, while the full lower lip was sensuously curved. Her skin was white as skim milk, yet lacking the transparency that so often goes with a fair skin. Although the day was mild she wore a coat of ocelot over her shoulders, the arms hanging loose, and under it a softly tailored suit of woollen material in a deep glowing shade of green that drew attention to the colour of her eyes.

Sharlie said, "Yes—my name is Raven."

"Let's be getting along, then," said the other girl, and turned and walked away.

Sharlie followed her to a low grey car with red upholstery; she eyed it critically, wondering whether it would soon become her charge. It was a famous make that she had driven, and liked. The girl, without speaking, swung herself into the driver's seat. Sharlie hesitated, not knowing where she was expected to sit, and with an irritable movement the girl leaned across to open the door beside her "Shove your suitcase in the back," she said.

Could she be Mrs. Ramswell? Sharlie had pictured a much older woman. This girl wouldn't want a chauffeuse. Possibly she was a married daughter? For married she must be, since the hand lying on the steering-wheel wore a platinum wedding-ring as well as a large squarecut emerald.

It was the first time Sharlie had been in Bath. She looked with interest at the attractive shop windows and presently with admiration at the beautifully laid out squares and crescents and wide streets that had been the kingdom of Beau Nash.

Still her companion drove in silence. Sharlie glanced sidelong at her profile, that wore a look of bored indifference, and at last ventured to remark shyly that she had had no idea that Bath was such a charming town.

"Think so? As far as I'm concerned London and Paris and New York are the only places in the world worth being in," was the discouraging reply. "I should go scatty if I had to live for ever in this part of the world!"

"Then—you're not Mrs. Ramswell?"

"*Me*? Lord, no!" The girl gave a short, unamused laugh. "I'm Nicola Freemantle. My brother is the Ramswells' son-in-law. My husband got himself put paid to in an air crash about six months ago and so I'm staying with them until I can find something fit to live in."

Sharlie, embarrassed, said no more. Probably the brusque way of talking, though it jarred, was Mrs. Freemantle's way of covering up her feelings. All the same, it was a relief to know that this was not her future employer!

Beyond the town they took a road that after climbing steeply ran along the side of a deep narrow valley. Rock roses fell in bright cascades over the walls of cottage gardens, every field and hedge was gold and silver with the flowers of spring, the copper beeches had not darkened yet to the less attractive liver colour of late summer but glowed rosily, touched with ruby and crimson, and chestnut trees, more massive than any Sharlie had seen, were lit by thick candles of white and pink.

Presently Sharlie saw that a mile or two ahead of them the valley divided into two, forming a Y-shaped fork. Standing on high ground between these two smaller valleys and facing down the main valley towards the now distant city of Bath, stood a large rambling Tudor house built, like every cottage and farmhouse in the neighbourhood, of mellow Cotswold stone and roofed with flat slabs of the same stone. It had the mullioned windows of its period. Behind, the rising ground was thickly wooded; on one side was a large walled garden with a range of greenhouses, and in front were lawns and terraced flower-beds that fell away to be lost in the trees and undergrowth climbing to meet them from the valleys on either side.

"That's Swanswick," her companion told her.

"What a lovely house it looks!" Sharlie exclaimed.

"Yes—if you like that sort of thing. Give me a flat in Mayfair and you can have all the Tudor houses in the world, as far as I'm concerned!"

A few minutes later they turned through lodge gates, crossed the nearer of the valleys by an old stone bridge and swept along a drive that at this time of year was a cool tunnel of green, walled by soaring tree trunks and sunlit undergrowth. Then they were out again in sunshine, sweeping round the side of the house they had seen from down the valley, and at last drawing up by its great oak door, fronted by two wide and shallow steps of stone.

It was so lovely a house and in so lovely a setting that to Sharlie its perfection seemed in those first moments scarcely real. Almost, she thought, one might expect the leading lady of some musical comedy to step through the door and break into song! But it was no stage star who emerged, but a sedate elderly butler, who took Sharlie's case from the car, and also several parcels which he handed to a maid who came behind him.

Madam, he informed Mrs. Freemantle, was in the morning-room and would be glad to see Miss Raven as soon as she arrived.

"I'll take her there myself," Nicola told him, and saying "Come on!" to Sharlie over her shoulder, set off at such a pace that the stranger had to hurry to keep up with her.

She led the way through a great hall on whose parquet floor lay Persian rugs in rich soft colourings, so fine and beautiful that Sharlie felt it almost sacrilege to walk on them and did her best to step instead on the polished wood. There were deep chairs, and Knole settees, covered in velvets and brocades. Even in her haste Sharlie could see that every article of furniture was fit for a museum, the pictures on the walls the work of great masters, even the superb curtains of damask and brocade worth a small fortune.

It would have been natural enough if at this moment all her thoughts had been bent on the meeting just ahead of her: the meeting with the unknown woman in whose hands lay her immediate future. Twenty-four hours ago she would have believed anything else impossible. Yet now, following Nicola Freemantle along a wide corridor, she was wondering, not "What is Mrs. Ramswell going to be like?" but *What would Richard think of this wonderful house?*

CHAPTER TWO

NICOLA FREEMANTLE opened a door at the end of a long wide corridor where a Chippendale mirror reflected a flower painting by an old Dutch master, and a superb marquetry tallboy was squired on either side by matching chairs.

"I've brought Miss Raven. Here she is!" said Nicola. There came no answer, for the room was empty.

"Mrs. Ramswell must have gone through to her bedroom. Wait here, will you?" Nicola said imperiously, and left the room by a door opposite the one by which they had entered.

Sharlie looked about her, intrigued by the surprising contrast between this room and the rest of the house as far as she had seen it. Elsewhere, everything had a strangely static look, as though it were never used nor moved. Each article of furniture stood primly in its appointed place; the lack of any papers, books, or personal belongings gave the place an air of being unlived in, waiting perpetually for a party that never happened. Everything was in perfect order, cushions plump and smooth, chair covers uncreased and fresh as though nobody had ever rested there, and although the place was furnished entirely with antiques, not one had been admitted that bore any traces of the usage of the years, no blemish in the shape of scratch or scar. Even the flowers had made her think "How expensive!" rather than "How lovely!" for they were perfect specimens of the greenhouse, not the garden, arranged with such studious care as to look more artificial than real. It was more like being in an extremely expensive interior decorator's showroom than in a home.

This room was different. It was a harmonious whole rather than the setting for a quantity of specimen pieces. Its contents blended happily together, obviously having been chosen for no other reason than because they gave their owner pleasure. One wall was filled entirely by glass-fronted bookshelves. Sharlie, looking at their contents, found they consisted of modern novels, travel books, biographies, as well as many classics and a number of books

28

on birds. A pile of books lay on a low table by a sofa that was drawn up near the window. Magazines and papers and a pair of gardening gloves were on another table near the door. A workbag lay on a chair, and there was knitting on the sofa. There were deep armchairs covered with flowered chintz, pretty and gay but by no means new; the curtains matched it. Many-coloured tulips in a glass accumulator tank made a bright splash of colour in a corner, and there was a great bowl of polyanthus on the table with the magazines. The watercolours on the wall were all of birds, exquisite studies of chaffinches in an apple tree a goldcrest on a larch spray, oyster-catchers on a shingle bank, mallard in flight. A small pair of field glasses lay by the knitting; evidently birds were an absorbing interest to the owner of the room.

The murmuring of voices ceased next door, and from the adjoining room came a slight woman with hair so silvery white as to appear luminous. Her eyes were blue as cornflowers, her skin had the transparency of extreme fairness; her features were delicate and regular. She was of medium height, but her slenderness made her seem taller than she was.

Searchingly she looked at Sharlie as she took her hand, murmuring a conventional greeting in a low, quiet voice. Her manner was formal and a trifle stiff. "I hope you had a comfortable journey?"

Nicola broke in before Sharlie could reply.

"Your shoes weren't ready. Was there something else you wanted me to bring? If so, it went right out of my head!"

"The fish, my dear! I do hope you remembered that?"

"Fish—that was it. Hudson will have to get it—I'm playing tennis with the Jacksons at half-past three and I've got letters to write before I go."

"Oh, *Nicola*! Hudson has that bee expert coming some time this afternoon. I can't send him. And Mrs. Tollworthy gets so temperamental if her menu is upset—"

Sharlie said quietly, "Can't I go and get it after lunch? I don't know Bath, but I could find the shop if you would start me in the right direction."

Mrs. Ramswell looked relieved. "That would solve the difficulty very nicely, though I scarcely like to send you off the moment you've arrived. However —Now you would like to see your room." She rang a bell. Nicola said, "Well, time to wash the little paws for lunch," and went away. Odd of her, thought Sharlie, that she should express no regret whatever for having forgotten the message she had undertaken for her hostess, nor offer to put matters right!

As Nicola left the room, a housemaid entered. Mrs. Ramswell asked her to take Miss Raven to her room, adding to Sharlie that lunch would be ready in about ten minutes. "I have arranged for you to have it with us in the dining-room, to-day."

Sharlie followed the maid back along the passage, up a wide staircase whose shallow steps of waxed oak were uncarpeted, to a small gallery open on one side to the hall. Out of the gallery ran a corridor with many doors. At the far end she ushered Sharlie into a small room whose windows looked across the terraced gardens down the long valley up which she had come from Bath.

Left to herself, she looked about her at the room that might be hers for months or years, or only for a night. It was a lovely room: the sort of room that she had seen in films or on the stage but never in real life. Ivory walls were scattered with silver leaves, the curtains were of silvery brocade lined with orchid silk, the bedspread and chair covers matched them and were piped with orchid. The carpet was orchid, fitting to the walls; the furniture was lacquered ivory, picked out in silver. The adjoining bathroom, too, was ivory and silver, with palest orchid towels and a fleecy bathmat of deeper orchid. It was all very lovely and impressive, but she found it difficult to image feeling quite at ease here. Would she ever dare to sit in one of those deep chairs, creasing its sumptuous brocade upholstery, or put her brushes and toilet preparations on that immaculate dressing-table? Her suitcase looked forlorn and out of place: she felt a little out of place herself!

She marvelled that a woman whose sitting-room expressed the personality of a book lover, a bird lover, a lover of flowers and needlework and gardening and simple homely pleasures, should have made the rest of her house a place of beauty that was costly and impressive, rich and ostentatious, as empty as a lovely woman without a soul.

Evidently Mr. Ramswell was away from home, or lunching elsewhere, for only three places had been laid for lunch. Nicola Freemantle came in late, without apology— strange manners from a visitor to her hostess! Ignoring Sharlie, she began a discussion with Mrs. Ramswell concerning friends with whom she had been telephoning. Once or twice the older woman changed the subject, bringing Sharlie into their conversation, but always Nicola harked back again at once to something in which the stranger could not join.

After lunch Sharlie went to Bath to fetch the forgotten fish. The car had better acceleration than any she had driven and was a joy to drive. She wondered whether Richard knew this part of the world, whether he, too, had driven along these leafy roads, had stopped his car where she was stopping now, to look at far blue downs framed by the trunks of giant chestnuts . . .

She saw him vividly in her mind as he had paused a moment on their walk through Mayfair's moonlit streets to light a cigarette, his shapely head bent above cupped hands, his thin dark face illumined by the flaring match that made a flickering flower of gold to bloom a moment in the ebony and silver world. She thought of things she would have liked to say to him, to ask him, knowing he would understand. She had suffered loneliness before, but never loneliness such as she knew now, for until meeting Richard she had never dreamed what real companionship could mean. And if, after one evening, it could mean so much, how deep its roots must strike after a longer knowledge!

The more she thought of it, the more she was convinced that he had felt as she did. Reason might argue that if this were so he would not have let their parting be a final one: instinct knew better. Then why, why, *why*—?

She told herself that speculation would lead nowhere, only keep the wound from healing. She must forget him— but it wasn't going to be easy . . .

On her return to Swanswick Jackson, the butler, met her at the door to take the fish, and tell her that Mrs. Ramswell would like Miss Raven to have tea with her in her own sitting-room at four o'clock.

Punctually at the appointed hour, armed with notebook and pencil, she went to Mrs. Ramswell's sitting-room, ready for the moment, which would probably come after tea, when she would be put through her paces, tested as to her speed at shorthand, ability to answer letters at her discretion, knowledge of the mechanics of a car.

She felt very much the employee on approval as she sat with Mrs. Ramswell having tea at a small table drawn up by the window, but soon forgot to be self-conscious and felt like any ordinary guest.

Mrs. Ramswell asked about her life before she had applied for the job at Swanwick, and somehow, despite the reticence of her manner, Sharlie must have sensed that she was interested and sympathetic, for she found herself telling of the ups and downs that she had known, the queer discoveries she had made regarding human nature, the odd, amusing experiences she had met with. They talked of gardens, of the ways of woodpeckers, and of books, and Mrs. Ramswell grew more animated as they discovered similar tastes in authors. Sharlie realised that the woman she had at first taken to be nearly sixty must be fully ten years younger. Her swift ease of movement as she rose to get a book, the freshness of her unlined skin, were far more youthful than the first impression given by her silver hair.

She said at last, "And now we ought to speak of what I have in mind regarding your duties here. That is, if you would like to stay when I have told you what I want."

The work, she said, would be elastic. Her husband was away a great deal, nearly always at mid-week, at the headquarters of his business in the Midlands. Sharlie gathered that he owned the controlling interest and was managing director of large factories that turned out enormous quantities of agricultural machinery which was exported all over the world. He had his own car; the one she had driven to-day was Mrs. Ramswell's—both were cleaned by an under-gardener.

She would be expected to give help with the work of a charity for which Mrs. Ramswell was honorary county secretary, to meet trains, do errands in Bath, deal with correspondence concerning the household and garden, possibly lend a hand in the estate office now and then, if they were shorthanded owing to illness or holidays.

"You have kept my letter regarding salary and hours off duty—though your free time would have to be as elastic as your work?"

"Yes."

"Then, having heard what would be expected of you, you will want to think things over before deciding whether you would like to come to me, or not," concluded Mrs. Ramswell. Not "to us," Sharlie noticed, but "to me."

She said, "But don't you want to try me out before we settle anything definite? You don't know anything about my capability—or otherwise!"

For the first time she saw a smile light Mrs. Ramswell's eyes, completely changing her expression. Until now, she had not realised the sadness and endurance written in her face.

"Your capability? You mean, how fast you can take dictation, and whether you can change a tyre, and if you know the difference between 'Yours truly' and 'Yours faithfully'?"

Sharlie smiled. "Well—that sort of thing, perhaps!"

"But those, to me, are very minor points. I want a girl of pleasing personality, with plenty of initiative, who will help to oil the wheels of this not always very easy household. Someone with her head screwed on the right way, who would be resourceful in emergency. Someone well equipped with common sense, and yet not too material. Someone with a sense of humour, who would be tactful with the servants. Someone on whom I could rely. And so I hope you will decide to stay here."

Sharlie was aware of two sensations: a warm tide of happiness rising in her heart, a wave of colour burning in her cheeks. She stammered, "I would always do my best, of course. But you can't tell—you've seen so little of me— you can't possibly—"

"I have seen enough of you to know the sort of girl you are!" She smiled again. "You must leave me to be the judge of that!"

"Then, if you really mean it, I would very much like to stay here."

"I never say a thing I do not mean.—And now, since everything is settled, you would like to have the rest of the day to yourself, I know. I shall expect you here, in this room, at half-past nine to-morrow morning. Until then, do as you please. Go where you choose, do anything you like. Mary will bring your dinner to your sitting-room when we have ours, at a quarter to eight. Tell her if you lack anything you want to make you comfortable.—Ah, just a minute! You must meet my grandchildren!"

Through the open window came the sound of treble voices, followed by a cry of "Gangy! *Gangy*! Here are we, so where are you?"

Mrs. Ramswell threw the window wider and leaned out. "Here am I, and here's Miss Raven, who has come to live with us."

On the drive circling the house Sharlie saw a dark girl in the uniform of a famous training college for children's nurses. Beside her was the small boy who had called for "Gangy," and in a cream-coloured pram sat a fat, wide-eyed baby girl of two years old, whose short hair curled in brown silken bubbles over her head.

Solemnly the little pair gazed at Sharlie. Then the boy asked, "Are you a lady or a girl?"

"Both," said his grandmother, before Sharlie could reply.

"She can't be both unless she's twins!"

"Now, George, don't argue," said the nurse repressively. Her uniform was immaculate, the children beautifully turned out; obviously she was an efficient young woman, but Sharlie was not attracted to her sallow thin-lipped face and small brown eyes like currants in a suet pudding, and was glad to see that George seemed oblivious of the admonition. He was a thin little boy of about five, with straight fair hair that fell in a fringe on his forehead, a short snub nose, and enquiring eyes, as blue as his grandmother's.

"Gangy, are you coming to play croquet with me?" he demanded, but the nurse said firmly, "Not this evening, George. You got so excited last night that it was nearly nine o'clock before you went to sleep."

"I weren't excited! It was just my eyes that didn't get that woolly feeling," George protested.

His grandmother said tactfully, "I was hoping you would help me in the rock garden."

"Weeding?" asked George suspiciously, then, with more enthusiasm, "Or can I look for slugs?"

"It would be the greatest help if you would look for slugs. I'll bring a tin to put them in."

"And give them to the ducks?"

"Yes, if there's time."

"What darlings!" Sharlie exclaimed, as Mrs. Ramswell closed the window and took up her gardening gloves. "Are they paying you a visit?"

An expression that was hard to fathom clouded the grandmother's blue eyes as she said quietly, "They live here now. They are my daughter's children. Their mother —is not with us any more."

Since Tuesday Sharlie had been getting to know the ways of her new post, and now, on Friday afternoon, she was going down to Bath to fetch a quantity of food and other odds and ends needed by the household for the week-end. Mrs. Ramswell had told her not to hurry back, if she would care to do some shopping on her own account, or see a film.

The day was warm and sunny, so she changed into a frock of deep blue linen, V-necked, with a white collar, white shoes, and a white bag, and left the house by a side door to fetch the car.

She had no doubt that her post was going to be a pleasant one, with plenty of variety. Most of the morning she was busy with letters and telephone calls, but yesterday she had driven Mrs. Ramswell to Gloucester to see a sick friend in a nursing home, and the day before she had driven the children and their nurse to a birthday party in a charming house some miles away.

Mrs. Ramswell was the most considerate of employers. The servants, who had at first been suspicious of her as a newcomer who might make trouble and put on airs, had been disarmed of their hostility by her pleasant manner and evident wish to make as little extra work as possible, and now their friendliness matched her own. The fat cook, temperamental Mrs. Tollworthy, took pains to send her tempting dishes. Jackson, the butler, told her of the most attractive ways to walk, and went after her with a mackintosh one morning when she had gone down to the kitchen garden with a message and was caught by a sudden shower. Mary had even volunteered to do her washing, "for I don't advise you to send anything that's fragile to the laundry."

Everything possible was done to make her comfortable and happy, and a week ago she would have been enchanted and elated to find herself so happily established. Yet now she felt no more than a mild pleasure and content at her good fortune. She couldn't feel acutely; she felt numb and jaded. Life seemed oddly savourless, a dish that needed salt to bring out its flavour—the salt of Richard's presence, or at least the anticipation of seeing him again one day.

Cullen, the under-gardener, had been polishing the car, so it was standing in the yard. She was reversing cautiously when through the purring of the engine she heard a voice calling her name, and stopped, startled, to see what was wanted.

Nicola Freemantle came up to the car.

"Didn't you hear me calling from my window as you passed?" she demanded irritably.

Sharlie switched off the engine. "No. If I had, I would have stopped, of course. I'm sorry you had to come after me."

"My brother will be coming on the five-fifty. I was going to meet him, but I'm going to cocktails in the other direction, and if his train were late I'd miss the best part of the party. So you'd better go instead. He'll be expecting me, so you will have to find him on the platform. Wait by the barrier and you can't miss him. He's tall and rather like me and he will be carrying a pigskin suitcase labelled Heighbrook." Turning on her heel, not waiting for an answer, she strolled away, humming to herself.

Sharlie made a little rueful grimace to herself as she started up the engine for the second time. She would have met the train quite cheerfully, even though it did mean missing the film she had wanted to see, if only the request had been pleasantly made, instead of given as a brusque command.

Nicola was the one fly in the ointment of her new life, with her imperious manner, and her dictatorial way of ordering Sharlie to get her a telephone number, as though the small word "please" had been omitted from her vocabulary. Still, Sharlie saw very little of Mrs. Freemantle, and probably the young widow would be going away before long; it seemed that she was only staying here while she looked for a flat in London, although as she had been here three months already, and doubtless found it pleasant to live in luxury that cost her nothing, it looked as though she were not exerting herself unduly over her flat-hunting. She went out a great deal with friends who called for her in high-powered cars, and seemed to lead a very gay life. Sharlie doubted if she would have lingered on here if she had not had ways of amusing herself in the neighbourhood, for life at Swanswick Hall itself was quiet and uneventful, though perhaps it grew more lively at the week-ends.

Sensitive to atmosphere, Sharlie felt a weight of sadness in the lovely Tudor house. She wondered what the cause of it might be. Possibly the return of Mr. Ramswell, who was expected home to-morrow for the week-end, might provide a clue. Possibly it was due to sorrow for the children's mother. Sharlie had at first thought young Mrs. Heighbrook had died when Gay, the little girl, was born, but something the nurse had said had made it clear that they had been living here only for a month or two, so probably she had died more recently, met with an accident, perhaps. Her name was never mentioned. Evidently her mother could not bear to speak of her. There was a son, Geoffrey, who was abroad at present on business for his father's firm. His photograph stood on his mother's bureau: a square face, practical and rather hard. With it stood a second photograph, of a dark girl with laughing, mischievous eyes and a mutinous mouth, who was presumably his sister.

Her shopping was a lengthy business. When it was done she parked the car, had tea in a quiet restaurant recommended by Jackson, then spent an hour exploring the old streets until it was time to meet the train.

She had no difficulty in identifying Randolph Heighbrook as he came towards her where she stood waiting by the barrier, for his resemblance to Nicola was remarkable. He had the same strange agate eyes, deep-set and heavy-

37

lidded under thin, irritable brows, the same hard upper lip and sensuous lower one, the same nose, finely cut, with sensitive, ill-tempered nostrils. He had Nicola's air of being highly bred, in a degree so marked that a well-known breeder of fox terriers who had travelled with him in the same carriage had been reminded by his appearance of certain dogs in whom temperament and stamina had been sacrificed to points and pedigree, with unhappy results.

In that short moment as he came towards her Sharlie was warned in a swift flash of intuition of something that in Nicola she had not detected; possibly in the sister it was lacking, or hidden by artifice; possibly in the brother it was more evident than usual in this unguarded moment when he was unaware of being observed. It was a decadence, a materialism that would mock at moral or spiritual values, a ruthlessness that would trample over any obstacle that might hamper him, regardless of the pain he might inflict on others . . .

There was no time to think about it now. She forced herself to smile as she went forward, saying, "I think you must be Mr. Heighbrook, aren't you?"

The ill humour that had darkened his face on seeing no sign of Nicola gave way to a smile that stretched the corners of his mouth but did not reach his eyes. Reluctantly she felt the charm that he switched on mechanically and was at the same time fascinated and repelled.

"I am indeed," he said. His voice was shallow and metallic. "I was just cursing Nicola for being late again! Are you her substitute? If so, I'm lucky!"

Briefly Sharlie explained the circumstances and led the way to the car. She had arranged the parcels so that there was room for him in the back of the car, but he said that he would drive and took the driving-seat before she could say anything. She didn't like it; she was responsible for the car, yet what was she to do? Silently she took her place beside him.

Nor did she like his driving. It was showy and erratic, and as she watched his hands grasping the wheel she had no sense of confidence. They were effeminate, narrow and long, and had peculiarly long supple thumbs.

She thought of Richard's hands, shapely and capable . . . She'd got to make an effort to stop thinking of Richard!

It was absurd that every avenue of thought should lead straight to a man of whose existence she had been unaware —how odd it seemed to think of any time in which she had been unaware of Richard!—barely a week ago. She tried instead to overcome her distrust of her companion, telling herself that it was unreasonable to dislike him on no evidence and that his young wife's death had probably thrown him somewhat off his balance. It must be painful for him to return here, where he had know happiness with her.

She said, "Another time, if I am sent to meet you, perhaps George will be allowed to come along, too. To-day, I didn't know in time."

"George? Oh, yes. George. Brats of that age usually do rather like a car ride, I suppose." He sounded unenthusiastic. "What happy chance has sent you to lighten the darkness of Swanswick? Dismal establishment, isn't it?"

It seemed an odd remark for him to make, considering that it was almost certainly his wife's death that had cast a shadow on the household that before her loss had probably been a happy one. Stiffly she said, "The furniture is wonderful!"

"M'm. I grant you that. Worth a pretty penny. Though personally I don't care for that museum stuff except for what it's worth. Give me something modern every time, whether it's a table or a picture—or a girl!"

Something in his insinuating voice made Sharlie feel acutely uncomfortable. To change the subject she told him of the party to which she had taken his children, describing Gay's excitement and delight when she had found a mouth-organ in the bran dip, and how George had spent all yesterday blowing bubbles with an outfit that had been his reward. Their father seemed uninterested, and broke in impatiently:

"What's the local chat? Any more burglaries?"

"Not that I know of. But I haven't been here long enough to know of any local happenings. I hadn't heard there had been any burglaries?"

"Hadn't you? It's been the talk of all the countryside for weeks! The fellow seems to time his robberies at the week-ends, when people have friends to stay, and so he gets a bigger haul."

" 'The fellow?' Isn't it a gang? Just one man?"

"Just one man. Must have colossal pluck and nerve!" He sounded full of admiration. Curious. And yet, not curious at all. Cunning and courage for the sake of gain would be just what one might expect him to admire . . .

"What does he take? Jewellery? Silver? Furs?"

"Nothing but jewellery. Easier to sell. He wears—they say he wears a mask. A well-made fellow, with an educated voice." He laughed. "All the old dowagers must be getting quite a kick out of it—wearing their best night attire in expectation of a visit from him!"

Sharlie was glad when arrival at their destination ended their conversation, which had done nothing to decrease the instinctive aversion she had felt at first sight of him.

Having garaged the car, she entered the house by the side door she usually used, and was going by a back staircase to her room so as to run no risk of meeting him when she heard his voice, raised in altercation with Jackson. He seemed to be protesting over being given a different bedroom from the one he generally occupied.

"But dammit, Jackson—if the Blue Room isn't occupied, why the devil shouldn't I have it, as usual?"

Jackson answered suavely, "Very sorry, sir. Madam gave orders that in future you will have the Oak Room, in the other wing."

"But isn't that adjoining Mr. Ramswell's rooms?"

"Yes, sir. I have no doubt that you will find it comfortable."

"That's not the point. The Blue Room is exactly what I need—exactly what I like! I—"

Sharlie passed on out of earshot. In her bedroom she found Mary, hanging up a dress she had been ironing.

"Thank you so much—how nice of you to do it for me! Tell me, which is the Blue Room?"

"The one next door but one to yours, miss. Mr. Heighbrook used to have it, but Madam gave orders for us to move his things to the Oak Room. That's in the wing at the far end of the house, near Mr. Ramswell's rooms. It's under the staff bedrooms, too, so we shall have to keep as quiet as we can—he'll make a rare to-do if we disturb him early! Mr. Heighbrook likes to lie long of a morning."

Sharlie was glad the solitude of her wing was not to be invaded. It seemed odd, she thought, for anyone to make so much fuss over the changing of his bedroom in a house where he was guest as well as son-in-law . . . The more she thought of him, the less she liked him. It was fortunate that she was unlikely to have any dealings with him.

At noon the next day, Saturday, she took several letters to Mrs. Ramswell's sitting-room for her to sign.

"Thank you, Miss Raven. I shan't need you any more this afternoon, but can you be available after dinner, please? My husband usually brings his secretary but she won't be coming this week-end, so if he does want to get off any urgent letters, it would be nice if you could take them, so that he'll have Sunday free."

"Of course," said Sharlie.

"There are some lovely walks—or if you'd like to go to Bath, Jackson will tell you about buses. I'm afraid it must be lonely for you here."

Sharlie assured her that she wasn't lonely in the least, and had been warned before she came here that the place was quiet and in the country.

"Well, when you've settled down we must try to find diversions for you, and some way of making pleasant contacts with people of your own generation."

After lunch she set out to explore the farther of the two small valleys that lay on either side of the house. She lay a long time on the sunny bank of a stream, listening to the murmur of the water and the singing of unseen birds, checking every thought that led towards Richard.

Once, she could have lost herself in the delight of giving free rein to her senses, abandoning all thought, to merge in colour and light, the pattern of leaves and branches, the harmony of running water and bird voices, the aromatic bouquet of the outdoor world. But now, a pleasure that she might not share with Richard was a pleasure halved.

It was after six when she returned to Swanswick. She went in as usual by the side door and was going towards the little staircase that was a short cut to her room, when a voice called her name imperiously, and Nicola came hurrying down the passage from the hall, looking furious.

"I've rung and *rung*, but Jackson doesn't come. Find him, will you, and say that people have come and we want drinks at once?"

"How many glasses?"

"Eight. Hurry, will you? We've been waiting ages. Really, it's *too* bad!" She flung away petulantly towards the drawing-room.

Sharlie went to the pantry, but Jackson was not there. Hearing voices from the servants' sitting-room she put her head in, and found Mary giving first aid to the parlour-maid, who had cut her thumb and was pale green.

Apologetically she said that she had come to look for Jackson. They told her he had gone to the lodge to fetch a parcel that had been left there by the bus, and should be returning any minute now.

"It's all right, never mind," said Sharlie. She had seen gin and orange juice and sherry in the pantry on a tray. Better to take them in herself than cause still more delay by waiting for Jackson to return—poor Margaret was obviously feeling far too sick and faint to undertake it.

She took glasses from a cupboard, hoping they were the right ones. Luckily the drawing-room door was open, for the tray was heavy and she needed both her hands. It was astonishing how much noise eight voices could make, and she was thankful that the talk and laughter did not abate as she entered. She was aware only of a blur of faces as she looked about her for a place to put the tray. A table near the door seemed the most convenient spot. Supporting as much of the tray as there was room for on the table, she held it with one hand and with the other tried to move a carved jade figure on a stand to make more room. It was heavier than it looked; she needed a third hand.

Somebody came and stood beside her. Somebody said, "I'll move it for you—that tray needs both your hands.— Why—*Sharlie!*"

Incredulously she looked up—straight into Richard's eyes.

CHAPTER THREE

SHARLIE stammered, "But you're not here—you're in Colchester!" then laughed, partly from sheer light-heartedness, partly at her own absurdity.

Richard laughed with her. "When I got back to Colchester I found that we were being moved to Rockmoor Camp, about four miles from here. We move in about ten days. So I came with Captain Brounlie to have a look-see. We're putting up at the Blue Boar, at Swilton, and he discovered friends staying there for the fishing. They'll be leaving with the mayfly. So they brought us along here so that we'll start off by knowing at least one household in the neighbourhood. Is that enough proof for you that I'm really here? Or must I show you my identity card?"

"I'll take your word for it," she said demurely.

Richard said, "I tried to ring you up, next day, at your hotel, but you were gone. Now that I've found you—"

Nicola's voice said smoothly, "Drinks at last!" She was beside them, then between them. Then she turned, stepping back as though by chance, so that Sharlie had to move nearer the door. "Drinks, people! Gather round!—I wonder if you'd help me, Major Heronshaw? Will you cope with sherry, if I deal out gin and orange?"

In the circumstances Sharlie felt that there was no alternative for her but to go. To Richard, over Nicola's shoulder, she said, "I must go now. Good-bye!"

"You can't rush off like this!" he said, and then, to Nicola, "I'd no idea I should find Sharlie here—"

"Really? So you know Miss Raven? How—unexpected!" Nicola's voice was sweet as honey, smooth as silk. She turned to Sharlie, looked her up and down, making her conscious that her linen dress was crumpled from lying on the grass, one arm scratched where she had caught it on a bush, her face flushed from the sun: making her aware of other people where a moment ago there had been no one but herself and Richard: a slim young man in uniform who was presumably Captain Brounlie, an older man who looked as though he had come here straight from fishing, two nondescript women and a third, with beautifully waved

43

white hair, charmingly dressed in black and white, talking to Randolph Heighbrook, who was listening with an expression of absorbed interest to what she had to say.

"Thank you *so* much for bringing in the drinks. I'll have to have a word with Jackson later," Nicola said to her. And then, to Richard, "We mustn't keep Miss Raven or we'll get her into trouble with our absent host. Business magnates don't like having their secretaries detained at other people's bidding!"

She smiled at Sharlie, who for the first time realised that, like her brother, she could turn on charm when she felt so inclined—but in her eyes was cold dismissal.

Sharlie said again, "Good-bye!" and fled, as Richard exclaimed, "But I say—Sharlie!—" It was impossible to remain a moment longer in the face of Nicola's determination that she must go.

She ran upstairs with a light heart in spite of being disappointed that she couldn't stay and talk to him. For he was coming to this neighbourhood. He'd actually be no more than four miles away. Above all, he had said, "*I tried to ring you up at your hotel, next day.*"

Going to her mirror, she stared earnestly at her reflection, wanting reassurance after Nicola's disparaging glances.

She found it. For the sun had warmed her skin to a becoming peach colour, and set gold gleams in her shining bell of hair, and happiness had lit stars in her eyes—and Sharlie knew, remembering the look in Richard's eyes, that it was these things he had noticed, not her creased frock nor scratched arm.

Someone was knocking at her door, and Mary entered. "Mr. Ramswell wants you in his room at half-past eight to take some letters. I thought you'd like to know at once instead of waiting till I bring your dinner."

"Oh—thank you, Mary! Will you show me where it is when the time comes?"

"Yes. It's a kind of little study place he has."

Sharlie called after her on a sudden impulse as she turned to go, "Oh, Mary! Just a minute! Have you a—a boy friend?"

Mary coloured faintly. "Well—not exactly, in a manner of speaking. But I'm going to the dance in the Hall, next

Wednesday, with Jim Cullen. You wouldn't know him—he's the under-gardener's brother. Works for Block, the builder."

Sharlie went to her hanging cupboard. Her clothes had been sent on from Yorkshire, only last night she had unpacked them. She took out a little frock of printed nylon. "I expect you've got a pretty frock, but this may come in useful for another time, if you would like it. It's always been a little—a little tight for me. It'll be too long for you, but you could shorten it, couldn't you?"

"Oh, *miss*—!" Mary was radiant, her round face transfigured. "I hadn't got a dress I really cared about, only my sister's that she gave me after she had the baby and put on so much weight that she couldn't get into it again. And though green's her colour it never did suit me. Oh, thank you *ever* so!"

Sharlie sang softly as she changed and washed and brushed her hair. She'd liked that dress. It hadn't been the least bit tight for her. But when one was so happy that it positively brimmed over, one just had to pass on something from the overflowing cup!

In her mind Sharlie had pictured Mr. Ramswell as a tall, distinguished figure with a scholarly stoop, a dreamer's eyes, a long, pale intellectual face; a man far more at home in a museum or art gallery than in his factory or office, a connoisseur of fine art to whom success in business had come in luck's course rather than in consequence of his own acumen. She had imagined him in the setting of a panelled study lined with first editions, with perhaps one superb picture over the fireplace.

The Mr. Ramswell of reality was the greatest possible contrast to the Mr. Ramswell she had pictured. He was short and thick-set, with a square pink face, small shrewd light grey eyes, and stubby hands. Nor was his study at all in keeping with the rest of the house: it was a cosy room furnished with a roll-top desk and shabby, comfortable leather chairs. The only pictures were of Highland cattle browsing by reedy lochs under the shadow of lowering mountains, and an engraving of "Monarch of the Glen." A jar of pipe cleaners and a fretwork pipe rack stood on the mantelpiece, with a marble clock, two brass camels, and a carved Swiss chalet.

He inspected Sharlie over the horn-rimmed spectacles perched on his small snub nose.

"You'll be Miss Raven. Just take down a couple of letters for me, will you, please." His intonation, rather than his accent, told of a north-country origin.

He dictated at a moderate speed, knowing exactly what he wanted to say, and saying it with neither hesitation nor afterthoughts.

"That'll be all," he said, when she had taken down a letter to the chairman of the local parish council and another to a firm who were to overhaul the central-heating system.

"Leave them here for me to sign some time to-morrow."

Sharlie rose to go, but Mr. Ramswell leaned back in his chair, joining his finger-tips together above his chubby waistcoat, and said, "Well, and what do you think of Swanswick?"

She said, sincerely, that she thought it lovely, adding that she had never seen such furniture and pictures outside an exhibition.

Mr. Ramswell chuckled, looking gratified. "That you haven't, I'll be bound! I had experts buying up the pick of everything that was for sale for eighteen months before we moved in here so as to be sure the place was furnished in the best of taste and with the best that money could buy.— You'll find it pays you always to get the very best you can afford, Miss Raven! Now, remember that advice!"

Sharlie smiled, and said she would, and went away partly enlightened in regard to one thing that had puzzled her since she came here: the strange discrepancy between the furnishing of Mrs. Ramswell's own rooms and the rest of the house. She knew now that Swanswick had been furnished with bought taste, and wondered why, since Mrs. Ramswell's sitting-room and adjoining bedroom showed a charming discrimination, and she evidently took pleasure in colour and harmony and had a real appreciation of old furniture. Why, then, had she had her home arranged by strangers rather than making it according to her own ideas—which were so different from theirs?

46

She typed the letters at once, and then, sleepy from her afternoon of lying in the sun, went to bed earlier than usual—but not to sleep. First she heard several cars arrive in swift succession. This was followed soon by laughter and hilarious voices calling to one another in the shrubberies and across the lawn below her window; evidently a party of the Heighbrooks' friends had come to visit them and hide-and-seek, or a treasure-hunt, or some such frolic was in progress, making sleep impossible until once more engines were switched on, and doors slammed, and the cars hummed away down the drive, and silence fell again on Swanswick.

She could not tell how long she had been sleeping when she was awakened suddenly. Moonlight streamed between her undrawn curtains, and the room, that had been filled with scented summer dusk when she had gone to bed, was bright as day. She lay alert, listening, wondering whether the sound that must have wakened her would be repeated. Presently an owl's cry shivered eerily through the night, and she relaxed; it must have been the owl that she had heard. She settled down again to sleep, then started up, for there was no mistaking the faint creak of a step on the little back staircase that went down near her room to a passage leading to the side door that she usually used.

Could Jackson have forgotten to lock the door? Had some intruder entered? Randolph Heighbrook's story of the burglar, never thought of since he told it to her, sprang to life. Could he have come here in hope of finding weekend guests with jewellery left lying on their dressing-tables, or with the idea of ransacking Mrs. Ramswell's room?

Until this frightening moment she had enjoyed the feeling of being in a small kingdom of her own, here in the wing whose only occupant she was. Now, for the first time, she regretted it. Her bell rang in a passage near the kitchen, out of hearing of the servants when they had gone to bed, and she had no other means of communicating with the rest of the house.

She scrambled hurriedly out of bed, feeling that she would rather face any chance of danger in her dressing-gown than cowering beneath the bedclothes. Her bathroom

47

door was open. Through its window, that opened on the side of the house, came the faint sound of the side door closing softly. Sharlie knew the hand that closed it must have done so at least once before, for if one didn't know the trick of easing it in a certain way, it shut with a sharp click.

Barefoot, she ran across the bathroom and looked out. No one was to be seen, but muffled and soft she could hear careful footsteps, and leant out as far as possible—then drew a long sigh of relief. For it was no masked figure that she saw, but Randolph Heighbrook, moving stealthily, keeping in the shadow of the house, his footfalls deadened by a pair of gym shoes.

Sharlie watched him disappear into the shrubbery, along the path that was a short cut to the garage. Then, laughing at her own momentary panic, she got back into bed.

She felt wide-eyed and wakeful, and instead of falling asleep at once lay puzzling over what she had just seen. At first she had taken it for granted that Randolph, feeling restless and unable to sleep, had decided to go for a moonlight stroll. And yet—and yet, it was unlike him to be so considerate of other people's slumbers as to wear those gym shoes. Odd, now she came to think of it, for him to own such shoes. She had been able to see them plainly in the moonlight; they were not tennis shoes, but were made of light-weight canvas, rubber soled, such as are sometimes worn by holidaymakers on the beach; not what one might have expected to find in the possession of a man who, unless she judged him wrongly, was as dandified in his taste as Randolph Heighbrook. Odd, too, that he had moved with such exaggerated caution, been so careful to keep well in the shadow of the house.

The more she thought of it, the more she was convinced that he was bound on some discreditable errand, for were it not discreditable, why all this stealth and secrecy? This was most probably the reason why he had objected to being moved from the Blue Room to one in another wing, where as well as being farther from the convenient side door, he was more likely to be heard by some light sleeper.

After speculating on the matter for some time, Sharlie came to the conclusion that he was probably engaged on an intrigue with some girl in the neighbourhood, and at last drifted into sleep again.

In spite of her broken night, Sharlie was up next morning in good time to go to early service in the village church, a charming little Norman building. After breakfast she wrote to Mona, letting her know that the luggage she had sent on had arrived safely, then went out of doors.

Going yesterday to the walled garden with a message for Wilson, the head-gardener, she had lingered to admire a fine display of polyanthus, and had told him she was very fond of gardening. He had answered, jestingly, that in that case she was very welcome any time to lend a hand with weeding—he was always glad of an addition to his staff! It would be fun, she thought, to take him at his word.

Accordingly, armed with a basket and a small fork she had discovered in a potting-shed, she opened a small green door set deep in the high wall and let herself into the enchanted world of scent and colour. The garden lay to one side of the house and in front of it, sloping to the south. It was for the most part given over to vegetables and fruit, but there were also beds of flowers planted for cutting. Darwin tulips, polyanthus, late narcissi and wallflowers, white arabis and golden alyssum made a brilliant patchwork pattern, filling the air with scent that blended in a heavy bouquet with the spicy odours of the currant bushes and the sharp, sweet, aromatic essences of herbs.

Along the length of one wall, facing south, there lay a wide herbaceous border where already fat green peony buds were slashed with pink and scarlet, the lowest flowers on the tall spires of the delphiniums were faintly tinged with blue, and the campanulas were hung with azure bells. Between the tall plants at the back and the fruit trees on the wall there ran a narrow path. From here she worked her way among the plants and set to work; in front, the bed had been kept reasonably tidy, but at the back the weeds had flourished during a spell of rainy weather earlier in the month.

Sharlie crouched there, weeding busily, pausing every now and then to stroke a peony's uncrumpling petal, or enjoy the poignant blue of a delphinium blossom, senses sharpened, pleasure infinitely more acute because after all

Richard had not left her life as suddenly as he had walked into it. He would surely telephone to her, or write, asking her to go out with him, arranging further meetings—she was certain of it. Not yet awhile, perhaps, but when the regiment had settled into its new quarters and the inevitable extra work entailed by the move had lessened.

Presently she heard the click of the wrought-iron gate in the wall nearest the house, followed by footsteps on the gravel, and approaching voices, and looking up, saw the Ramswells strolling towards her. Having already wished them both good morning when she met them on their way to breakfast as she returned from early service, Sharlie did not move, but went on with her self-appointed task. A short path cut the border in two halves, and led to a seat set in a yew arbour against the wall. To this seat they took their course, Mrs. Ramswell pausing now and then to pull a weed or behead a dead flower. Sharlie, not realising that the campanulas from among whose roots she was disentangling bindweed were providing perfect camouflage for her blue dress, had no idea they had not seen her there. She went on weeding, lost in her own thoughts, till Mrs. Ramswell's raised voice caught her ear, following apparently on something her husband had been saying.

"You wouldn't listen to me at the time of Averil's marriage. Time has proved that I was right. Won't you, to please me, listen to me now?"

"You're too unworldly in your outlook to be any judge of these things. There are only two things in this world worth possessing. Money and breeding. I began life with neither. But I made the money, and I bought a son-in-law with breeding, and I want my grandchildren to be brought up with every advantage that I lacked at their age. I want them to grow up knowing the right people. And it gives the house a tone, if you know what I mean, to have the future Lord Frostenden spending his week-ends here, and his sister staying with us months on end. Through them, all manner of people come here that would never bother with a pair of old fogies like you and me."

Horrified, Sharlie realised they had not seen her. To make her presence known would be embarrassing for all of them now that she had heard so much not meant for her. Better remain hidden, taking care to hear no more.

So she crouched lower still behind the taller plants and put her hands over her ears.

"Do you really think it's any advantage to the children to grow up among the rackety crowd Nicola and Randolph bring here? Last Sunday, when all those people turned up before dinner, one of them was actually giving George sips of his cocktail. A child of barely five!"

"Oh, well, it maybe wasn't very wise, but it doesn't often happen and it was the Duke of Allerdale that did it, for I saw him from the window."

Mrs. Ramswell made no comment, and for several minutes they sat in silence. At last her husband asked her testily, "Well—what is it you want?"

Sharlie, suffering agonies of cramp among the campanulas, tried to move cautiously into a less uncomfortable position, and in doing so lost her balance. To save herself from falling over she had to take her hands from covering her ears, so that she heard Mrs. Ramswell's answer.

"I want our house to be a home, not a cross between a museum and a cocktail bar for the Heighbrooks and their friends. I don't want Randolph to come here so often, and I want Nicola to leave here altogether. And above all I want Averil to come back to us. Her place is here—"

Quickly Sharlie placed her hands against her ears again, and heard no more.

"Averil has made her own bed and must lie on it. A woman's place is with her husband. I told her so, and you, too, and I'm not a man to change my mind."

"To change one's mind is not a sign of weakness but of strength. It takes courage to admit one may have been mistaken, cut one's losses, reconstruct the pattern of one's life. Always I've sensed something ugly, something *wrong* about both Nicola and Randolph—"

"You must remember Randolph is the children's father. And we'd lose a lot if he and Nicola weren't here. None of their friends would come here for the love of you and me!"

"Their friends! They have no real friends. Just a gang of gold-diggers who come here for the food and drink they get. Oh, Tom—why can't you be content with knowing all the pleasant, ordinary people in the neighbourhood that we might have as friends, the people more like ourselves?

51

My father was a country doctor. Yours was a village black-smith. Why not stop trying to be grand? Why bother about people who only come here for what they can get out of us?"

"We want our grandchildren to start higher on the ladder than we did ourselves. We want them to have every possible advantage."

"Indeed we do! But what advantage will it be to them to start by making contacts with a crowd of people who have an utterly material outlook and a low standard of behaviour? Their own father will be the worst possible influence for them in a year or two."

"Their own father will be Lord Frostenden one day."

"If I could only make you see it isn't *who* you are that matters, but *what* you are! Not what you *have* that counts, but what you *do!*—Tom, do consider what I ask. Do let us rid ourselves of these two parasites and make a fresh start. Let's give up trying to impress the world with our possessions—"

"Even if you were talking sense, d'you realise that Randolph has a hold on us? Tell him to clear out, and he could retaliate by taking away the children."

"He would let us adopt the babies legally if he were paid enough. I quite agree that he will always have a hold on us until they're ours by law. He hinted as much, once, when I put my foot down, and said I wouldn't have him here if he were troublesome."

"Why, what had he been up to?"

"Pestering one of the maids. Mrs. Tollworthy complained of it to me. Not pleasant, having one's own son-in-law, a guest in the house, making love to one of the maids!"

"The aristocracy have different ways from ours . . . The Heighbrooks are a social asset that we can't afford to lose. Not yet awhile, at any rate. We'll think about it, maybe, when we've got more of a footing in the county. If I could get a seat next election on the County Council I would meet more of the right kind of people on my own. But for the present I've said my last word, Eleanor, and that's final!—That's a fine lot of gooseberries coming on."

"Yes. We're having the first tart for lunch to-day." For a few minutes longer they talked about the garden, then rose to go indoors.

On the lawn Nicola and Randolph and half a dozen of their friends were drinking cocktails and excitedly discussing the details, real and rumoured, of a burglary that had taken place last night at Pomfrey Court, where Lady Pomfrey had been robbed of all her jewels by a masked man who was reported to have entered by a ladder taken from a potting-shed and taken them from her dressing-table while she slept.

"How do they know that he was masked, then, if she didn't wake?" Somebody was asking, when Randolph interrupted.

"Hell! My tedious in-laws are upon us. Prepare to exude charm, all of you, from every pore. I must stay in Papa-in-law's good books at all costs—Hul*lo*, sir! Coming to join us in a drink?" He smiled down charmingly at Mr. Ramswell as though his father-in-law were the *one* person in the world he had been longing to see. "Let's see—who do you know? I don't think you've met Lady Angela Transom, have you? Or Major Crofton-Wildermere? I think you know everybody else."

A pretty girl who didn't know the difference between a Gainsborough and a Van Gogh, asked wide-eyed, "Oh— are you Randolph's father-in-law? We've just been envying you your *marvellous* pictures." A dapper young man wearing a double-breasted waistcoat and an orchid in his buttonhole said, "Yes, by jove! Not to mention your still more marvellous bwown shewwy, sir!"

"Ha! Very glad you like it. Don't mind if I have a glass of it myself, now that I'm here. How about you, Eleanor?"

But Mrs. Ramswell had gone quietly indoors, back to the private world she had built up about herself of her own secret thoughts and interests, in which to find a sanctuary from the other side of life.

When they had gone, Sharlie straightened her cramped limbs, and took her tools back to the potting-shed before going in to lunch. Although her eavesdropping had been unintentional she felt guilty: yet it was impossible not to think of the little she had overheard.

So it was Mr. Ramswell's choice, and not his wife's desire, to have the house "a cross between a museum and a cocktail bar"! . . . She was glad that Mrs. Ramswell did not, apparently, care greatly for her son-in-law nor for his sister.

Who, wondered Sharlie as she washed her earthy hands, was Averil, whom Mrs. Ramswell wanted to return here?

The days slid by. In her free time, alone, Sharlie explored the lanes and woods round Swanswick. She went by bus to hear a Chopin recital by Kathleen Long in Bath. Another week-end came and went. Randolph and Nicola had a bottle party on the Saturday evening, to which Randolph caused a photographer to be sent from London by the *Prattler*—much to the gratification of Mr. Ramswell, who posed between a minor actress and a peeress who, although he did not know it, was about to be divorced for the third time. Again, that night, Sharlie heard Randolph leaving the house stealthily, this time soon after midnight.

And every time she heard the telephone ringing its imperious summons, Sharlie asked herself with quickened pulse, "Can this be Richard?" And every time she saw the postman in the distance, or heard the bell ring at the time when he was due, she thought, "He may be bringing me a letter from Richard!"

But the telephone was always someone wanting Nicola, or the fishmonger to say that after all he couldn't let them have the soles, and the only letter that came for Sharlie was one from Mona's mother, hoping she was happy, and saying she must come back to them if ever she wanted a holiday or a rest.

News travels quickly in the countryside, and so she knew, within a few hours of their arrival, that the Midlothian Hussars had come to Rockdown Camp. Surely she would hear from Richard any day now!

Four days, then five, then six went by, and still she had no word of him. The long suspense began to tell on her, making her irritable over trifles that she would not normally have minded, and inclined to start at any sudden noise. She was impatient with herself.

And then one dull grey morning as she was finishing her solitary breakfast, the telephone rang in her sitting-room, and Jackson's voice said from the pantry, "There's a call for you, miss, but I thought you might have gone to Madam's room. I'll put it through to you at once."

"Oh, thank you, Jackson!"

Waiting seemed eternity. All manner of goblin faces she had never noticed before peered at her from the pattern of the curtains as she stood there clutching the receiver as though it wanted to escape her, telling herself it probably wasn't Richard at all, but that shoe shop in Bath about the Glastonbury boots she'd ordered.

At last a man's voice asked, "Is that Miss Raven? Just a minute, please, sir—miss I mean," and Sharlie knew that it wasn't the Bath shoe shop after all, and the grey day seemed suddenly full of promise, as though any moment the sun would struggle through the clouds—for in a minute she would be hearing Richard's voice.

More quickly than she had expected, she heard his crisp "Hullo?" and said demurely, "This is Mrs. Ramswell's secretary speaking."

Richard said gravely, "Oh, I see. Then will you take a message for Miss Raven, please?"

"With pleasure!"

"Then will you tell Miss Raven Major Heronshaw has been extremely busy since he saw her, but would be very glad if she could manage to have tea with him to-day at the Regency Hotel in Bath at four o'clock?"

"I'll ask Miss Raven. Will you hold on, please?"

She flew downstairs to Mrs. Ramswell's sitting-room. It was empty. She knocked on the adjoining bedroom door, but had no answer. Then, as she wondered desperately where to look next, she saw her through the window, spraying a bed of Karen Poulsen roses for greenfly. She ran out.

"Good morning! Oh, please, would it be all right if I had my free afternoon to-day instead of to-morrow? Or do you want me specially for anything to-day?"

Mrs. Ramswell, who disliked driving herself, had been going to ask Sharlie to take her in the afternoon to Dorchester, but the sight of the young radiant face looking at her so anxiously made her change her mind.

"Certainly! Have to-day instead, by all means," she said, and went on with her spraying, glad that her pretty secretary looked so happy, but hoping that it didn't mean she was involved in a romance that might lead soon to marriage. Even in this short time she had grown to rely on her, and though another girl might be equally efficient, it would be difficult to find anyone with such a sympathetic personality, such kindness in her eyes, such friendliness in her smile.

Sharlie ran back upstairs. "Good morning! This is Sharlie speaking. Thank you so much for asking me to have tea with you this afternoon. I'd love to come."

"Good. How about bringing Mrs. Ramswell's secretary along with you? She sounded rather nice, I thought."

"Oh, no! I don't think you'd like her at *all*. She's horrid. She steals peanuts from bird tables," said Sharlie earnestly.

"H'm. I'm very fond of peanuts. I'll have to ask her to come out with me by herself, one of these days. She might be worth knowing.—Four o'clock at the Regency? Will that suit you?"

"Splendidly."

"Good. I'm afraid I have to dash off to a conference at five, so don't be late if you can hep it, will you? An hour is none too long."

After lunch she manicured her hands, painting her nails with deep rose lacquer that was becoming to the warm peach laid by the sun upon her creamy skin, and matched her lipstick. Then she changed into her favourite navy and white outfit.

She set out in plenty of time to catch an earlier bus than was absolutely necessary, for to run any risk of being late was unthinkable, and this was not a day for hurrying. All morning the sun of early June had poured down, filling the valley with shimmering heat, drawing the scent from the long border of Mrs. Simkins pinks under the windows in delicious heady waves. But it was cool in the green tunnel of the avenue. Bees were humming in the limes, and sunlight filtered through the heart-shaped leaves making a dappled pattern of emerald and gold.

"*An hour is none too long,*" Richard had said. It might mean very little. It was the sort of polite remark anyone might make. And yet—and yet his voice had sounded as

56

though those six words had meant more than their actual sense . . .

The drive gates opened on an empty stretch of road midway between the village and a group of farm cottages nearer Bath. One bus stop lay outside the village inn, another by the cottages. Sharlie hesitated for a moment, then decided to walk towards the cottages and wait there in the shade of a yew hedge.

A car stood near the gates, as though waiting for someone. As Sharlie began to walk along the road she heard the engine being started. A moment later the car overtook her, passed her, stopped a few yards beyond her. A girl leaned out: a dark girl with a determined mouth and troubled eyes: a girl whose face was somehow curiously familiar. Sharlie went on towards her, supposing she was going to ask the way, prepared to say the inevitable "I'm sorry, I'm a stranger here!"

The girl asked with a strange urgency, "Are you the secretary at Swanswick?"

Startled, Sharlie answered that she was.

"Then will you please, *please* get in the car and come with me, somewhere where we can talk?"

She must be quite unbalanced, Sharlie thought compassionately. She can't have any possible reason for wanting to talk to me in private. If she did, why not have come to the house?

She said, "I'm very sorry, but I'm meeting somebody in Bath at four. I've got to catch the bus that's due in a few minutes. Won't some other time do instead?"

"I'll take you anywhere you like in time for your appointment, but I've *got* to speak to you. I've waited so long that I'm simply desperate. I heard of you five days ago from Mrs. Wilson—you know, the gardener's wife. I came straight over to the inn at Rillbrook. Every afternoon I've waited where you saw me waiting now, hoping you might come out." She opened the door of the car. "Do *please* come!"

"But why—?"

"Oh—I forgot. Of course, you don't know who I am! It seems so odd for someone not to know me, here. I'm Averil Heighbrook. I'm the Ramswells' daughter. George and Gay are my children!"

CHAPTER FOUR

INCREDULOUSLY Sharlie stared at Averil Heighbrook. Square chin like her father's, dark hair combed back in loose shining waves, rebellious mouth, troubled hazel eyes that one could imagine filled with mischief, lit with laughter, in happier circumstances than were now, apparently, her lot: the likeness to the photograph on Mrs. Ramswell's bureau was unmistakable.

How was it that she had believed the Ramswells' only daughter to be dead? What was it Mrs. Ramswell had told her? Groping in memory, she remembered the words used:

"My daughter . . . is not with us any more."

It had been left with her to construe them as she pleased. She stammered, "I—didn't realise you were alive!"

The other girl said bitterly, "I'm not alive. I'm dead to all of them at home.—Get in, will you? I want to turn into a side road where we're less likely to be seen. I don't want anyone to know I'm in the neighbourhood."

Sharlie got in beside her. A quarter of a mile along the road in the direction of Bath they turned into a narrow lane, with unclipped hedges growing high on either side. That traffic seldom came this way was evident from the grassy surface of the track. A few yards from the entrance Averil stopped the car and switched the engine off.

"Tell me—how are the children?"

"Very well, both of them. George is thrilled because he's just been given a bit of garden of his own. It's about six feet square. He says he's going to grow only pink flowers in it."

George's mother laughed. "He always did like pink best! And Gay? When last I saw her she was just beginning to say a few words."

"She chats away nineteen to the dozen now, though I can't always make out what she's saying. George always seems to understand her, though!"

Averil took out a platinum cigarette-case from her bag and offered it to Sharlie, who refused, then took one herself and lit it, blowing the smoke out through her nostrils, tossing her hair back when she had shut her bag in an impatient way she had.

"Well, now—before I tell you what it is I want you to do for me, I'd better tell you the whole story."

Sharlie said quickly, "Don't tell me anything you may regret!"

"As far as I'm concerned there's nothing that the whole world isn't welcome to know . . . My father is a self-made man, as they say. My mother married him for money, because *her* mother was desperately ill with lung trouble and her one chance of living was to go to Switzerland . . . It did prolong her life a few months longer, I believe. However, that's old history. The point is, that being unable to give Father more than liking, Mother has always felt she'd got to make it up to him in other ways. She's always let him have his way in everything, no matter how much it went against the grain. Never argued. Seldom expressed any opinion of her own. When I was a child I used to rather despise her for it, not knowing the reason, nor the self control it must have taken. But though she meant it for the best of motives, it didn't work out well in ways. Father began to think, in time, there could be only one opinion in the house, and that was his. Well—I grew up taking Father at his own valuation, and thinking Mother sweet but rather futile. Father used to talk to me a lot about how nobody thought anything of you unless you had money and position, and of how I'd got to make a marriage that would give me the position, as the money side of it was all right! I don't think Mother realised for some time what was happening to me. When she did, she did her level best to put some sense into me, by slow and tactful stages. But it was too late. By then I was so chockful of all manner of false values that there wasn't room for any sound ones."

Averil was smoking in quick, nervous puffs. She flicked an inch of cigarette ash through the window. While her head was turned away Sharlie glanced surreptitiously at her watch. A quarter-past three—she was all right for time. She ought to reach the Regency quite easily by four even if they didn't leave here till twenty to.

Averil went on, "All this long story must be deadly boring for you, but I want to put you in the picture, so that you'll know just how it all arose . . . When I was barely eighteen, a few months before I was due to leave school, Mother was rushed into a nursing home for an emergency operation. The staff at Swanswick were quite capable of carrying on on their own, but I was longing to leave school, and so I made a great display of daughterly devotion and insisted that I must come back to run the house. Daddy was quite pleased that I should, and so I had my way. I usually did, in those days! . . . It wasn't as exciting as I'd hoped. We came here from the north eleven years ago—five years before this happened, but though people had called, they hadn't done much more about us. Swanswick was really rather like one of those National Trust houses, with us tucked away as caretakers in our own quarters. One expected to see the furniture and pictures railed off from the admiring sightseers. People came once, and marvelled, but they didn't come again, so it was pretty dreary for me until one day we went to Newbury races, and some man Daddy knew was talking to Randolph, and introduced us. We asked him to come back with us for dinner, and ten days later we were engaged. Father was enchanted! It was exactly what he'd wanted for me. Randolph hadn't a bean, but that didn't matter—he was an Honourable and Lord Frostenden's only son. It wasn't only the prospect of being Lady Frostenden one day that dazzled me, though—I really was crazy about Randolph in those days. Head over heels in love with him."

Averil paused to light a second cigarette from the stub of her first one.

"He has tremendous charm," said Sharlie, glancing at her watch again. Half-past three. "I'm afraid we'll have to leave here in ten minutes. I simply must be at the Regency by four," she said. The other girl nodded shortly, and went on with her story.

"Mother came back from the nursing home a fortnight before we were going to be married—we only had a month's engagement. For the first time in my memory she opposed Father in something he had set his heart on. She said I was too young and inexperienced to know my own mind, that we ought to have at least a year's engagement, and that I ought to have the chance of meeting lots of other men before I married. I know now, though I didn't at the time, that she kept telling Father she had an intuition that Randolph was no good, that all his charm was just a thin veneer and didn't mean a thing, but Daddy wouldn't hear a word against him. Randolph had summed him up and was playing a succession of trump cards in the shape of strings of impressive relatives and friends. Some of them had pretty shady records in addition to their titles, but of course Father had no idea of that."

"What about your brother? How did he take it all?"

"Oh, Alan was at Oxford. He's always been the cat that walked on his lone. Since we were in the nursery I've never known what was in his mind.—Well, after honeymooning in Venice we settled down in Eaton Place to live on the extremely generous allowance Father gave me. Randolph had wanted a marriage settlement, but Father had the sense at least to keep the purse strings in his own hands. He offered Randolph a job in the firm, but Randolph said he'd rather stand on his own feet and make his way without help. The fact was, as I very soon realised, that he had no intention of settling down to business hours. He did make a certain amount of money by fits and starts, though how, I never knew. He lost a good deal gambling . . . From the day we came back from our honeymoon he gave up the pretence of having married me because he was in love with me. He still turned on the battery of his charm occasionally when he wanted to get something out of me, but mostly he made no bones about being bored with me. He liked women older than himself. I was far too trusting and ingenuous in those days! So from the beginning I was disillusioned and unhappy. Things went from bad to worse. At first he wasn't actively unkind, but after a bit I must have got on his nerves. He lost no opportunity of jibing at me, hurting me, humiliating me. Yet in a way, against my will, I was still infatuated with him. Every now and then we'd have a passionate reconciliation, he'd turn on all his old charm and I would hope against hope that things were going to be better in the future. But they weren't—though I was happier for a few months after George was born. At last I couldn't stand it any longer. I came home to Swanswick, told my parents the whole story, said I wanted to divorce Randolph—I

61

had evidence, all right—and was sure they'd have me back. Mother was on my side, of course. But Father was appalled. He wouldn't hear of it. He'd bought me a position in Debrett and I must keep it, willy-nilly. So I went back to Randolph—Father said he'd cut off my allowance if I didn't. We had another of those exhausting reconciliations that didn't last, although I honestly did try my best to make a go of it. Finally, when Gay was nineteen months old—three months ago—I took the children and their nice elderly nannie to rooms in Cornwall, in a farmhouse. I left a note for Randolph saying I'd pay three-quarters of my allowance from Father into his account—Father needn't have known that I'd left Eaton Place for more than a holiday. But there's a sadistic streak in Randolph, a love of power that's the result, I've always thought, of being neglected and not wanted much as a small boy. His mother had no use for either of her children; she was mad on hunting, lived for that, and racing. He came and took the children away from me—packed them and Nannie into the car one day when I'd gone to the village, shopping, and brought them here, to Swanswick. What he told my parents, I don't know. Father cut off my allowance at once, and said I wasn't to set foot inside the gates unless I was prepared to go back to Randolph. He dismissed kind old Nannie, who adored the children and was fond of me and would have given me a chance of seeing them now and then, and engaged a hard young woman who knows all about psychology and calories and nothing about loving them, and gave her orders that I must never see them. I did try, once, but there was a scene—she hustled them away, and George was upset, and cried—" She bit her lip. "I can't do that. It isn't fair to them."

"How can they prevent you from seeing your own children?"

"Having walked out on their father I'm in a difficult position as regards my 'rights' over them . . . Mother wrote me a heartbroken letter when it all happened, and I gather Father made her promise not to write again."

Sharlie said, "I'm terribly sorry to interrupt you, but I wonder if you'd mind telling me the rest on the way to

Bath? I can't be late—it's rather important to me not to be."

Averil tossed back her hair impatiently. "Don't worry. I'll get you there in time . . . The position is now that Father's practically trying to starve me into going back to Randolph—"

"But I just can't understand his attitude! Surely it's your happiness that matters to him more than anything? His only daughter—"

"Yes. But he wants me to be happy in *his* way. Not mine. He's convinced he knows what's best for me—and that what's best is for me to be Lady Frostenden in due course. I know it seems incredible, but it's true. Now listen. You must be wondering why I'm telling you all this. I want you to do something for me. I want you somehow to think out a way of bringing the children to see me now and then."

Sharlie made a quick gesture of refusal. "I can't! I—

"I knew you'd say that. But you can. You must! I shall go crazy if you don't! Use your imagination! Think what it means to me, never to see them, not to know anything about them—and they're growing up so quickly! You could easily invent some reason for taking them out in the car. The nurse must have some time off. You could volunteer to take them for a picnic. Who looks after them when she goes out?"

"She hasn't been away from them since I've been here. I think she has a week-end once a month, and then your mother looks after them with Mary's help."

"That would be your chance! You could offer to take them off her hands one afternoon and I could meet you with a picnic tea."

As she talked, Averil had been gazing straight in front of her. Now she turned to Sharlie a face so lit with hope, eyes so bright and eager, that it was almost more than Sharlie could bear to disappoint her.

She said, "I'm sorrier than I can tell you. But you must see that I can't do it. I can't be disloyal to my employers. I know it probably sounds priggish and tiresome—but I simply *can't*!"

Averil seized her wrist. "Oh, please! You must! You were my one hope!" she said imploringly. "I shall go crazy if I can't see them, and I can't think of any other way . . . I'd even do as Father hopes I will, and go back ignominiously to Randolph, only it would be no good. There's nothing worse for children than to bring them up in an atmosphere of rows and ugliness and wretchedness. I'm not quite selfish enough for that. Won't you, just once, do it for me?"

"No. But I tell you what I'll do, that would be better than nothing. I could write to you regularly, a sort of diary of their doings, and post it to you every week. I could take snapshots of them, too.—Now we simply *must* go. As it is, I'll be a few minutes late, and I did desperately want to be in time. We can arrange details as we go."

For a dreadful moment Sharlie was afraid that Averil was going to refuse to leave without further discussion. She said, "But I— Oh, well—!" Then with compressed lips began to back the car out of the lane, so fast that Sharlie instinctively gripped the side of the door. Luckily no other car was passing and they left the lane in safety and shot down the main road.

"You'd tell me little funny things they say? And let me know at once if one of them were ill?"

"Of course I would . . . I'm wondering if it wouldn't be best to tell Mrs. Ramswell I've been talking to you, and what I'm going to do. I'm sure she wouldn't mind, and unnecessary secrets are such a mistake."

"Better not. It might upset her.—Oh, I don't know! I'll leave it to you."

Sharlie wished she wouldn't drive so recklessly, swinging out wide as she took her corners, cutting in between a lorry and a bus that laboured uphill.

Averil said, "Tell her, if you tell her anything at all, I'm working as receptionist for Betty Sherren's brother. He's a doctor in Wimpole Street. Mother will be wondering how I'm managing for money. I did send her my address, but when I wrote I hadn't a job . . . If ever you change your mind about fixing up for me to see the children, send me a wire. David's an angel, he'd let me off any time at a moment's notice. I'll post you my address this evening. Your name is Raven, isn't it?"

Mechanically she said, "Yes. Sharlie Raven." Mechanically she answered, as far as she was able, questions about George and Gay—whether George ever spoke of her, whether the new nurse let them have a night-light—George was frightened if he woke in the dark. But though her heart was wrung with pity for the unhappy, self-willed girl beside her, it was of Richard she was thinking: Richard, who would even now be waiting for her, looking at his watch, perhaps thinking her unpunctual and unreliable.

She wondered after whether it was because Averil sensed her thoughts that she drove so speedily, or if she were alway as reckless as this afternoon. She said at last, "I don't know if you're hurrying specially because I'm late, but honestly, I'd rather get there a few minutes later still, than run the risk of never——"

"—of never getting there at all," she had been going to say. But the words died in the screaming of brakes, the crash and grind of metal on stone, as Averil took a corner far too quickly, in the middle of the road, swerved to avoid a car coming towards her, also on the crown of the road, skidded, and with a sickening jolt and lurch landed in a ditch, against a wall.

For a moment time seemed to stand still. The silence seemed more sinister than the noise it followed. Then there came a clatter of running feet, the shrill sound of excited voices as several people who had been invisible before mysteriously appeared, apparently from nowhere. An elderly woman with a shopping basket, a younger woman carrying a baby, a couple of children in their early teens, and a middle-aged farm labourer stared with anxious curiosity at the two girls. Sharlie swallowed, unclenched her shaking hands from the door they had been clutching, and with an effort managed to smile reassuringly at them.

Beside her Averil said in a shaken voice, "Gosh! That was a narrow squeak! What about the other car?"

The labourer said, "They're all right. The gen'leman's comin' for to see how you be farin' ."

The "gen'leman" was a commercial traveller who, when his anxiety was relieved, was exceedingly irate with Averil. She had caused him, he declared, to buckle his mudguard on a gatepost. Small thanks to her that matters were no worse! He'd want her name and address for his insurance company.

65

Averil retorted that he, as much as she, was in the wrong. Fortunately at this juncture an A.A. scout appeared and took charge of the proceedings.

Sharlie had been jarred and shaken; her head was aching. She leaned back in her seat, resting her head on her hand. Richard's words were echoing in her mind: *"An hour is none too long . . ."*

They wouldn't have even an hour together now. He must be thinking she'd forgotten he had asked her to have tea with him . . . As though she could! If only she could let him know now what had happened, so that he wouldn't wait and wonder and finally leave the Regency at five o'clock not knowing why she had failed him.

Then she had an idea. She asked the A.A. scout, "Is there a telephone box near here that I could use?"

He told her there was an A.A. box at the corner, and gave her the key. Five minutes later she was describing Richard to a girl with a sympathetic voice, and surprisingly soon after that Richard was saying, "Sharlie? What's all this about an accident? Are you all right?"

Briefly she told him that a friend had been driving her to Bath, and what had followed.

"Sure you're all right?" he persisted.

"Perfectly. Just a bit wobbly at the knees! But I'm afraid there isn't any hope of reaching you before five."

"Even if there were you'd far better go home and lie down. You're bound to be a good deal shaken up. Do keep quiet for the rest of the day. Will you?"

"Probably."

"I wish you'd be a bit more definite than that!"

"All right, I will." Even in her disappointment at not seeing him, it was comforting that he was concerned about her.

"No hope that you can come another afternoon this week instead of to-day?"

"Not a hope. I have one afternoon a week, as well as Sundays, and this was it."

"M'm. I haven't got many free moments myself, but one must eat! And one can occasionally squeeze an hour between things.—I say, Mrs. Freeland—Freemanson—what's her name?"

"Do you mean Mrs. Freemantle?"

"That's it. She rang me up just after I'd been talking to

you this morning, and asked me there to tennis on Sunday afternoon. I said I'd go. Any chance of seeing you?"

"None at all. I'm Mrs. Ramswell's secretary, not a guest!"

"I know. But even so I'd hoped you might be somewhere on the scene. Too bad. I'm sorry."

"I'll have to go now."

"How are you going to get back to Swanswick?"

"In my friend's car, I expect. I don't think it can be damaged too much to be able to carry on under its own steam. Good-bye!"

"Good-bye. I still hope you'll be visible on Sunday. If you are we must fix up another meeting. If not, I'll ring you up, or write."

Back at the scene of the accident Sharlie found a breakdown lorry, summoned by the A.A. scout, had pulled the car out of the ditch, and that it had suffered no worse damage than the loss of a good deal of paint from the side that had scraped against the wall, and a badly crumpled mudguard.

She asked if Averil would mind driving her back to Swanswick as it was now too late for her to go to Bath. Averil was full of penitence for causing her to miss her appointment, and drove to a point on the road near the gate but where the car was out of sight of the lodge.

"You'll tell me every single little thing you think I'd like to know about the children? And send me snapshots as soon as you can take them?"

Sharlie assured her that she would.

"I believe it would be better not to say anything to Mother about having met me. Then if father does find out, she can say she knew nothing about it. I don't want her to have to fight any battles on my account."

"I expect you're right," said Sharlie. As she walked slowly back along the green lime-scented tunnel of the avenue, she was reflecting ruefully that if Mr. Ramswell did find out that his wife's secretary was in communication with his daughter, there was little doubt that she would immediately lose the post she liked so well, and which above all was in the same neighbourhood as Richard. Yet she was convinced that, although to have arranged for Averil to see the children would be disloyal to her employers, she would be doing no wrong in sending her news of George and Gay. She couldn't, wouldn't go back on her promise to the distracted young mother, no matter what the cost to herself might be.

The following Saturday morning, as Sharlie and Mrs. Ramswell were discussing ways and means of filling a vacancy that had occurred in the list of speakers at the Women's Institute, Nicola came in. Not bothering to bid Sharlie good morning, she said to Mrs. Ramswell, "I did tell you, didn't I, that I've asked some people to tennis to-morrow afternoon? I thought I'd better remind you in case you wanted Miss Raven to fetch cakes from Bath."

"You didn't tell me, Nicola. I should be glad to know in good time of any arrangements you may make for entertaining here, so that the servants' outings may be considered. Miss Raven will be busy this afternoon. You'd better go yourself to get some cakes."

Nicola looked taken aback but said, "Oh, very well."

"You should be back in time for tea if you catch the bus that leaves the village just after two," said Mrs. Ramswell pleasantly, making it clear she did not expect Nicola to take the car. "How many people have you asked?"

Nicola hid her resentment and surprise at being questioned regarding the party she proposed to give, as she had given many others, in this house where she was guest but was accustomed to behaving as hostess.

"Nine, so far, counting Randolph and myself. Yolande Lebois was coming, too, but she has sprained her ankle. I must do some telephoning and get another girl. Ten is the best number for two courts."

As she turned to leave the room Mrs. Ramswell stopped her. "One moment, Nicola!" She turned to Sharlie. "Do you play tennis?"

"Yes—I love it!"

"Would you like to play to-morrow afternoon?"

Sharlie, embarrassed, said, "Oh—yes! But I—" She looked uncomfortably at Nicola.

While the brief exchange had passed between the others, Nicola had been doing some rapid thinking. She didn't at all like the new air of authority in Mrs. Ramswell's manner—almost as though the worm were going to turn at last. Perhaps she *had* been going a bit far lately, taking things too much for granted, treating the house too much like an hotel. It suited her extremely well to live at Swanswick, free of cost, and never better than at the moment. For she must marry again, since earning her own living held no attraction for her and her income was too small to buy her the expensive way of living she enjoyed. Yet to find the ideal husband wasn't going to be too easy. One possible candidate was attractive but had no money; another was a millionaire but also a deadly bore; a third, who was good-looking and rich and danced divinely, was notoriously a philanderer. This Major Heronshaw who had come to Rockdown seemed to have more advantages as a possible husband than any man she'd met for many a long day. Reputedly wealthy, his dark, enigmatic good looks were of the type that most attracted her, and his apparent indifference to herself was piquing. She must alter that . . . Now, of all moments, she must run no risk of having to leave Swanswick! Better to put up for the moment with a small annoyance than risk the security of her tenure here. Wiser to smooth the ruffled feathers of her hostess, if ruffled they were, than risk the loss of any of the advantages Swanswick had to offer. No need to worry about this pretty nobody—mere prettiness had no chance nowadays in competition with polished poise, and grooming, and sophistication. And probably the girl's idea of tennis was mere pat ball in comparison with Nicola's own finished style, that was the result of competent coaching since she was a child. And if she did get a bit above herself, well, one could put her well and truly in her place at some more auspicious moment than the present.

So, for the benefit of Mrs. Ramswell, Nicola gave the young secretary one of her most charming smiles—and Nicola's smile could be particularly charming when she pleased—and said, "Yes, do play with us! Lovely to be saved the bother of getting another girl. How silly of me not to have thought of you before!"

Shortly before noon on Sunday, Nicola put her head round the door of Sharlie's sitting-room. Sharlie, who was writing a letter, looked up, surprised by this unusual attention.

"May I come in?" asked Nicola, her manner so pleasant that Sharlie felt it had been horrid of her in the past to suspect the young widow of being deliberately disagreeable to her. It wasn't fair to tar her with the same brush as her brother, either. Probably the poor girl was merely miserable when she seemed aloof, and curt at times from sheer unhappiness.

"Yes, do. Won't you sit down?" she said, moving some sewing from the most comfortable chair.

Nicola perched instead upon the table, swinging her slim legs with their spiky ankles, and lit a cigarette. "It looks as though we're going to have a lovely afternoon for our tennis!" she remarked.

"Yes, it does look promising," Sharlie agreed. Funny, how she could never seem to feel at ease with Nicola.

"What are you going to wear? We mustn't clash!" said Nicola. "I saw two sisters last week wearing frocks that positively screamed at one another. Lemon and corn colour. Do let's avoid that risk, at all costs!"

Sharlie was surprised by this interest in her attire. After all, even if their frocks did clash, they wouldn't be in such close contact as all that. The men's white flannels would be there as well. She said, "I haven't decided, yet."

"You lucky girl! You must have lots of choice, then," said Nicola. "Do show me what you've got. I adore seeing clothes!"

Sharlie was more astonished than ever. She often wondered how it was that Nicola contrived to have so many smart frocks and suits. Her own far simpler and less costly wardrobe couldn't possibly interest the older girl, whose taste and mode of living were so different from her own. She tried to pass the matter off by saying lightly that she had nothing worth seeing, only a very few, very ordinary garments!

Nicola persisted. "Let me have a look at them."

In face of such determination it was difficult to refuse without seeming churlish. Reluctantly Sharlie led the way to her bedroom and flung wide the wardrobe. "There! A very modest collection!" she declared, and after a moment would have closed the door again, but Nicola put out a long pale hand and lightly touched a washing frock.

"You're fond of blue!"

70

"Yes. And if one's rather short of money, one's got to have one basic colour. Blue is a good one."

Nicola touched Sharlie's only afternoon frock, of printed Tricel in muted pastel colours. "Pretty," she said.

"I'm glad you like it."

"Were you thinking of wearing it this afternoon?"

"For tennis?" Sharlie was surprised. "Well, no. I'd thought of a white linen." She indicated two plain frocks with pleated skirts.

Nicola raised her eyebrows. "One of those? Oh . . . You *do* realise it's going to be a party, don't you? Not just a four for a knock-up?" She took the Tricel frock from its hanger, held it against Sharlie. "Terribly becoming to you . . . Well, I'll leave you to your letter-writing." She tossed the frock on the bed and went away, leaving Sharlie looking at it undecidedly.

Nicola had made it obvious that she thought the white frocks too plain for this afternoon, and that something smarter, such as the tricel, would be more suitable for the occasion. Nicola had far more experience in such matters than herself. And yet she couldn't imagine playing energetic tennis in that frock! It would look all wrong, out of place on a court, to her own way of thinking.

Still undecided, she asked Mary when the housemaid brought her lunch, "Mary, what do people wear when they come here to tennis parties?"

"The young ladies, do you mean? Just plain white, linen or pique mostly, like the two you have yourself."

"Mrs. Freemantle, too?"

"Oh, yes! I've just been pressing her white pique for this afternoon. The laundry sent it back not to her liking, so it was 'Press this for me, will you, Mary?'—never thought of doing it for herself, and me with extra work at the weekend, and Mr. Heighbrook never out of his room till nearly twelve!"

Light dawned painfully on Sharlie. So Nicola had been trying to lead her on to make an exhibition of herself, so that she would appear ridiculous and overdressed this afternoon! Tears stung her eyes. Why should she be so spiteful and unkind to someone who had done her no harm, and could in no way rival her?

71

She wouldn't take part in this hateful party where she wasn't wanted! She would send a note now to Nicola by Mary, making some polite excuse . . .

Then, as she sat down at the writing-table, second thoughts prevailed. Once already this week fate had cheated her of a meeting with Richard. It would be childish to cut off her nose to spite her face!

Slim in her white slip, she brushed her shining hair, remembering with increasing confidence an episode of the previous August.

School tennis, and after that an occasional game with friends had been her only experience of the game until last summer. Then, as luck would have it, a man whose name was famous in the world of tennis happened to be staying nearby while Sharlie was at York. Happening one day to see her with three other girls playing tennis, he had strolled up to them when they had finished playing, commenting on their play, and volunteering sound advice.

The others had thought it "frightful cheek!" of the ugly stranger in the late forties to poke his nose in where he wasn't wanted. Only Sharlie had thought it nice of him to bother, and lingered when the others went indoors, asking for advice about some stroke of hers that never quite came off. And he had told her that if she were really keen he'd give her a few hints another time.

Since it was obvious that he knew what he was talking about, she had replied that she would be very grateful. For the next week or two they had gone off together when they happened to be simultaneously free, and he had coached her on one of the courts of a preparatory school whose headmaster had given them permission to use it when they chose, the boys being on holiday. It had amused and pleased him to help the girl who tried so hard as well as having natural aptitude for the game, and was so charming to him though she had no notion who he was, nor that the lessons he was giving her for nothing would have cost her what to her was probably a small fortune if he had been giving them professionally.

The other girls had laughed at Sharlie, saying good-naturedly that she must be hard up for a boy friend, to bother with the middle-aged tennis-player!

Only when he had left York did she tell them, greatly to their envy, what she had only learnt herself on saying goodbye; that he was Ralph Dobell, of Davis Cup fame . . .

She was glad now for that episode, as she slipped into her white linen frock with its short pleated skirt. The knowledge that Dobell had thought her worth the trouble of coaching gave her fresh confidence and courage.

She waited in her room until she heard a car arriving, and looking out saw two girls accompanied by two men she had seen here before talking and laughing on the drive with Nicola and Randolph. A moment later a second car, an open one, came round the corner of the house. Richard was driving. Another man was sitting by him, and a third sat behind.

Sharlie took one last look at herself to make sure no final adjustment was necessary. Gravely her dark blue eyes looked back at her.

She made a face at her reflection.

"Smile, can't you? You're going to a tennis party—not the dentist!"

The mirrored face laughed back at her. Holding her head high, she ran downstairs.

CHAPTER FIVE

THE tennis-courts lay below the house, and to the left of it, the garden being on the right. As Sharlie joined the others they were discussing how to play. Richard was standing with his back to her; she recognised the men who had come with him as Captain Brounlie and the lad he had told her was Copper Kendall, one of his subalterns, when they were dining together at Franchini's.

Nicola gave no sign of seeing the newcomer, though she was facing her as the younger girl came down the path. Sharlie stood hesitating on the outskirts of the group, feeling schoolgirlish and gauche. Then Richard turned to toss his jacket on a seat, and saw her.

"Sharlie! So you're coming to play, too, after all! Good!" he exclaimed.

Everyone turned to look at her. Nicola could no longer pretend to be unaware that she was there. She swept her up and down with an appraising glance, expressionless, showing none of her annoyance that her spiteful little plan had failed and the secretary, instead of wearing the printed frock that would have been so out of place upon the tennis-court, looked charming in a crisp white frock, her glossy hair held in place by a wide band of deep blue velvet echoing the colour of her eyes. Tiresome, too, that the girl and Richard Heronshaw had known one another previously. Nicola wondered what was the extent of their acquaintance or friendship, promising herself that she would find some means of nipping it in the bud—or if it had gone beyond the budding stage, would end its blooming.

She said, "Oh, there you are, Miss Raven!"—implying by her tone that Sharlie had kept them waiting. She told the others, "Miss Raven is Mrs. Ramswell's secretary. She's deputising for poor Yolande Lebois, who's sprained her ankle. Too bad, isn't it!" This time the implication was that Sharlie was an indifferent substitute, asked reluctantly to fill a gap because no one better was available. Nicola made no introductions. Having informed the others of the secretary's name and position, she had done enough; there was no need to tell the Raven girl with whom she played.

They had already tossed for who should sit out first; the lot had fallen on Major Musbury, a tall man in the thirties, whose reddish hair was already receding. He had been one of the quartet who had been the first arrivals. Nicola took it for granted that Sharlie should join him, and the others all trooped off to play.

Sharlie and Philip Musbury sat side by side in two deckchairs. His one absorbing interest in life was racing. When he had discovered that his companion had no opinion as to whether Jumping Jehoshophat had a good chance for the Leger, and didn't even know that Young King Cole was favourite for the Gold Cup, he abandoned all pretence of interest in her, answered her attempts to find some subject of mutual interest with the briefest mono-syllables and sat in moody silence, watching small dark Lydia Kellaway, who knew the Racing Calendar by heart and could have stood up to a gruelling examination on Ruff's *Guide to the Turf*.

Presently Nicola sent them off to play together against Copper Kendall and Lydia Kellaway, while she sat looking on with Ronald Brounlie in animated conversation. Their laughter rang in Sharlie's ears, mocking her own recent failure in the art of making small talk. Nor was her self-confidence increased by Major Musbury's trans-formation from gloomy silence to cheerful bantering as he walked with Lydia on to the court, leaving her to follow with Copper. After they had tossed for service, he and Lydia continued their gay repartee across the net, joined now by Copper, for several minutes before he tossed the balls to his waiting partner. It was herself Sharlie blamed for being gauche and awkward, instead of their bad manners.

It was the first time she had played tennis this summer. Her first service smashed into the net; her second, in her anxiety not to serve a double fault, was accurate but slow. Lydia sent it skimming to land just inside their back line, where Major Musbury missed it. As the game began, so it continued. Sharlie, tense and ill at ease, felt she could do nothing right. Her timing was all wrong, her aim inaccurate, she felt clumsy and awkward. Nor was her partner's attitude helpful. He seemed more interested in chaffing Lydia across the net than in backing up his partner's efforts:

and she, instead of realising that she was playing with an ill-mannered and selfish partner, too preoccupied with his infatuation for Lydia to be considerate to Sharlie, saw herself in her humility as an unwanted outsider, a nonentity so lacking in personality that the others treated her as though she wasn't there.

When they had been beaten six two, six one, Philip called a perfunctory "Thanks, partner!" and joined the others at the net, where they continued some laughing argument they had begun during the last game. Sharlie walked alone, with bent head, back to the chairs, wondering why she had been playing so badly. It was horribly disappointing. Being ignored and—yes, humiliated—wouldn't have mattered half so much, mightn't in fact have happened, if she had shown her old form . . .

"Pride comes before a fall," she told herself, "it serves me right for wanting to show off." She was thankful that Richard had not been a witness of her bad play and of what she felt to be her failure to join with the others.

Ronald Brounlie, rose to help her as she was pulling on her deep blue cardigan, and would have drawn her into talk, but Nicola prevented him by continuing to tell him some tale of a mutual friend as though no newcomer had joined them, and perforce he had to give her his attention. Sharlie took a chair a little way apart from them, wearing a bright fixed smile. She'd look as though she were enjoying every moment of this hateful party, if the effort killed her.

"Time to play once more before tea!" Nicola said as the other players finished their third set. She was well pleased to find that, as she had hoped, the girl who had been forced unwanted on her party was little better than a rabbit. Thinking out her plan of action, she had decided that her best move would be to make Sharlie play with Richard. No man enjoyed the handicap of an incompetent partner; he would like Sharlie none the better after suffering from her ineptitude on the court.

"Let's see . . . Ronald, you and I will take on Richard and Miss Raven. Randolph, you arrange another four.— Dear me!—What a lot of R's!" she exclaimed.

Sharlie felt her lips go dry, her heart beating in uneven, heavy thuds as she took off her cardigan. If only she were playing as she'd played last summer after Dobell had coached her! If only she could walk on to the court light-heartedly, instead of being filled with dread of letting Richard down!

Beside her Richard's voice said quietly, "Not tired, are you? You're looking rather white."

She shook her head. "I'm all right. But I'm afraid you're going to find me a bit of a handicap. I'm playing vilely! Worse than ever in my life, I think."

"Not *really*?" Richard said. "How shattering. I mean, this is a matter of life and death, isn't it? We're not just playing to enjoy ourselves or anything like that!"

Sharlie looked up, and met the laughter in his eyes. Suddenly all her being was flooded with delicious happiness. No matter how badly she might play, it wouldn't matter. It wouldn't matter if Nicola still contrived to keep her hovering on the chilly fringes of the general talk, excluded from the laughter. Nothing mattered save the lovely knowledge that she and Richard looked at life from the same angle, loved the same things, shared a secret wordless understanding . . .

Last time she had walked on to the court she had been tense from self-consciousness caused by the knowledge of Nicola's cold, critical eyes watching her. This time she felt buoyantly carefree.

"Their service," Richard said. "I expect you'd rather have the right court, wouldn't you?"

She nodded.

"Attagirl!" said Richard, going to the net.

Deliberately Nicola delayed her first service, fiddling with her belt, smoothing back an imaginary piece of hair, and for a moment, as she waited, nervousness took Sharlie in its grip again, as had been Nicola's amiable hope.

Then it came, stinging and swift, cunningly placed. She took it with a brilliant backhand drive that sent it spinning to the back of the court, well down the centre. Nicola called "Mine!" and hit it into the net.

Richard returned her service with a hard shot to the lefthand corner of the court, from where Ronald sent it back. Richard volleyed it. Ronald volleyed back, past Richard's head.

77

Lithe and swiftly, Sharlie ran. The ball landed just inside the left-hand corner of the court. She sent it skimming between their opponents . . .

"Love thirty," said Richard. "Pity you're in such bad form, partner!"

Something happened then to Sharlie. The joy of movement took possession of her. All that Dobell had told her, all that she had so laboriously practised, became instinctive, no longer a matter for conscious effort. Body and mind moved together in perfect harmony.

Copper Kendall paused in pulling off his sweater. "By Jove! There's hard hitting for you! Can't make out what's happened to that girl—what's her name?—Sharlie—"

The others lingered, then decided not to play, they'd watch, instead. It didn't look like being a long set, anyway.

It wasn't. The score was six one, five love, fifteen forty, when Sharlie sent the winning stroke flashing down the court to land an inch inside the black line, skimming so hard and fast that Nicola's fierce dive was unavailing.

"Thank you, partner!" Richard said. "Wonderful of me to beat them, considering the fearsome handicap you imposed on me!"

She met his eyes, and laughed. "Thank goodness I was playing better this time than at first," she admitted.

Nicola was saying to Ronald Brounlie that she didn't know what in the world had happened to her game—she had been playing abominably.

"You were playing very well. We were outclassed, that's all," said Ronald cheerfully. As they walked together off the court he said to Sharlie, "That's a wizard backhand stroke of yours—looks so deceptively gentle!"

"Yes—Sharlie's a dark horse," said Richard, as he helped her with her cardigan.

The others had gone ahead of them towards the house. Nicola said graciously to Sharlie, "Do join us in the dining-room for tea, Miss Raven!"

"Thank you so much," said Sharlie pleasantly, giving no sign of her amusement at the men's expressions of surprise that any other alternative was possible. Poor girl, she thought compassionately, how tragic that her unhappiness over losing her husband should have had this effect on her, made her all spikes and claws and bitterness . . .

78

Tea was served buffet fashion in the dining-room. The parlourmaid poured out, while Jackson handed round the cups. Sharlie would have handed sandwiches, but Richard took them from her. "I'll do that."

Copper Kendall said, "No, let me, sir," and they were left together. Nicola lost no time in separating them, telling Richard that she specially wanted him to see a fine old map of the neighbourhood that was hanging near the window. There she gathered a little group about them. Ronald Brounlie, blue-eyed, clean-shaven, more a naval than an army type, came to where Sharlie stood by herself near the door, and made pleasant small talk.

Presently Richard called across the room, "Sharlie! What was the name of that old street in York—Whip-ma-some-thing? Do you remember?"

"Whip-ma-whop-ma-gate," she told him. Everybody laughed.

"There's a name rather like it here. Come and look." So she became part of the group, too. The others called her Sharlie, following Richard's lead—even Randolph, who had never called her anything but "you" before, as though even the effort of remembering that her name was Raven was too much trouble.

"I'd no idea that you were such a star turn on the tennis-court," he said. "You'll have to play with me when we go out again, to compensate for all these cakes I've eaten!" Sharlie could feel Nicola's annoyance, and was sorry, in her own pleasure, to be a source of irritation.

A lull fell in the general talk, broken by Lydia Kellaway, who had apparently just returned to the neighbourhood after a short absence. "Somebody tell me all the local doings!" she demanded. "What's been happening? Any more burglaries?"

A chorus answered her.

"My dear! Haven't you *heard*? All Lady Pomfrey's jewellery—"

"And Mrs. Tremsett's pearls—"

"And not a single clue, though the pearls were the eighth local burglary in three months—"

Richard said, "I wonder how much longer the fellow will get away with it. He's bound to slip up, one of these days!"

"It might remain an unsolved mystery, like the Jack the Ripper murders," Randolph said. "Must be a man with pluck and a cool head."

"There's probably more than one man, although only one has been seen," Major Musbury suggested. "Probably a second fellow waiting with a car."

"Do you suppose he's armed?" Lydia wondered.

"Yes—Mrs. Tremsett woke and saw him, tall and slight and wearing a black mask. He pointed a revolver at her when he saw she was awake, and whispered that if she roused the house he'd shoot. The poor soul lay there trembling for at least ten minutes before she dared to leave her bed and wake the servants. By the time the police came there was no sign of anyone. She hadn't heard a car, either."

"I wouldn't mind wagering that he's single-handed. Must be exciting to go off into the night alone and creep about an unfamiliar house, not knowing what lies hidden in the dark—disaster, or a rich reward! He must have guts, whoever he is," said Randolph. "One can't help rather admiring the fellow!"

Sharlie said, "I don't think there's anything in the least admirable in the sort of courage that is used for personal gain at the expense of other people. I can't see anything heroic about theft. In any circumstances it must be mean and sordid."

There was a general murmur of assent, interrupted by Randolph.

"You can't deny it must take pluck—"

"Armed against any defenceless person who might try to stop him?" said Richard scornfully.

"He mayn't be armed at all. It may be just some toy weapon he uses as a bluff," Randolph argued.

You could see, thought Sharlie, that the moral aspect of the matter meant nothing whatever to him. Curiously she looked at him, reflecting that one didn't feel that he was positively bad, but simply empty of all good. Randolph returned her gaze. Startled by the anger in his eyes, she averted her own quickly.

Nicola broke in on the discussion by suggesting a return to the tennis-courts. The tension broke as they abandoned teacups and went out of doors again.

As they left the front door side by side Richard exclaimed, "I nearly forgot—" and slipped a hand into the pocket of his jacket to bring out a note. He handed it to Sharlie.

"I'd meant to give this to the butler for you if I didn't see you. I—"

Behind them Nicola called, "Oh, Richard! Do tell me—"

"Read it and let me know the answer when there's an opportunity," said Richard, turning back to Nicola.

Sharlie walked on by herself reading the note. Would she, asked Richard's clear firm writing, go with him that evening for a meal to a little inn he had discovered where they fed one rather well? If so, if she would let him have a verbal answer by the bearer of the note, he'd send her word when he was leaving. They would drop the men he would be bringing with him, at the mess, and then go on together.

Sharlie thrust the note deep in the pocket of her cardigan as Nicola said, "Will you sit out this time, Miss Raven?"

She settled herself in a deck-chair, caring not at all that Randolph, looking sullen and ill tempered, said no more of wanting her to partner him; indifferent as to whether she played again or not, now that she could dwell in happy anticipation of the evening. Richard, as he laid his jacket on the chair next to her before going off to join a men's four, looked at her questioningly.

Sharlie nodded. "Thank you—I'd love to!"

"Good!" He looked pleased.

Sharlie played once more. Afterwards, Nicola came up to her.

"Thanks very much for helping us out. We needn't keep you any longer—Major Musbury has to go, and it's much cooler now, we shan't need a relief."

She nodded in dismissal.

Sharlie, as she turned away, said, "Oh, good—I'm going out this evening, and I was afraid I mightn't have time first for a bath."

Never more than now had she appreciated the delight of having her own bathroom, the delight of making preparations in the luxurious setting of her charming room. Leisurely she bathed and changed into fresh underwear.

Finally she slipped into the printed Tricel frock in which Nicola had hoped she might make an unsuitable appearance at the tennis party, and waited by the window so as to be ready to join Richard when the others came up from the tennis-courts.

Jackson had brought down drinks, iced fruit cup in a giant glass jug, and an array of bottles. To Nicola he murmured that Mr. and Mrs. Ramswell had gone out unexpectedly for dinner, Mr. Ramswell's brother having telephoned from Gloucester, where he had been delayed by a slight mishap to his car. They would dine with him there and bring him back to Swanswick for the night. Although the butler did not care for Nicola he was punctilious in his service.

Until now Nicola had never asked her friends to dinner nor to lunch; one reason being that the presence of the Ramswells would have cramped their spirits and behaviour, another, that to take too many liberties might jeopardise her comfortable position here. This seemed too good an opportunity to miss! If Richard stayed for dinner, they might wander after in the scented quiet of the gardens. Randolph was quick to take a hint—he'd leave them to themselves. She would wear the white-and-emerald model from Koski Soeurs, as yet unpaid for: all the more reason to make good use of it.

When Lydia Kellaway broke up the party, saying she was dining out, Nicola lingered behind the others. "Oh, Richard—I just want to ask you—"

Richard turned back.

"Yes?"

"Can't you stay and dine with me and Randolph? If you let the others have your car, we'd run you back later."

"How very kind of you! But I'm afraid I can't as I'm fixed up already for this evening. Perhaps you'll let me come another time."

"Of course! I'll ring you up." Nicola was more than provoked that Richard couldn't come. It might be long enough before she had another opportunity of asking him, and having in the first place marked him as an eligible quarry, his original attraction for her had mounted to a powerful infatuation, whetted, owing to the perversity of her nature, by his apparent indifference to her: an indifference she was determined to overcome. Walking beside him towards the house, she spoke of plays and films in Bath, asked him if he liked the theatre and cinema, gave him every opportunity of inviting her to go with him to one or the other. Richard did not take it. Undeterred, Nicola suggested that perhaps next week-end he would dine with her and Randolph at the Regency. "We're only guests here, and one must be careful not to abuse one's privileges! So we often do our entertaining elsewhere."

It was untrue, and Randolph, overhearing her, glanced at her sidelong in cynical amusement. Nicola looked back at him blandly. Richard said it was extremely kind of her, but it was difficult for him to make plans far ahead.

They gathered by the front door, exchanging farewells. Jackson was waiting there in case his services were needed. Richard caught his eye.

"Oh—would you tell Miss Raven I am leaving?"

Jackson looked beyond him. "Miss Raven is already by your car, sir."

Turning, he saw Sharlie, who had come from the side door, hoping, for some undefined reason, to make her departure with him as inconspicuous as possible. Over her frock she had slipped a light coat of a deep blue colour. In contrast to the heated tennis players she looked cool and charming.

Richard and his two companions, having finished their farewells and thanks, joined Sharlie at the car, and a moment later they were speeding down the drive.

"Will you forgive me if I keep you waiting for five minutes? A clean shirt—" Richard said.

Ronald and Copper made their apologies for not waiting with her; they must hurry to change to be in time for dinner in the mess. As she waited Sharlie's happiness was faintly tarnished by the memory of the look on Nicola's face as she had seen Sharlie waiting beside Richard's car. She'd had a feeling, all along, that it would have been better if Nicola had not seen her leave with him, and had wished it had been possible to suggest meeting him at the gates, but to do so would have invested a perfectly harmless outing with an air of furtive secrecy. In any case, she told herself, it was absurd to think that Nicola could mind—and if she did mind, then she had no right to!

She wasn't even Sharlie's employer. Besides, in her free time she might go where she pleased, with whom she liked—and she had known Richard before either of them had set foot in Swanswick. It was absurd to feel uncomfortable because of that strange menacing expression Nicola had worn! . . . Better to think of something pleasanter, such as the letter she had written earlier in the day to Averil Heighbrook, telling her of the children's latest doings: how they had been given a sand-heap, in which George built castles, while Gay preferred to turn out endless pies and puddings from her little set of moulds. How George had learnt to whistle two distinct and separate notes. How Jackson had been teaching him to fly a home-made kite. How Gay could sing "Three Blind Mice" quite recognisably . . . She wondered how that tangled tale would end, and whether ultimately Averil would return to Randolph so as to be with her children. One couldn't, somehow, picture those two settling down to happiness together, or indeed to anything better than perpetual storms . . .

Richard said, "Sorry I've been longer than I said. I found a telegram that needed a reply.—Now for the Plover's Rest!"

By winding lanes he drove her, where wild roses strewed the hedges "like semibreves in a wild, ancient tune," through villages whose garden walls were thickly thatched, finally down a narrow road worn deep between the fields by feet of men and beasts through many generations to a small ancient inn whose windows looked across a lawn that sloped down to a little river. It was the haunt of fishermen, a quiet place, unspoilt by modern innovations saving those that made for comfort. The walls were Cotswold stone, mellowed by the sun and storms of many a bygone year. Stonecrop made a yellow patchwork on the stone slabs of the roof. A red-faced smiling man, hearing the car, came to the open door, whence came the mingled odours of good cooking and a wood fire.

He made them welcome, saying that they would have the place to themselves. The guests who were at present staying there had had high tea and gone off to the river, where they would remain until it had grown too dark for them to see their lines, returning at some unknown hour to the cold meal that would be left ready for them.

"Your dinner will be ready in a quarter of an hour. Meanwhile, you'll find chairs in the garden, and if you'd care for me to bring a glass of sherry——?"

So they sat together sipping sherry in the garden, where the air was sweet with new-mown grass and southernwood and roses, and there was no sound but the gentle murmur of the river. Presently they strolled down to the water's edge and looked where weeds lay quivering like long green floating hair against the pale chalk bottom, and an agitated waterhen called to her family of soot-black fluffy balls to hide among the reeds for safety.

Summoned to dinner by the landlord, they found their table laid in readiness by a window in a charming panelled room with a huge open fireplace, and moulded plaster ceiling. A smiling girl served them with savoury brown soup, grilled trout that had, she told them, been caught that morning in the river, roast chicken, juicy and tender, with new potatoes and the first of the green peas, and gooseberry fool.

"You'd like your coffee in the garden, I expect?" the girl suggested, and they said they would, telling her at the same time that it was the best meal either of them had enjoyed as long as they remembered. She flushed with pleasure. "We do our best to please!"

"What a discovery you made when you first came here!" Sharlie marvelled. "Pure magic—and that *heavenly* meal!"

"Yes—it's a good spot. I found it quite by accident one day when some fellow who was directing me to a short cut told me to turn left when he meant right, and so I landed up at the Plover's Rest instead of Little Huckleby! I telephoned them yesterday to say I might be coming here this evening with a guest, but wasn't certain. Otherwise we mightn't have fared quite so well, though adequately, I've no doubt."

The bats came out and wove their flickering invisible patterns in the scented dusk, the river sang its gentle song, as old as time, as new as each new day, and still they sat there making fresh discoveries about one another, as many another couple hovering on the brink of love had sat before them in the same spot.

The word ambition had been mentioned. Richard asked her, "What does ambition mean to you, personally? What do you want out of life? What *does* a modern girl want?"

She answered slowly, "Being 'modern' is concerned with ways of living and thinking. But it can't touch fundamental instincts. And I believe women live by instinct far more than by reason, and a woman's instinct is to want the same things that her forbears wanted in Victorian days—or for that matter, in the stone age!"

"Such as—?"

"Husband, home, and children. Loving and being loved."

"Sharlie—you're so sweet! You make it quite impossible to go on resisting you—"

Sharlie had been sitting with hands clasped behind her head, face tilted to the sky, unconscious of the lovely line made by her throat and lifted chin against the dark yew hedge beyond. She dropped her hands now in her lap, and turned her head to look at him. All her life long she would remember that one moment out of time when their eyes met, and Richard's, that in the past had often seemed to her so enigmatic, were suddenly revealing.

" 'Resisting' me? But why?" she asked.

"Because—" he began, then shook his head. "Not yet," he said. "It's a long story. And there are some things that one may spoil by rushing at them. Let's leave it till another time, I think. Don't you?"

She longed to cry, "No! Tell me now! Even with the whole of life lying ahead of us, let's not waste one single precious moment of it!" Yet in a way she knew that he was right, and that when one was certain of the ending, the period of anticipation, of delicious suspense, was very sweet. When it was over, one could never have it back. So she said, smilingly, "I think it's often a mistake to hurry things."

Her hand lay on the arm of her chair. Richard covered it with his for a brief moment, then lifted it, dropped a kiss lightly in her palm, folded her fingers over it. "Keep that for me, will you?"

Sharlie uncurled her fingers, peering in her palm, matching his gravity with her own. "Will it mind being washed?"

"Not in the least, so long as you avoid carbolic soap."

"I'll try not to forget," she promised him. They laughed. Then Richard rose. "It's time I took you back."

They scarcely spoke during the homeward drive. Only when they turned in at the gates of Swanswick Sharlie asked if he would take her to the side door, as it was the nearest to her own quarters and she preferred to use it.

"Good night! And thank you for a lovely evening and the best meal I've had for ages!" she said when he had duly drawn up by the side door. Would he suggest a time and place for their next meeting? Or must she again endure days of suspense, listening for the telephone, watching for the postman?

"I've got to be away most of this week on a course. I wonder—could you manage to meet me in Bath for dinner on Friday? I'll be passing through on my way back to Rockdown?" Richard asked, and her heart missed a beat from happiness and relief.

"On Friday . . . That's the evening I nearly always have to meet Randolph Heighbrook at the station. But if he comes as usual by the five-fifty, and his train is up to time, I don't see why I shouldn't manage it. Mrs. Ramswell never wants me in the evening. But if he came by a later train, I couldn't. Would it be too late for me to let you know on Friday morning?"

"You won't be able to get in touch with me. I'm not quite certain where I'll be most of the day on Friday. You could leave a message for me at the Regency, though."

"I'll be in Bath in any case on Friday afternoon, collecting week-end shopping. I can leave a note for you with the hall porter."

"Good idea. Round about half-past seven, if you can come?"

A moment later Sharlie stood alone, listening to the sound of his car dying away down the drive, unconscious of the eyes that watched her from the window of a room where Nicola was in the habit of writing her few letters. This morning she had left her bag there. Going to retrieve it on her way to bed, she had heard the approaching car, had known it must be Richard bringing Sharlie back, and switched the light off so that she might watch them unperceived.

Standing pressed against the curtain, well to one side of the dark window, she could see them clearly in the dusk; Richard's dark head bent towards Sharlie, Sharlie's face tilted to look at him. Her lips were pressed together in a thin hard line, her eyes were bright with anger, and she dug her nails into her palms, hearing them plan another meeting.

She felt that if he bent his head still further, if he kissed Sharlie, it would be impossible to control the seething anger struggling in her for expression. Yet when Richard got back into the car without so much as shaking hands with Sharlie, Nicola told herself that their real farewell had probably taken place elsewhere, and felt no better.

She stood a long time in the darkened room when Sharlie, having locked the door, had gone up quietly to bed, clenching her hands, wondering how best to come between the man she wanted and the girl she mentally termed a presumptuous little upstart. It would be easy to frustrate their plan to meet on Friday evening, by telling Randolph that she wanted him to catch a later train. But that would only be a temporary measure. Surely she could think out something that would have a lasting effect in separating them?

She went at last to look for Randolph, and found him in his bedroom, sitting in an armchair with his feet propped on another, reading a thriller. On a table at his elbow stood a decanter three parts filled with whisky, a syphon, and an empty glass.

"I thought you'd be in bed. You keep late hours. No wonder you look washed out sometimes!" she observed.

"You're not exactly what I'd call an early bird yourself, this evening."

"I started bedwards quite a time ago, but something cropped up to delay me." Nicola perched herself on one arm of the chair on which his feet were resting, looking down at him. So placed, facing one another, the resemblance between brother and sister was striking, so similar were the thin strong brows above their heavy-lidded eyes, the sharp, high, slanting cheekbones, the two noses, delicately cut, with high curved bridges, and the full, sensuous lower lips: so similar, too, their strangely blended look of ruthlessness and weakness, decadence and distinction.

"Listen, Rando," Nicola said, employing the old name of nursery days, "I want something. And I want it badly. And unless you help me, I'm not going to get it, by the look of things."

"And if you don't, there'll be hell to pay. *I* know. Well —what d'you expect me to do about it?"

"Give me a cigarette."

Randolph tossed her one; followed it by his lighter. Nicola lit it expertly, breathing out twin smoke streams through her nostrils. Then she made a chain of smoke rings, staring reflectively at her brother.

"How long do you suppose we shall be able to go on like this?" she asked at last.

"Sponging on my in-laws, you mean? It's hard to say. Once or twice lately I've fancied Mrs. R. was getting a bit restive."

"Me, too. And if we have to clear out, what's the next move? What do we do for the useful commodity known as money?"

"Oddly enough, I'm not too badly off, these days. And you and I have always hung together. While I've got any boodle, you're all right."

"Honour among thieves. At least we've got that merit. How unlike you to have ready money. How d'you manage it?"

Randolph gesticulated vaguely with his cigarette-holder.

"One picks things up, you know, in London Town!"

"And have you picked up so much that a wealthy brother-in-law wouldn't interest you?"

"M'm. Better than a poor one, any day. What's all this leading up to, anyhow?"

Nicola blew another smoke ring. Then she told her brother what it was she wanted of him.

CHAPTER SIX

ON Wednesday morning the telephone rang in Sharlie's sitting-room while she was having breakfast. Jackson, speaking from the pantry, told her Dr. Sherren would like to speak to her, from London.

At first the name conveyed nothing to her. Then she remembered that Sherren was the name of the doctor for whom Averil Heighbrook was acting as receptionist, the brother of her school friend. A moment later a pleasant voice asked, "Is that Miss Raven?"

"Yes!"

"David Sherren speaking. I think it's better not to make explanations on the telephone. Does my name mean anything to you?"

"Yes. I quite understand."

"I have to come to Bath to-day for a consultation, and I wondered if it would be possible for you to have tea with me this afternoon? I'd very much like to have a talk with you."

"Luckily it's my free afternoon, and I was going to Bath in any case. It couldn't be more convenient!"

A time and place of meeting were arranged, and Sharlie returned to her egg and bacon, wondering what he could have to say to her, and what he would be like. She welcomed any means of hurrying the time until her next meeting with Richard on Friday evening. It was too soon to ask Mrs. Ramswell by what train Randolph would be coming, so she was still uncertain as to whether she would be able to meet Richard in time for dinner, but she had "a feeling in her bones" that all was going to be well. Only once since she had been here had Randolph said he would arrive by the later train, and then had wired to say that after all he would be on the earlier one.

Again she heard his voice: "*Sharlie—you're so sweet! You make it quite impossible to go on resisting you—*"

Again she felt his hand, vibrant and firm, covering hers briefly . . .

When she had finished breakfast she went to the nursery, where she had become a welcome visitor. Thawing the unfriendliness of the nurse had taken time and patience, but she had finally achieved it by ignoring her offhand manner, lending her magazines, and listening patiently to the endless saga of her feud with Mrs. Tollworthy, the cook.

The children flung themselves on her with shouts of welcome, at which the nurse looked none too pleased. The smile she gave the visitor was a sour one. Ruefully Sharlie realised that although she gave no sign herself of any affection for the children, she was jealous of their liking anyone else.

George cried, "Look! I got a parcel! It's a book. *The Swiss Family Robertson*—"

"Robinson, I've told you twice already, George," said the nurse.

"Well, I *said* Robertson! It's in words of one sybullul so's not to be too hard to read. I'm going to learn to read today."

"I got a pahcul, too," said Gay, waving a pink rabbit.

"And it's not a birthday nor it isn't Christmas!" said George.

"They came from London. I expect Daddy sent them for a nice surprise," said Nannie. Sharlie had other ideas, suspecting it was Averil who had sent them, but she made no comment.

"It's a lovely book," she told George. "They get wrecked on a desert island and have all sorts of adventures."

George looked anxious. "Do they get safe home again?"

She told him quickly, "Oh, yes! They have a lovely time and there's a happy ending."

He looked relieved. He couldn't bear sad stories and had wept inconsolably over the death of Cock Robin.

Averil would be pleased, thought Sharlie, to hear of their excitement over the parcels. She must tell Dr. Sherren every little detail she could think of, as well as writing her usual account of them to their mother. Probably that was why he wanted to see her, so as to take first-hand news of them to Averil.

She stayed with them until it was time for her to go to Mrs. Ramswell, building a little house of bricks for Gay's pink rabbit, spelling out with George the first few sentences of his book, a simplified edition of which each word was divided into syllables by hyphens for the benefit of small

91

readers, and taking mental note of all they said, so as to remember it this afternoon.

Dr. Sherren had arranged with her that they should meet inside the entrance of the restaurant where they were going to have tea. They had no difficulty in recognising one another; Averil had described Sharlie to him on her return from their first encounter, and he went up to her as soon as she came in.

He was fairish and clean-shaven, with steady grey eyes. His height was average, he was slightly built, and there was nothing noteworthy in his appearance. And yet the moment he had said "You must be Miss Raven, aren't you? I'm David Sherren," and taken her hand in a firm grip, Sharlie knew him for a man of personality, a man who would be staunch and helpful in a crisis and a loyal friend, a man whom one could trust.

They found a table in a quiet corner and he ordered tea. When Sharlie had poured out he said, "You must be wondering why I troubled you to come here, so I'll get straight to the point. I don't expect nor want you to betray a confidence. But can you tell me if you think there's any chance that Averil's parents may let her live with them again at Swanswick, so that she'll be with her children?"

"I'm sorry. If I could, without disloyalty to the Ramswells, I would help you. But I've no idea whatever. I see partically nothing of her father, and Mrs. Ramswell has never mentioned her to me, except just once. Then she said, 'Our daughter is not with us any more.' I thought she meant her daughter was dead . . . It was the greatest surprise to me when Mrs. Heighbrook told me who she was that day she waited for me by the gate!"

David Sherren smiled. "She told me about that.—I'd hoped you might have gathered some sort of impression of the possibilities for Averil, from the general atmosphere of her home?"

Sharlie shook her head. "It's difficult. I only know that Randolph and his sister are very much at home there. If Averil came back, the situation would be quite impossible unless they had some sort of reconciliation."

He sighed. "I suppose so. One would have thought Heighbrook might have had the decency to leave the coast clear for her. Surely she has the first claim on her own home! Extraordinary that her parents take Heighbrook's side instead of hers!"

"Extraordinary. But I gathered from her that her father hopes to starve her into doing as he wants and rejoining her husband. Apparently he was infuriated that she hadn't made a success of the marriage that had been such a triumph, socially, from his point of view."

"Yes, so she told me. It's fantastic!"

"Yes. Life often is fantastic and incredible. I'm always coming across situations that would seem wildly improbable if a writer used them in a novel. In your profession you must see behind the scenes in so many lives that fantasy must be an everyday affair to you!"

"Yes. But it's different, you know, when it affects someone you—like a lot. One would have thought her mother might have helped her more."

"I've wondered about that, too. But apparently her mother gave in in everything, for years, to Mr. Ramswell, because she felt it was her duty. Now he's so domineering and autocratic that he won't listen to any arguments. And 'he who pays the piper calls the tune'! Mrs. Ramswell has no money of her own. I do know that she's said all that she can on Averil's behalf, but without money she can do nothing practical to help. She knows her husband better than you or I. Perhaps she has some plan of influencing him gradually. One can't tell."

"No," he agreed, "one can't tell. And knowing only a fraction of the story, one can't blame.—What do you think of Heighbrook and his sister? I've never met either of them."

"I don't like them, I'm afraid. And yet I'm sorry for them. I've gathered from what Averil told me, and from one or two things they've let fall, that they must have had a wretched childhood. Their parents were away from home continually racing. They loved gaiety, and in summer they used to take a house in London for the season, and left the children in the country in the care of a series of indifferent nurses, none of whom stayed long. Children do need stability so badly!"

David nodded. "Yes. They need to grow their roots in an atmosphere of security and love."

"Roots! It's odd that you should use that word, for I was thinking the other day that neither of them seems to have grown any. I can't explain quite what I mean . . . they seem so volatile and unstable. And I think perhaps having to fend for themselves too much when they were children has given them a feeling that they're up against the world and have to grab what they can get, regardless of the cost to other people."

"I daresay that is so. In adult life most people tend to pass on what they gleaned in the receptive years of childhood. Their father was a very wealthy man at one time, but he betted very heavily, and took to gambling to retrieve his racing losses, which were serious, and finally went bankrupt—had to sell the family estate. Probably Heighbrook and his sister were embittered by that, on top of the indifference of their parents when they were small, and try to get their own back now by callous behaviour to humanity in general. It's not such an uncommon reaction as you might suppose! Hard, though, on those who come in contact with them." He sighed. "All this is cruelly hard on Averil. In childhood she was given everything she wanted. Fate was kind. Too kind. She met with none of the difficulties and opposition that we all need to develop the qualities that help to face disaster. None of the ups and downs that give us gradual introduction to real trouble. And to meet with it so suddenly has hurt her badly. She has no philosophy, poor child, to help her. So she kicks against the pricks and hurts herself still more. If only one could help her!"

He is in love with her, thought Sharlie. He is in love with her, but would do all he could to hide it from her, because she was storm-tossed and bewildered and he would never want to influence her. And in any case, one could see that David Sherren would not want to build his marriage on the foundation of divorce. Oh, what a sorry tangle!

Sadly she said, "When people are in serious trouble no one can do much to help. But just to know one's friends are sorry, and would help if they could, *does* help! . . . As a nation we're too much given to reserve, I think. Silent sympathy may be all very well, but sympathy expressed is infinitely better. If it can't be spoken, it should be written. It can do no harm, and may do untold good."

"You're perfectly right. The same applies to praise and admiration. Why save them up, as we too often do, till somebody is dead, when they would have given such pleasure and encouragement in life?—I would have brought Averil with me, but I wanted to have a talk with you alone, to see if we could think out any plan of action, any way of letting her be with the children, that would not involve returning to her husband. Knowing what I do of both of them—though in his case it's only hearsay—I can't think that a reconciliation would ever work."

"I'm afraid not. I'll let you know if the situation should change in any way, or if I have any bright ideas. But you must remember that my first duty is to Mrs. Ramswell. I couldn't betray a confidence."

"Of course. That's understood."

"Will you tell Averil that you met me?"

"Yes, as soon as I get back."

So, though she would be writing soon to Averil, Sharlie told David of the children's pleasure in their parcels, which he told her Averil had sent, and added various little details that would be of interest to their mother.

When he had left her to drive back to London Sharlie sat a long time in the cool, quiet dimness of the ancient abbey, instead of going to a cinema, as she had planned. She was in no mood now to watch the unrealities of a film. The story on the screen would have seemed artificial in comparison with the complications of real life that were uppermost in her mind. David Sherren, calm and wise and understanding, could have given Averil so much that she lacked to make for happiness, helped her to find the qualities she needed to make a happy married couple. But as matters stood, she could see nothing ahead of them but sorrow. And supposing Averil fell in love with David— had already learnt to love him? What more likely, when her work for him must bring them constantly in contact?

Gradually peace of mind returned to her in the tran- quility of the old church where so many had come before her with the burden of their sorrows or to give thanks for deliverance from their troubles. Most happenings, she was convinced, worked out eventually for the best if only one could learn to take the long view. Ultimately, Averil and David would find happiness in the way intended for them, she was sure of it . . .

She returned by bus to Swanswick sooner than she had intended. Mary, having seen her from a window, came to her room. "I thought you were going to be out for dinner?"

"I'm afraid I changed my plans. I don't want to be a bother, but I wonder if you'd bring me a boiled egg, or whatever is easiest?"

"We can do better than that, I should hope!" Mary said, and presently returned bearing cold chicken, salad, and a fruit jelly.

"I've got an iron on, and that frock you're wearing could do with a bit of a press. Got crushed in the bus, I shouldn't wonder. If you'll give it me I'll put it right. It won't take me a minute," said Mary, as she set the tray on the table and drew up a chair.

Sharlie's heart warmed with the girl's kindness. Such small happenings made some of the brightest colours in life's patchwork. She was smiling to herself, remembering it, when she went out presently to the garden, meaning to weed a bed of wallflower seedlings, in an out-of-the-way corner, that she had noticed were in danger of being smothered by chickweed. To her surprise, when she arrived there scarcely any weeds remained, and Mrs. Ramswell, kneeling by the bed, was clearing the last corner.

"Oh—you've forestalled me! If you'd come half an hour later you wouldn't have found a trace of chickweed! I'd noticed it, too!" Sharlie exclaimed.

"At your age you should be doing something gay of an evening. Not toiling in someone else's garden. How very nice of you to bother," Mrs. Ramswell said, rising and drawing off her sturdy gardening gloves.

"I enjoy weeding. It's fun, when plants are being strangled, to set them free.—I'll take that basketful of chickweed to the hen-run, shall I?"

"We'll take it there between us."

The hen-run lay beyond the garden, on the far side from the house, sheltered from the east and north by the garden wall and a small copse of beeches. When they had scattered the contents of the basket among its inhabitants, much to their delight, Mrs. Ramswell said that she was going for a stroll before returning to the house, and turned away, along a path skirting the beeches. Something in her solitary figure suddenly struck Sharlie as being desolate and forlorn, reminding her of the lines of patience and endurance set about her mouth, the loneliness in her eyes. Impulsively she ran after her.

"Shall I come with you?"—Then she was horrified by her own temerity. Probably Mrs. Ramswell liked her solitude and preferred her own companionship to that of her employee, who was to all intents and purposes a stranger to her, even though they had lived for several weeks under the same roof. She stammered, flushing, "But perhaps you'd rather be alone—"

"Indeed I shouldn't! I'd like nothing better than your company, if there's nothing you would rather do."

So they fell into step together. On one side the beech trunks rose in smooth grey columns like the legs of marching elephants caparisoned in emerald. On the other, a field sloped down to the little river. Birds were singing in the tangle of the woods beyond it. Ahead of them a green woodpecker flew crying his strange call, "Yaffle-yaffle-yaffle!" And presently they heard him drumming on a tree trunk like a miniature machine-gun. The air was sweet with clover.

They talked, pitching their voices low. Mrs. Ramswell told Sharlie of the phantom Roman army that was said to march along this little valley and across the hill beyond it by an ancient track still to be seen, on moonlight nights. Sharlie told her in return of a tiled pavement recently excavated not far from York. They spoke of books, and ghosts, and music. Then a cuckoo flew across their path, calling his clear mechanical song.

"*Hateful* bird!" Sharlie exclaimed. "I never know why poets look on cuckoos as romantic—horrible parasites that they are!"

"I know. I used to feel as you do. But like many another evil, the cuckoo has his part to play in the scheme of things. The balance of nature would be gone if every cuckoo in the world were suddenly blotted out of life."

"Yes . . . Do you really think that applies to all evils?"

"I am sure of it. Everything has some purpose in the universe. Some seeming evils—like the cuckoo—exist as I said, to preserve the balance of nature. Others, that physical or spiritual or mental strength may be acquired in overcoming them."

"It's a comforting theory."

Circling the copse, they strolled down the back avenue towards the house. High in the lime trees bees went murmurously about their business of collecting honey.

Sharlie said, "How I do love the scent of limes!"

"If only June could last for ever," Mrs. Ramswell murmured.

"Oh, but how we'd miss the other eleven months!"

"One could very well spare some of them. December, January, February, March—yes, you may have my share of those!"

"I love them," Sharlie protested. "Cosy evenings by the fire, hearing the wind howl when one's lying snug in bed, the ring of frosty ground, bare trees against a winter sky, a firelit room, the scent of the first hyacinth—I could go on for ever!"

"I wonder if you realise how fortunate you are in loving all the little things of life? Colours and shapes and smells and birds and flowers——"

"You love them, too!"

"Yes. But I had to learn to love them. My senses are far less acute than yours. I had to sharpen my perceptions, teach myself to hear and see and feel. You'll find, in time of trouble, that all these little things become to you what sand is to the ostrich. That is, if you use them wisely."

In time of trouble . . . Sharlie, in the radiant certainty that for her love was approaching its fulfilment, felt warm compassion for the lonely woman who had missed so much, and had to bear her trouble by herself.

"You mean one can take refuge in the loveliness of every day? Bury one's head in the sand of gardening and books and music and the seasons?"

"I mean just that."

"Thank you for telling me. I shall remember."

The glimpse behind the barrier of reserve that Eleanor Ramswell had built up about herself had been very revealing. Sharlie could imagine, pitifully, her gradual withdrawal from the major happenings of life, that had for her proved so unsatisfying, into the world she had created for herself: how she had schooled her mind to dwell on what she read, on history and ornithology, and found companionship and solace in the company of birds and flowers, music and books and vanished races.

Sharlie longed to penetrate still further behind that barrier of reserve, to tell her she had talked with Averil, and that her daughter was with good friends: longed for her to ease her mind of the burden of anxiety and worry she must feel on Averil's account by talking, pouring it out to a sympathetic listener. But to mention Averil might be to make worse trouble later for her mother: should Mr. Ramswell come to know the secretary had been in communication with Averil, he would at once suspect his wife of having instigated it. Far better that she could deny that they had ever mentioned Averil's name.

Sharlie prayed that night: *"Help me always to realise my own good fortune, to be aware of my own happiness and be thankful, never taking it for granted."*

At an hour when she was usually still asleep, Nicola came next morning to Mrs. Ramswell's room. Sharlie was filling in a form with flag-day returns in connection with the charity for which Mrs. Ramswell was county secretary, while the latter went through the morning's letters.

Sharlie had already asked if it would be convenient for her to be out to-night for dinner, after she had met Mr. Heighbrook's train, and had been given pleasant and prompt consent. "I'm so glad for you to be going out. It must be dull for you, cooped up in the country. Youth needs young companionship, and I'm afraid we offer you very little distraction here."

"I love being here!" Sharlie had assured her.

Nicola bade them each a separate good morning, which was unusual; generally she ignored Sharlie. She said, "I've heard from Randolph. He'll be coming by the later train this time, the one arriving at seven-forty."

Sharlie felt sick and stunned with disappointment. She had so looked forward to this evening, had been so sure that it was going to be a milestone, and the happiest milestone so far, in her life. And now it wasn't going to happen, after all. She hadn't realised until this moment how she had been counting on it, living for it.

Mrs. Ramswell said, "Oh, what a pity. Sharlie is going out for dinner." She had substituted the more friendly "Sharlie" in place of "Miss Raven" for the past few days. Lack of practice in self assertion made her hesitate a moment. Then she added, "You had better meet Randolph yourself, Nicola. We can have dinner later."

Sharlie had expected an outcry, protests that Nicola was going to a cocktail party and couldn't possibly leave in time to meet the train. To her astonishment—and truth to tell, to that of Mrs. Ramswell—Nicola said with her most charming smile, "Yes, as Miss Raven—or may I call you Sharlie, too?—is going out to dinner, that's much the best plan. And I think we won't come back to dinner. Mrs. Tollworthy does hate having it late, doesn't she? We can easily have a meal in Bath."

Mrs. Ramswell, secretly much surprised by this immediate and willing acceptance of her suggestion, said that there was no need for them to be out for dinner, but Nicola was insistent.

"Indeed we will. One mustn't impose too much on your marvellous staff. And we'll enjoy a frolic on our own for once!"

Wonders would enver cease, thought her astonished hostess. This was the first time in several months that Nicola had shown the slightest concern for the servants. Unhesitatingly she had asked hordes of people to drinks or tea and tennis of a Sunday, regardless of the household staff's time off duty, had been unpunctual for meals, and stayed in bed of a morning so late that Mary had had a rush to get her room done before lunch, and had many a time been delayed on her free half day owing to the long time it took to set in order the litter of clothes, cosmetics, magazines, trinkets, and what not that Nicola left scattered in her wake. One ought to make allowances for bad training in youth, but it was difficult when one was prejudiced by resentment on account of one's own loved child: difficult, too, to appreciate this more thoughtful attitude on Nicola's part when one remembered previous selfishness. She said, "Well—if you really mean it, I'm sure Mrs. Tollworthy would be pleased!"

"Of course I mean it! And it would be too bad if Sharlie had to miss her dinner engagement."

"I *do* think it's kind of you!" said Sharlie gratefully. She wondered if Nicola guessed this evening was for her a very special occasion, and was being kind because of memories of the time when she herself had been deliciously entangled in the early stages of romance. Those memories must hurt now almost intolerably. No wonder she was unkind at times: the sight of other people's happiness must be so painful in the face of her own loss.

She would have liked to wear her dinner dress; a number of people did wear long frocks for dinner at the Regency, she knew. But she would have felt ludicrous travelling so attired in a country bus, and so she wore instead the frock that she had worn when she had dined with Richard at the Plover's Rest. Mary had pressed it for her in the afternoon, though she had protested that she would do it for herself. The housemaid had flushed up becomingly.

"I'd like to do it for you. I only wish I could do more. Jim's asked me to go with him steady and we're hoping to get married some time next year when we've saved a bit towards the furniture. And it's all thanks to you because I look my best in that nice dress you gave me!"

"Oh, what nonsense, Mary! Jim would have fallen in love with you if you'd been wearing pea-green trimmed with puce! It's nothing to do with me! But I *am* glad for you!"

And she was all the happier for the housemaid's happiness as she walked to catch her bus. She wanted all the world to be as happy as herself. She was in love with life, in love with all humanity that evening. Happiness radiated from her, deepening the deep blue of her eyes, setting her mouth in sweeter curves, making her walk even more buoyant and lissom, so that people turned to look at her, and the old ones smiled a little wistfully, and the young ones envied or admired, and all of them felt happier for seeing her.

Richard was waiting for her in the lounge of the Regency. He was sitting in a corner, watching the door. He rose as she came in, but stood where he was, so that no one else should take the sofa he had secured, instead of coming to meet her. It was strange, she thought, how seeing him so, among a crowd of strangers, increased her sense of intimacy so that she felt as though she had known him always, knew instinctively all that she had not had the time nor opportunity to learn.

Richard said, "Good! First I was afraid I'd find a note here saying you couldn't come. Then I was afraid you might get held up at the last minute, and every time a page appeared I half expected him to bring me a telephone message saying you couldn't meet me after all."

"I very nearly couldn't! Randolph Heighbrook is coming by a later train than usual, and if I'd had to meet him this would have been impossible."

They sat together on the sofa. A glass half filled with sherry was on a table by Richard.

"I didn't wait for you before having a drink," he apologised. "I've had a strenuous day, and this was badly needed! What will you have? Sherry or a cocktail."

"I don't want anything. Don't hurry over yours—I'm not as ravenous as all that!"

"So someone else has gone to meet the train?"

"Nicola Freemantle is going. She was most awfully nice about it."

"Was she? Somehow I haven't taken to that young woman."

Sharlie, warmly grateful to the girl who had made it possible for her to be here now with Richard, was forgetful of past slights and lack of kindness.

"Haven't you? I think she's so very attractive. She has such distinction, and she wears her clothes so beautifully. One would notice her anywhere. And I do think she has tremendous charm."

"I didn't think she was particularly charming to you that day at tennis!"

So he had noticed Nicola's cavalier treatment of her! Sharlie was glad, but said, "She must be very unhappy. It's quite a short time since she lost her husband. Grief does have the effect of making some people embittered and—and edgy."

"M'm. That's one way of looking at it, certainly!"

Most girls, thought Richard, would have borne Nicola a grudge for her behaviour at that tennis party, when she had seemed to him to lose no opportunity of snubbing and humiliating Sharlie. It was typical of her to regard the affair so generously.

Idly he asked, "And Heighbrook? What d'you think of him?" For himself, he couldn't stand the fellow at any price. Wouldn't have trusted him a yard. It would be interesting to know how Sharlie judged him.

But Sharlie's gratitude to Nicola made her feel she owed her loyalty, even to the extent of being charitable about her brother. So she said, "I can imagine that he mightn't be a man's man. But to most women I should say he is unusually attractive. That family has more than its fair share of charm, if those two are a fair sample! And I should say that any girl whose dream of married bliss was to undertake the reformation of a rake would fall head over heels in love with Randolph!"

Richard stubbed out his cigarette. "Think so? No knowing what will appeal to a woman!"

Sharlie smiled back at him. "None. We're unpredictable!"

"How about eating?" Richard suggested.

The head waiter, as he led them to their table, said that Richard had been wise to book it in advance, for they were unusually busy, and had reluctantly been turning guests away.

Sharlie looked about her at the crowded room as Richard ordered dinner, seeing the other diners through a golden haze of happiness, wondering whether Richard would explain, over the meal, those cryptic words of his that had been haunting her since first she heard them: *"You make it quite impossible for me to go on resisting you—"* or would wait until they were alone, having halted on the homeward road to walk together down some woodland path or quiet lane where he might tell her what he had to tell in a secluded peace.

Then the blow fell that was to wreck the evening's happiness. For in the doorway she saw Nicola and Randolph, tall and striking and well-bred, looking about them with a blend of arrogance and expectancy. Quickly she looked away.

God—let them leave here quickly, without seeing us . . .

But Nicola had already seen them. Followed by Randolph she came towards their table, leisurely and yet too

103

fast, so that Sharlie was unable to tell Richard, who was having a discussion with the wine waiter, of their approach: her murmured "Nicola and Randolph are here—they're coming to join us—" was lost under the waiter's wordy praises of some wine. He looked up in astonishment as Nicola's deep husky voice exclaimed:

"So *this* was your dinner engagement, Sharlie! What a piece of luck for us! I didn't book a table, and there's not one to be had, and Randolph hasn't had a bite to eat since lunch. So may we—?"

No matter what he might have felt, Richard had no alternative but to say, "Of course! Do join us!" —hoping he looked more pleased than he felt.

Waiters came, bringing chairs and laying two more places; it would be rather a tight fit, but they would manage.

Nicola was wearing emerald, intricately cut, yet with an effect of simplicity. She looked superb: not beautiful, but distinguished, striking, and supremely well groomed.

Across the table her eyes met Sharlie's in a long look of triumphant mockery. In that revealing moment Sharlie knew, as surely as though Nicola had told her in so many words, that her apparent kindliness in offering to meet Randolph's train, then have a meal with him in Bath, had not been kindliness at all, but a design to suit her own ends. Somehow she must have found out that Sharlie would be dining here with Richard, and had decided to come here with Randolph, probably meaning to join them afterwards for coffee in such a way that it would be difficult to refuse their company, and to stay with them for the remainder of the evening. Fate had played into her hands by making it impossible to get a table, so that she and Randolph had had a good pretext for asking if they might join forces with Sharlie and Richard without delay.

The studied malice of it robbed her for a moment of speech, or any sensation save incredulous anger. Then she looked at Randolph, and saw from the amused, sardonic, sidelong glance he gave her that he was aware of what had happened.

Why, why, *why*—? she asked herself. But there would be time enough to work out that bewildering problem later on. Now she must decide on her immediate course of action.

She wouldn't give the slightest clue to what she felt. She would be as gay as though to have her *tête-à-tête* with Richard suddenly turned into a foursome were the most delightful happening in the world. She would behave as though the Heighbrook brother and sister were the two people in all the world that she most desired to see at this particular juncture. If they had hoped to witness her disappointment, it was they who should be disappointed!

Catching Richard's eye, she smiled at him, a radiant smile, intended for the benefit of the other two.

Then she turned to Randolph, her face still lit with gaiety.

"What quite incredibly good luck that you came here, instead of to the Majestic or the Pulteney or—oh, any of the others! It would have been too maddening to have heard to-morrow that we'd missed each other!" she exclaimed.

Randolph looked at her a moment with narrowed eyes. Then he smiled back at her, and this time there was no mockery in his eyes, but admiration, undisguised.

"I quite agree with you. Too tragic."

Richard turned away to talk with Nicola.

CHAPTER SEVEN

WHEN she had recovered from the shock of disappointment caused by having what should have been an evening spent alone with Richard turned so unexpectedly into a foursome, Sharlie found the episode not without redeeming features.

It was fun to feel herself and Richard linked together as conspirators determined not to betray their annoyance at the intrusion. She was secretly amused too, by Randolph's evident wish to ingratiate himself with her. Previously she had only seen him exercise his undeniable charm on others. Now he concentrated all of it on herself, made her the centre of his interest and attention, carried on a low-voiced conversation that somehow conveyed the flattering implication that the others were of no account, since it was only she who mattered in his estimation. Flattering, too, the way he turned his shoulder on Nicola, who sat on his other side, as though wishing to exclude the others from his talk with Sharlie.

Making pretence of being completely taken in, she played up to him, fencing gaily with him, parrying his repartee, exchanging sally for sally, listening demure and wide-eyed to his flattering insinuations. It must be gall and wormwood to Nicola to see how, far from succeeding in her scheme to spoil Sharlie's evening, she had to all appearances added to her enjoyment.

Much as she would have liked to catch Richard's eye from time to time, she judged it wiser to refrain from doing so. Randolph was no fool. Better not to run the risk of giving him the slightest reason to suspect she was bamboozling him for her own amusement. So throughout the meal she carefully refrained from the exchange of even one conspiratorial glance with Richard. Later they would laugh together as they speculated as to the reason for this unwelcome intrusion on their evening.

Nicola nipped general conversation in the bud, taking it on herself to answer some remark Richard made across the table to Randolph, murmuring to him in a low husky undertone, excluding the others from their talk. Sharlie longed to hear what they were saying; it was with an effort that she kept her attention fixed on Randolph . . . Probably Richard found it equally hard to seem whole-heartedly absorbed in Nicola!

At last the waiter brought the final course: an ice for Sharlie, mushrooms on toast for the others. Soon, she thought thankfully, dinner would be over. Surely when that time came Nicola and Randolph must have the grace to leave them to themselves!

Across the table she intercepted Nicola's glance sliding from Randolph to herself before it turned again to Richard. Momentary foreboding chilled her. With an effort she shook it off. She must have been imagining the mockery and triumph she had thought she saw in those cold agate eyes. For why should Nicola feel jubilant, since the girl whose evening she had planned to spoil, for some strange reason best known to herself, had given no slightest sign of being disconcerted, far less disappointed?

They had coffee at the table, knowing it might be difficult to find places in the crowded lounge, since other diners had already left the restaurant and the best corners would have been snapped up.

Sharlie's heart leapt joyfully when at last, through Randolph's talk of the latest musical-comedy star, she heard Richard asking for the bill. At last, she thought, the endless seeming prelude was drawing to its close. Soon the real evening would begin . . .

Randolph, when the waiter brought the bill, became more absorbed than ever in his description of the tall young red-haired dancer who was making such a hit in "Pins and Needles," feigning oblivion of the fact that Richard was taking out his notecase. Nicola murmured that she and Randolph must pay their share, but her protest lacked conviction, and Richard, glad enough to have the chance, inopportune though it might be, of returning hospitality, would have none of it.

"Well, since we've dined with you, you must let us have our turn of playing hosts! There's dancing every Friday in the Regency Rooms, adjoining here. Quite a good band, too, considering that it isn't a London one. Let's all go on there, shall we?" Nicola suggested.

Randolph was suddenly silent—almost, thought Sharlie, as though his sister's words had been a cue. Nobody said anything. Then Nicola, ostensibly to all of them but looking at Richard, said, "Well? What about it?"

"Sounds a good scheme to me!" said Randolph.

Sharlie was silent. Surely, she thought, Richard would make some excuse, would say he'd got to get back early to the mess, so that they could leave here without more waste of time, drive into the country, be alone again together.

But Richard made no pretext for refusing Nicola's suggestion. Turning to Sharlie, he asked her, "How about it? Would you like to dance?"

Their eyes met, but in his she saw no message, only a cool, impersonal question. So after all he did not long, as she had longed, all evening, for the time when they would be alone again: if he had, he could have settled it all so easily in a word or two. And she had been so *sure* . . .

She forced her stiff lips to the curves of a smile, and the reluctant muscles of her face to the semblance of pleasure, hoped that her eyes did not betray the desolation in her heart, as she said brightly, "It would be fun, unless you're tired, after your long day?"

He did not take the loophole of escape she offered him, but answered in a hearty voice, "Tired? Not a bit of it!"

So it was settled. She must shut out thought: time for that later on, when she was solitary in the haven of her bedroom. Meanwhile she must concentrate on keeping up the stale pretence of gay enjoyment, only now there was a difference: now she must pretend to Richard, too, instead of knowing he pretended with her. It was a game no longer, but a matter of pride, that nobody should guess the bitterness of her disappointment.

Not for a moment did it occur to her that her assumed interest in Randolph might have deceived Richard as well as Nicola, and that in fact she had been doing exactly what the other girl had hoped for.

Several couples were already dancing when they arrived in the ballroom adjoining the hotel, together with more new arrivals. When they had taken possession of a table at one end of the long room, Richard turned to Sharlie. "Will you dance this with me?"

At once her spirits soared. To dance with him would be the next best thing to being alone with him. She had been dreading that he might ask Nicola first, but now she told herself that she had been exaggerating everything, making mountains out of molehills, imagining without the slightest cause that there was something different in Richard's attitude towards her.

Her smile was radiant as she said, "I'd love to!"

Randolph laid his half-smoked cigarette in an ashtray, not bothering to stub it out, and held his arms out to his sister, without a word. Nicola slid into them and they glided away together, perfectly matched and well aware that they were attracting considerable attention by their expert dancing and distinctive good looks.

He said at last, "Well?"

"It went off really better than I'd dared to hope. She played right into our hands. You were superb, of course. You must have given the impression of being heavily smitten with her—to anyone who wasn't in the know!"

"M'm. It was easier than you might suppose. She's by no means unattractive."

"Oh, quite appealing in her way, I grant you. Not at all your cup of tea, though."

Randolph made no answer.

Sharlie and Richard were alone together in a world of rhythm and music and enchanted movement, drifting, eddying, floating on the current of the waltz. For a moment Sharlie was as happy as though Nicola and Randolph did not exist. Then Richard said, "Great luck, wasn't it, those two turning up like that?"

She looked at him, and in his eyes could read no sign that he had spoken ironically. So she had misread him. He'd been pleased. He hadn't minded in the least about the interruption of their solitude . . .

She said enthusiastically, "*Great* luck!" They spoke no more until the dance was over and they went back to their table, to be embroiled in laughing argument with the others over the respective charms of two much-bedizened young women Nicola had nicknamed Marmalade and Apricot from the colour of their hair.

As soon as the music started Randolph asked Sharlie to dance. She went with him with every appearance of alacrity. Richard looked after them for a moment before asking Nicola to dance with him.

"I'd love to, presently. But do you mind if I just finish this cigarette first?"

They sat looking on. Nicola made amusing and at times ribald comments on the dancers that made Richard laugh, although he was in no mood for laughter; her tongue was witty as well as caustic. Sharlie and Randolph swung past them. Randolph's head was bent to Sharlie's, he was murmuring something in her ear; their cheeks were close to one another.

Nicola said, "Naughty of those two to use us as their cat's-paws! I wonder if they realise the transparency of their little plot!"

"How do you mean?"

"Well, it's so obvious, isn't it? The poor sweets have to be so careful, though they tell me the King's Proctor isn't quite the ogre that he used to be. I'd no idea what was afoot when Randolph asked me if I'd meet his train and dine here with him, but obviously when Sharlie had fixed up to meet you here, she must have told him and they hatched this little plan. As soon as I saw you and Sharlie I knew why Randolph had been so insistent on coming here—but one can't blame them, can one?"

Richard said, "I am afraid I haven't the faintest notion what you are talking about." His voice was unperturbed, but Nicola, glancing at him sidelong, saw the twitching of a muscle in his cheek, and that his hands were tense, and knew that he was less indifferent than he would have cared for her to know. She hesitated for a moment. Supposing he and Sharlie were already engaged—? But she had gone too far now to draw back, and besides, nothing venture, nothing win! She'd take a chance.

Assuming an expression half rueful, half amused, she said, "Oh, dear—have I been letting the cat out of the bag? I thought, as you're an old friend of Sharlie's she'd have told you. But she's right, of course, to be discreet." Rapidly she went on talking, in lowered tones, keeping her eyes fixed on his face, candid and wide. Richard's expression was of polite interest, as though he listened to a piece of not particularly striking news about a casual acquaintance.

Did he care? Or didn't he? she wondered. Then she saw his hand clench until the knuckles were white. Well—many a man had been caught on the rebound!

"Surely, at dinner, you must have noticed how absorbed they were in one another?" she ended.

Richard's white teeth showed in a smile that did not light his eyes. "Must I? I was rather absorbed myself, you know!" he parried.

Nicola flashed him a provocative glance. This was going well, far better than she'd dared to hope. What line should she take now? Gay, witty camaraderie? or sympathetic feminine charm?

"Poor Randolph. I've been so worried about him. No one can possibly imagine, without going through the experience, the tragedy of an unhappy marriage." She sighed. There was a far-away look in her eyes. Watching her reflection in a distant mirror she was well pleased with the result. "Still," she murmured, "one does learn from one's disasters!"

Richard shrugged. His lips were cynical. "Some lessons are better never learned."

Nicola hoped she looked as wise and wistful as she intended.

"Never to turn back the pages—always to look forward—those are things worth knowing," she breathed. Subtly she had linked them in a bond of similar disillusion.

The orchestra swung the foxtrot to its close. Nicola said urgently, as they watched Sharlie and Randolph cross the floor towards them, "You won't tell Sharlie what I've told you? I'd no idea you didn't know already. She would tell Randolph, and he can be rather frightening when he's angry! Wait, and let her tell you of her own accord."

"I won't say anything."

"You promise?"

"Certainly."

Sharlie, joining them, heard the last words, the appeal in Nicola's voice, the reassurance in Richard's; sensed the atmosphere of some mutual understanding from which she was excluded; wondered if she were imagining things because she was so disappointed, or whether Richard was really avoiding meeting her eyes?

Randolph said cheerfully, "Drinks, I think, don't you?" —summoned the hovering waiter and without consulting the others ordered champagne. Sharlie asked if she might have orange squash instead.

Brother and sister exchanged a cross-fire of amusing repartee while drinks were served. Only Sharlie and Richard remained silent, saying no more than was essential for civility.

When the next dance began Randolph rose, holding out both hands to Sharlie. "This one with me?"

She hesitated for an instant, waiting for Richard to say, "Hi! It's my turn to dance with Sharlie!" or something of the sort, but he was silent.

"Come, it's a good tune, we can't waste it! Heronshaw will understand—won't you, old boy?" said Randolph.

Richard said expressionlessly, "Perfectly."

Sharlie took Randolph's meaning to be that Richard would understand it wasn't very amusing for brother and sister to dance together more than once or twice. Well—that had nothing to do with her and Richard, into whose evening they had gatecrashed! But since Richard made no protest she must go with Randolph with as good a grace as possible. Next time, Richard would be sure to ask her before Randolph had a chance.

But when the next dance came, Richard made no move, engrossed in talk with Nicola. And when the next dance came, and the one after that, it was the same thing. Sharlie spent the remainder of the evening dancing with Randolph, a fixed smile on her lips, bewilderment and misery in her heart. It was as though she were divided into two separate entities. One of them laughed and talked with Randolph while the other sat apart, solitary, agonised.

"But you can't be *certain* that there isn't any Loch Ness monster! The most unlikely things are possible!"

. . . *What can have happened between me and Richard? What can have gone wrong?* . . .

"I don't agree. It's fun to speculate about a mystery. It would be dull if all of them were solved and there were no room left for wondering!"

. . . *Can it be something I have said, or done, unknowingly?* . . .

"I'm sorry to disappoint you, but I'm not a scrap afraid of mice! Fish are my weak spot. There's something so—so *sinister* about a large fish. I think the acquarium at the Zoo is far more frightening than scores of mice!"

. . . Or am I making mountains out of molehills, being silly, because it matters so much? Shall I be laughing at myself this time to-morrow, wondering what on earth I was depressed about?

But at the evening's end it was brought home to her only too clearly that the rift between herself and Richard was not of her imagining. Randolph said to him, "Nicola and I are going straight back to Swanswick. No point in your coming out of your way to bring Sharlie back, we can look after her! Unless you'll come along, too, and have a nightcap?"

It would have been so easy for Richard to reply that he must see his guest home for himself, although he wouldn't have the time to spare to come in for a drink. That would have left them free to linger on the way, if he had wanted to. Sharlie caught her breath, waiting for him to speak.

He did not look at her. "Thanks very much," he said to Randolph. "I ought to get back right away. So if you'll take Sharlie?"

"Nothing I'd like better!" Randolph answered.

When Nicola and Sharlie had collected their belongings from the cloakroom, they all walked the few yards to the hotel's car park. Nicola fell behind, fumbling with the catch of her bag, and Richard waited for her. Randolph slid his hand beneath Sharlie's elbow, drawing her ahead.

"Looks as though my glamorous sister has made something of a hit!" he said.

"She's so attractive," Sharlie answered. She hated the touch of Randolph's fingers on her arm, yet did not like to draw away from him, feeling that to do so would seem to magnify a trifling incident.

Richard stood with the two girls as Randolph unlocked the Swanswick car.

"Do come to tennis on Sunday afternoon, won't you?" Nicola asked him. "Not a party this time, it's bad luck on the servants if we're too gay at the week-ends! Just a four."

Richard hesitated before saying, "Thanks very much. I'd like to."

"All aboard," called Randolph from the driver's seat.

Sharlie said to Richard, "Good night, and thank you so much. It's been fun!" They shook hands, a conventional gesture that seemed strange between two people who an hour or two before had been on terms of friendly informality.

One last vestige of hope fluttered in Sharlie's heart. Would Richard ask her now if she would come out with him again?

But Richard only said, "Good night. Nice of you to come." Their eyes met for a moment. Then she turned away and got into the car, taking a seat behind, though Randolph wanted her to sit with him in front. Nicola lingered, talking to Richard in what to Sharlie's straining ears sounded a confidential murmur.

"I shall sit behind," she said at last, in louder tones and Richard opened the door for her. Finding Sharlie already in the back, she exclaimed, "But you must sit in front with Randolph! I insist!"

Sharlie was taken aback by this unusual solicitude.

"Honestly, I'm perfectly comfortable here—"

"Nonsense, my dear. Now come along!"

So to save further argument Sharlie clambered out again and moved in beside Randolph, who welcomed her with, "That's more like it!"

Nicola said something Sharlie couldn't catch, to Richard; her voice held a note of indulgent amusement. Sharlie wondered whether it were the moonlight that made him look so white and haggard, or if he were very tired?

Nicola said innocently as they turned in at the gates of Swanswick, "You're very silent, Sharlie. Didn't you enjoy yourself?"

It was nearly over now. In a few minutes she would be blessedly alone. She'd make one final stand to save her pride.

" 'Enjoy' is far too mild a word. I adore dancing! I'm a little tired, that's all," she said, so cheerfully that Nicola was silenced, if not altogether deceived.

Sharlie wondered how in the world she could have been so dense as not to see at once what was so obvious, once one realised it: that Nicola's reason for breaking in on her evening with Richard was that she wanted him for herself, either because he was comfortably off, or simply for dog-in-the-manger motives.

Surely, oh *surely* Richard, who had had considerable experience of the world, couldn't have been attracted by her superficial charm, must have seen through her artificial appeal?

Instinct had told her that he loved her. Richard was neither fickle nor capricious. Therefore he must love her still. What *could* have caused this sudden, one-sided estrangement?

Logic reasoned, "If he had loved you, why should he have danced with Nicola all evening, made no attempt to bring you home, made no suggestion of another meeting with you? No . . . It's a case of wishful thinking on your part. Richard was charming to you—no denying that. Probably he liked you quite a lot. But Richard never said one word to you of love. You must have magnified mere trifles into matters of importance, misconstrued mere liking into something greater, built a fragile chain of circumstantial evidence to make a case that fell to pieces when the time of testing came."

Instinct argued piteously, "That's not true, I *knew*—"

Logic remorselessly retorted, "Then apparently you knew wrong. And you betrayed too much to Richard of your feelings, and so he judged it wiser to draw back, out of what might have become a difficult situation for you both . . ."

"I believe that girl will cry her eyes out," Nicola told her brother presently, over sandwiches and drinks, and was surprised and made uneasy by his answer, "Well, if she does, it's a damned shame."

It would be a tiresome complication if he had fallen for Sharlie. Not that his infatuations ever lasted long, thank goodness!

"Is Little Brother going all tender-hearted? Wonders will never cease!" she mocked.

After a moment he grinned back at her. "Not as you'd notice! But she's a taking piece."

"Not half as taking as your charming sister when her mind is set on something."

115

"You're a devil, Nick—but an attractive devil, I'll grant you that."

They smiled at one another, well pleased with their evening's entertainment.

Nicola was wrong in thinking Sharlie would cry herself to sleep. Some troubles go too deep for tears. She went to bed dry-eyed.

Sharlie woke next morning heavy-eyed and with an aching head, for she had passed a restless night. Mrs. Ramswell commented on her pallor with concern.

"You look so pale to-day, my dear! Aren't you feeling well?"

Sharlie assured her that she was perfectly all right. "We danced last night, and I suppose I'm out of training for late hours and crowded rooms."

Then would she, Mrs. Ramswell asked, mind having nursery meals to-day? She had completely forgotten that Nannie had asked ten days ago if she might have this week-end off, and as it happend Mr. Ramswell would be coming home for the week-end in time for lunch, instead of after tea, as usual, and disliked having his usual routine disturbed.

"Of course. I'll take them on entirely, if you like," Sharlie offered. "I should enjoy it, honestly!"

She meant it. George and Gay were an engaging little pair, and the care of them would distract her from dwelling on her own affairs.

"I hope I needn't ask you to do that. I do enjoy having them to myself, without Nannie! But if it's difficult—if my husband wants me to go out with him——"

"Then you can rely on me to be your deputy," Sharlie assured her.

The morning's post happened to be a small one, but it included a letter for herself from Averil. She slid it into her pocket to be read later, when she had dealt with the morning's correspondence. She wished Averil would not write to her, for she was afraid that one day Mrs. Ramswell might meet the postman and take delivery of the letters, which as a rule were sorted by Jackson, and recognising her daughter's writing on an envelope for her secretary, conclude that they were carrying on a secret correspondence—which was true, of course, although that correspondence was on lines involving no disloyalty, in Sharlie's mind, to her employer . . . It was all very complicated and troubling.

Later in the morning she drove Nannie to Bath to catch her train to London. The children came, too. George had promised to take care of Gay on the homeward journey.

"We'll be as quiet as two little mouzes!" he assured his grandmother earnestly when she expressed doubts as to whether they should go.

"If you really are two 'mouzes,' not a pair of rampageous tigers, we might stop on the way home by Buckley Brook and play there for a while," Sharlie told them, a proposal that was received with cries of rapture.

Nannie said sourly that she knew what *that* would mean. Wet feet, and colds for her to deal with when she got back on Monday. Sharlie, watching the happiness on two small faces banished by anxiety, said soothingly that she would see to it that their shoes were kept quite dry, and wondered why a woman who appeared to have no love for children should have taken training as a children's nurse. She said as much, tactfully, on the way to Bath.

"What made you take up nursery nursing, Nannie? Did you choose it for yourself, or did your parents plan it for you?"

Nannie made answer primly that she had taken nursery training because the sort of people who could afford a trained nurse for their children could afford to give her "luxury in nice refined surroundings, if you see what I mean. And, of course, it's not like being really in domestic service. Naturally I'd not demean myself by *that!*"

So this, thought Sharlie, was the sort of woman they had put in charge of two impressionable babies—this silly creature with her material set of values, who thought she would "demean" herself by doing housework! Mary, who took a real pride in her polishing and scrubbing, was worth ten of her. How long, she wondered, would the children be at the mercy of her shallowness, her utter lack of tenderness and understanding? And how would they develop, brought up lacking a mother, with a dissipated father who took no interest in their well-being, by a grandmother whose good sense and taste were overruled by their snobbish, vulgarly materialistic grandfather?

The little pair sat "Good as two mouzes" on the homeward road until they reached the hump-backed bridge of Buckley Brook. There Sharlie drew the car in to the side, and they went down the bank to where a winter flood had left a miniature sandy beach.

"And now," said Sharlie, "we'll take off your shoes and socks. That's much the surest way to keep them dry!"

Ecstatic squeals greeted this suggestion. "Nannie *never* lets us!"

"Perhaps you've never been in this sort of place on such a lovely sunny day with Nannie," said Sharlie tactfully. When their twenty wriggling little toes had been released and George and Gay were happily engaged, Gay in building a sand castle, George in digging a channel to surround it from the stream, she settled down to read the letter she had received that morning from their mother.

She sighed when she had read it, slipping it slowly back into its envelope. Sentences and phrases stood out in her memory, etched there in Averil's impetuous writing.

I simply can't go on like this, cut off indefinitely from the children . . . I can't think of any solution other than divorcing Randolph, if I can only get the necessary evidence. . . . It isn't my own freedom that I hope for, though legally divorce would set me free, so long as Randolph and I are in the same world I could never feel truly released from marriage with him. I suppose it's the result of being descended from a long line of Quakers on Father's side . . . David is being wonderful, so understanding. If only there were something he could do to help, he would, but no one can . . . So I'm seriously considering employing a detective to keep track of Randolph. I suppose it's asking too much of you to suggest that you would tell me if you knew of any local evidence that might help? It's hateful, but what else am I to do if ever I'm to have my babies back again?

Yes: it was too much to ask of her. Too much to ask that she should involve herself in anything so sordid and repugnant to her. Yet was anything too much, she asked herself, anything that one might do to help George and Gay towards a happy, normal growing-up with the young mother who adored them? How hard it was sometimes, in this most complicated world, to steer the wisest course—how difficult to read the dictates of one's conscience!

George called to her. "Look at the water running round the castle! It would drown the enemy if they fell in!"

"Yunning yound ve tastle!" Gay echoed.

For the remainder of the day she gave herself up to the care and happiness of the children, having nursery lunch with them, taking them for a picnic tea in the woods near the house, reading the book Gay called *Peter Yabbit* to them later, when, in pale blue dressing-gowns, they had their supper of milk and biscuits at a table in the nursery window.

After her own evening meal she wrote a non-committal letter to Averil, telling her of the day's doings but making no comment on what she had written concerning a divorce. Then she went to bed, earlier than usual. She lay awake for some time, thinking of Richard, hoping Nicola would ask her to make a fourth at tennis to-morrow: refusal would be soothing to her smarting pride.

Soon after midnight, as she was at last dropping off to sleep, her mind was switched to other matters by the faint creak of a step on the back staircase, followed a few moments later by the sound of cautious footsteps below her window. So Randolph was off again on one of his mysterious nocturnal expeditions. Probably, were she to tell Averil, there would be little difficulty in obtaining evidence for divorce. Yet the idea of playing spy was utterly repugnant to her. She fell asleep still undecided as to whether to withhold help in other people's matrimonial affairs was the wisest and most sensible course, or whether, having regard to the future of the children, it was merely selfish isolationism?

No invitation to play tennis was forthcoming. From Mary, Sharlie gathered that Lydia Kellaway was coming to lunch and would be staying on to make a fourth. Mr. Ramswell was going out this afternoon, so Mrs. Ramswell would be free to enjoy her grandchildren by herself. Sharlie offered to help in putting them to bed, but was told apologetically that she would not be needed. "I do so enjoy having them all to myself, and it so seldom happens!"

She decided to go for a long bicycle run, out of earshot of the tennis players, and away from the knowledge that Richard was so near yet out of reach. She kept her bicycle in the garage. It was a new one, and she kept it carefully, so it was annoying to find the mudguard splashed, the wheel-rims stained with mud, though she had cleaned it thoroughly last time she put it away.

Cullen was washing down the car. She told him, "Someone seems to have been borrowing my bicycle!"

Cullen was a Scot from Yarrow. "Have they so?" he asked, his quiet Border voice lifting the sentence at its end. "It's funny, now, you should be saying that, for Mary used to keep her bike where yours is now. She used to say that someone was for ever taking it, but I just thocht it was imagination till she found the mudguard badly buckled. Since then she's had it in what used tae be the laundry."

"It looks as though I'd better keep mine there, too."

"Maybe so," Cullen agreed. "Mary'll tell you where she keeps the key. There's nobody else uses the place."

Could the borrower of bicycles, Sharlie wondered as she pedalled along the avenue, be Randolph? One couldn't picture him, immaculate and debonair, using a bicycle when a car was available, but he left the house so stealthily that it was obvious he did not want his mysterious nocturnal expeditions known, so possibly he took a bicycle as being soundless, and less conspicuous. Well—he should find hers no longer available, next time he wanted it!

She spent the afternoon exploring by-roads that wandered along little lonely valleys where the undergrowth grew lush and tangled in the woods, and women picking fruit in farmhouse gardens waved a friendly greeting as she passed. Here she would loiter until it was reasonably certain that the tennis-court had been deserted for to-day and Richard had gone. Her eyes were heavy still with unshed tears, her heart ached from its hard core of wounded pride. The pageant of the countryside in June gave her no pleasure now.

At the hour when labourers come home a man, sunburnt and young, came past her on his bicycle as she rested by a gate. A girl in a blue overall, a baby in her arms, was waiting for his coming in a cottage garden. Taking the baby from her, he set it on the seat of his bicycle, which the mother guided. Slowly they went up the path, pausing to take notice of the apple crop, and how the peas were swelling. Then the door closed behind them.

At last the tears stung Sharlie's eyes. Pride suddenly seemed of small account, feather light in the balance against the man one loved, his child, his home, his garden. Folly to hold herself aloof, denying herself and Richard the opportunity for a new beginning. All her life she might regret it, if she put her pride before her love.

There might be time still, if she hurried, to meet Richard on his way back to the camp from Swanswick . . .

Ten minutes later she reached the lodge gates. She had no means of knowing whether Richard had already left: all she could do now was to pedal slowly along the avenue, and hope.

Midway between the gates and the house, she heard a car coming towards her. Her heart gave a sickening lurch, then began racing wildly. This must be Richard! Or if it were only Lydia, then Richard must be following soon.

She saw that it was Richard's car. Surely he would stop —he couldn't fail to stop!

The car slowed down as it approached her. He was going to stop . . . Relief surged through her heart. She told herself that everything was going to be all right . . .

A tweed-clad arm waved to her, a voice called, " 'Evening, Sharlie!" Richard drove slowly past her. . .

When she was hidden from him by a bend in the avenue she dismounted, and stood listening to the sound of his engine fading in the distance, till it died away and there was only silence left.

CHAPTER EIGHT

NEVER had Sharlie felt so utterly devoid of hope and happiness as in the days that followed. She lived mechanically, working feverishly in the garden when Mrs. Ramswell had no further need of her, since work distracted one from thought, and every thought led now along an avenue of pain. Everything seemed poisoned by her bitterness against Nicola, who had deliberately come between her and the happiness she might have found with Richard.

The more she thought of it, the more she was convinced that it was due to something Nicola had said that Richard's attitude towards herself had suddenly altered. What this could have been she could not, for some time, imagine. Not once did it occur to her that Nicola might have hinted of an understanding between herself and Randolph. Even if it had occurred to her, she would have dismissed the notion as fantastic. Finally she came to the conclusion that Nicola had let fall some enlightening remark, apparently casual, as to Sharlie's feeling for Richard himself. One could imagine it so well, that lazy, husky voice, saying something like: "Poor Sharlie! Really, you know, it's hardly kind of you to tamper with her young affections —though at twenty-three she should have learnt to hide her feelings better!" Or perhaps: "D'you think it's fair to Sharlie to philander with her?"—opening his eyes abruptly, cheapening what had passed between them, nipping in the bud all chance there might have been that further meetings might have changed his liking for her into something deeper. What more natural, if this had happened, than that he should feel it wiser, kinder too, to see no more of her?

If their relationship had been clarified, if he had ever said one word of love to her, she would have ignored the claims of false pride, written to him pleasantly and briefly, telling him that the truth, no matter how unpalatable, would be preferable to this unexplained withdrawal. In the circumstances this was not possible. She must endure his silence as best she could.

It was a painful effort to foregather with the children daily in the nursery or garden, be cheerful with George and Gay, and tactful with their sour-faced guardian, so as to be able to send constant news of them to their mother; an effort to listen attentively to Mrs. Ramswell's description of a family of wagtails she had seen from her window mobbing a crow; an effort to make pleasant small talk with Mary when the housemaid brought her meals; an effort not to give short answers, not to resent other people's happiness.

One evening when rain fell in streaming veils that shrouded all the distant view, Mary, bringing Sharlie's tray, made some trite remark about the weather. Sharlie, sick at heart, answered her curtly, then at the hurt look in the housemaid's eyes said quickly, "Mary, I'm sorry! I'm—I'm going through a bad patch, and it's made me thoroughly snappy and disagreeable. Do forgive me!"

"There's nothing to forgive, miss. We all get our ups and downs, and when you're feeling down you think you're never going to be up again. It does make you a bit short, I've been that way myself." She said no more, but later showed her sympathy in small kindnesses; a Victorian posy, carefully arranged, as she had seen it demonstrated at the Women's Institute, put on Sharlie's table; a muslin bag with dried verbena leaves laid beneath her pillow.

The little episode had opened Sharlie's eyes, showed her where she was drifting. She realised that she was at a cross-roads in her life: her present attitude would affect her ever after. She had got to think things out.

"I'm going for a walk," she said to Mary, when she came to clear away.

"Out, in this rain? It doesn't look like clearing, either! Wouldn't you be better indoors, with a nice book?"

"I enjoy walking in the rain, so long as I'm suitably dressed for it."

Presently, in mackintosh, sou-wester, and stout shoes, she let herself out by the side door and followed the back avenue where a cart track branched away from it to meander through the fields. The air was freshly odorous of wet earth and leaves. Rain pattered in the trees and whispered in the grass. Sharlie thrust her hands deep in her pockets, lifted her face to the grey skies, and faced the future.

When, an hour later, she re-entered the side door, Mrs. Ramswell called to her. "Is that you, Sharlie?"

"Yes. Did you want me? I'm so sorry—"

"I only thought it would be nice to have a word with you. It wasn't urgent in the least, and Mary told me you had gone out walking. You must be soaked, my dear!"

"Not really. Only a bit wet on the surface. I'll change my shoes and be with you directly."

Two cups and a steaming jug were waiting on a silver tray on a low table by the fire when, a few minutes later, Sharlie entered Mrs. Ramswell's room.

"A fire! How lovely!"

"Isn't it? If a fire were rare and costly people would flock to see it, rave about the beauty of its living, leaping, life and colour. But because fire is a miracle of every day, we take it as a matter of course.—Have some hot chocolate. I made your damp condition an excuse for having it. I love a hot drink at this hour!"

"Why don't you have it regularly, as you like it?" Sharlie suggested.

"I don't quite know, unless subconsciously I'm trying to postpone the hour of being an old lady as long as possible."

They sipped the hot sweet drink in a companionable silence. At last Mrs. Ramswell said, "Sharlie, I don't want to pry. But for the last few days you haven't been yourself. I've had a feeling that you are unhappy. I do hope it isn't anything to do with your life here? You've no idea how having you has helped me. From the beginning you have fitted in so perfectly."

"I'm glad if I have pleased you . . . I *am* rather unhappy, but it isn't anything to do with being here."

"There's nothing I can do to help?"

"There's nothing anyone can do. I must work out my own cure."

Eleanor Ramswell stifled a sigh, looking at Sharlie's shadowed eyes and wistful mouth. "Ultimately we all have to do that. But if I ever can help, promise you'll let me know?"

"I promise. It does help, just knowing someone *wants* to help!" said Sharlie gratefully.

"You're looking tired. It's time you went to bed.—First, though, I must remind you of a poem that is useless when one's unhappiness is the worst sort of all—unhappiness for someone else. But when one suffers solely on one's own account it gives one fresh courage. At least, I have found it so."

Going to a bookcase, she found at once the book she wanted, an anthology of verse. "Here it is." She handed it to Sharlie opened at Henley's "Invictus." You know it already, I've no doubt."

"Yes. But I had forgotten. Thank you!"

"Take it to bed with you. Good night, my dear!"

When she was alone, Eleanor Ramswell sat a long time gazing into the fire. If only one could share the fruits of one's experience! . . . but one couldn't. One could only indicate the signpost to the tree of knowledge where they might be gathered . . .

In her own room, Sharlie read the half-remembered lines, from the first verse:

> *Out of the night that covers me,*
> *Black as the pit from pole to pole,*
> *I thank whatever gods may be*
> *For my unconquerable soul.*

to the last:

> *It matters not how strait the gate,*
> *How charged with punishments the scroll,*
> *I am the master of my fate:*
> *I am the captain of my soul.*

Yes: it was true. Anything was endurable so long as it concerned oneself alone. Nothing could destroy one's personal integrity, no one could rob one of the power to rule one's thoughts and shape one's spiritual and mental destiny. Nothing, save one's own folly or weakness. No one, save oneself.

She would be strong. Hate was a boomerang, destroying the hater, not the object of his hate. She would not allow hatred of Nicola to take possession of her, to her own injury.

Unhappiness might be made a weapon of destruction or a tool for building. She would use hers constructively. She would not let it warp her nor embitter her, making her the instrument that caused unhappiness for others.

Her aching heart ached still, but bitterness and despair had given place to fortitude and courage when at last she fell asleep.

An early catalogue of bulbs was in the post next morning. Sharlie and Mrs. Ramswell spent a happy hour in planning scent and colour for the dark days of winter, discussing the respective merits of grape hyacinths and scyllas, and agreeing that while poetaz narcissi were fun to grow in pebbles and water, hyacinths were loveliest of all.

Sharlie was typing the completed list, smiling as she pictured the scented trusses of star-shaped flowers, when Jackson came to tell her "Mr. Heighbrook has telephoned to say he will be coming this evening by the usual train."

"To-day? But this is only Thursday!"

It seemed, however, that Randolph was coming a day earlier than usual. Nicola, asker by Mrs. Ramswell if she would meet his train, replied that she was going to a cocktail party. So it was Sharlie who set out with some reluctance after tea. She did not wait for Randolph on the platform, but sat in the car until the train came in, then stood beside it so that he would find her at once.

"Hullo, honey! I believe you're even prettier than last week-end!" was Randolph's greeting. Sharlie ignored it.

"So you've come back a day earlier than usual." Obvious, but one had to make some remark and she could think of nothing better.

"Yes. Couldn't stay away from you a moment longer." Sharlie ignored that, too, but Randolph persevered.

"Missed me?"

"Very much. The bath water is several degrees hotter when you're away."

"I don't believe you take me seriously!" he lamented.

"Does anyone?"

"We'll let the matter drop until you're in a better frame of mind.—Well, what's the local chat? Any more burglaries?"

126

"Wartle Manor, last week-end. Jewels, and a gold toilet set, they say. It's odd, how all these burglaries happen at the week-ends!" Relieved that he had abandoned his attempted flirtation, she became expansive. "If I were the police. I'd shadow everyone who's known to come regularly to the neighbourhood from Friday to Monday . . . I wonder if they do?"

"I wonder . . . H'm, I wonder." He threw back his head and laughed, rather theatrically, Sharlie thought. "Do you suppose that car behind us is a police car, sleuthing us?"

"This is Thursday," Sharlie pointed out.

"How right you are! . . . Look, let's be serious."

"I am being serious."

"Not in the way I'd like. Why is it that I don't see more of you?"

"Why should you?"

"Because I want to."

"And I suppose your own 'want' is your criterion for everything."

"I don't know any better one. And what I want at this particular juncture is for you to say you'll dine and dance in Bath with me one evening. Friday or Saturday, as you please. Will you?"

Sharlie's first instinct was to refuse, pleasantly, but very definitely, but she bit back the words before they reached her lips. If, disregarding her antipathy towards him, she feigned a friendliness she did not feel, mightn't there be an opportunity of persuading him to leave Swanswick, let Averil have the children, even use his influence with his father-in-law to bring about a reconciliation between parents and daughter?

Randolph interpreted her silence as indicating that she would ultimately accept, but was meanwhile playing the feminine trick of keeping him guessing. She must be humoured and persuaded; it was part of the eternal game between the sexes.

"Ah, now, my sweetie, say you'll come!" he coaxed her. "Have a heart and be a honey—not an acid drop!"

His similes were so absurd that Sharlie burst out laughing. Randolph took his left hand from the driving-wheel and laid it on her lap. "You'll come!" he said triumphantly.

Sharlie replaced his hand upon the wheel. "I'll come, but only on condition that it's understood I'm not your sweetie *nor* your honey, and I don't like being pawed."

" 'Pawed!' What a crude expression!"

"It's a crude action," said Sharlie dryly.

"Well, if I'll sign an undertaking to refrain from crudity, you'll come? Which night? To-morrow or Saturday?"

"To-morrow." A week-end was none too long to accomplish all that she would like. If she made good headway to-morrow, there would still be Saturday and Sunday.

"It's a date. The Regency?"

The Regency. Setting of the evening that had begun so happily and for her had such a sorry ending . . .

"I—could we go somewhere different?"

"The Regency *is* appallingly respectable," he agreed. "We'll find a brighter haunt."

"It isn't that. I like respectability—"

"You *like* respectability? . . . H'm. Not a bad pose, now I come to think of it, for Bath. Original, these days."

Sharlie said no more. Randolph's glib repartee and spurious charm gave her a curious sensation of talking with someone slippery, someone who wasn't really there at all: a tiring feeling. To-morrow evening, she reflected ruefully, she would have to keep her wits about her.

Sharlie told Mrs. Ramswell in the morning of her plans, although her evenings were her own and what she did with them was nobody's concern: something frankly told seemed normal and above board, while if discovered by chance it had a flavour of furtiveness and secrecy.

Mrs. Ramswell answered rather blankly, "Oh! . . . I hope you'll have a pleasant evening." For a few minutes she was silent, while Sharlie checked the tradesmen's books. Then she said hesitantly, "Sharlie, I—it isn't any of my business, but you're very young—" She broke off, as though not knowing how to continue.

Sharlie said gently, "Thank you. It's very kind of you to bother about me, and I do appreciate it. But I truly don't think you need worry. I've got my head screwed on the right way—at least, I hope so!"

Eleanor Ramswell's eyes were kind, but troubled still. "I know you have, my dear. It's not your head I'm worrying about!"

Sharlie smiled. "My heart? That's not at all in danger, I assure you. I'm thoroughly inoculated against trouble of that sort."

"Are you? My own girlhood was so ignorant and sheltered that I find it hard to realise how well equipped your generation is to deal with life." Sharlie was glad to see that she looked reassured.

Randolph, driving to Bath in the car he shared with Nicola, told Sharlie he was taking her to a new place he had heard of. "The Green Lizard. They say it's not at all bad for a provincial restaurant."

They parked the car, then walked a short way down a narrow side street. Here in the spacious basements of a vast Regency house two enterprising ex-servicemen had opened a small restaurant run on the most modern lines with cabaret and dance floor. The house itself was let in flats to a firm of solicitors and a dentist.

The restaurant was walled with mirrors, tinted palest peach, in which every woman was reflected so becomingly that she felt her best—a promising beginning to any evening! The tablecloths were peach pink, the glass pale sparkling blue, the china blue, ringed round the rim with several silver circles. The waiter who came to take their order was pleasant and efficient, and he served them with an excellent variety of hors d'oeuvres.

"A fairly promising beginning," Randolph said.

"Yes. It's a charming place."

"M'm. Not too bad, is it?—Considering it's not in London."

Sharlie, though intensely irritated by his contemptuous attitude towards everything provincial, was grateful for the opportunity it afforded her for mentioning the matter uppermost in her mind.

"As you're so fond of London, I rather wonder that you ever leave it! To anyone of your cosmopolitan tastes I should have thought country week-ends must be so boring."

"Believe me, they are! Or were, until you came. But my papa-in-law has a firm hold on the purse strings, and as the purse in question is a pretty fat one, well—" he shrugged—"I take the diplomatic course. Who wouldn't?"

Sharlie nodded pensively. "And yet, you know," she said musingly when they were eating sole cooked with shrimps and cream, "I feel you've taken the wrong turning somewhere. Got in the wrong groove.—Do forgive me if I'm being too personal!"

"You couldn't be," he reassured her, flattered. So she wasn't going to be as difficult as he had thought . . . Always a good sign when the conversation took a personal turn! "Tell me, what sort of 'groove' d'you see me in?"

Sharlie appeared to be considering it. "I don't see you fitting in a groove at all. I should have thought you were adventurous and independent. I should have thought you wanted freedom from responsibilities for years to come. I should have thought you'd have regarded children and the ties of domesticity as shackles; chaining you to humdrum ways when what you crave for is excitement and variety."

"You know, you're right! You're absolutely right! Now how the devil did you hit the nail smack on the head?"

Smiling, she shrugged her shoulders. "Sometimes one does just know a thing like that! Besides, it's rather obvious that your children don't mean very much to you."

"They mean no more to me than if they were that waiter's brats. I don't suppose I'd know them if I saw them in the street. That shocks you, does it?"

It did, but Sharlie wasn't going to tell him so.

"Not exactly. What does shock me is, that though you don't want George and Gay their mother hasn't got them. Children do need at least one parent."

Randolph's whole face suddenly altered, became harder, sharper, scored with bitterness as his eyes narrowed and his lips tightened. "I had none, to all intents and purposes. I see no reason for putting myself out so that the brats can have a better start than I did."

Sharlie realised, too late, that she had blundered: knew that the hurt Randolph had suffered from neglect in childhood had left a scar that warped him, made him see life crookedly, made him resentful of all happiness, even to the pitch of grudging his own children what he himself had lacked. Quickly she tried another tack.

130

"I should have thought you were the last person to cut off your nose to spite your face," she murmured pensively.

"Meaning?"

"You hate these country week-ends. You're bored with your in-laws and you regard your children as a nuisance. I can't imagine why you don't break away from all of it and make a fresh start."

"So you think I'm sticking it simply to queer Averil's pitch. There's a lot more to it than that."

Yes, thought Sharlie, there's luxury that costs you nothing, and a wealthy father-in-law who makes it worth your while not to remove the kudos of your well-connected presence from his house!

The time had come to change the subject: to pursue it might lead Randolph to suspect she had an ulterior motive. Lightly she said, "Isn't life complicated!—What a delicious meal. I do think it was clever of you to discover this attractive spot," and smiled at him disarmingly.

"Nicola said it wasn't too bad. She came here the other night with Heronshaw," Randolph told her.

Richard had brought Nicola here! Already, then, she had succeeded in her deliberate intention of attracting him. Richard, who only five days earlier had said, "Somehow I don't take to that young woman."

She wouldn't think of it. She couldn't bear to think of it . . .

She said that she supposed Randolph went out a great deal in London, and asked which restaurants were most popular at the moment. His face relaxed again, but Sharlie had decided to abandon any personal topic for this evening. It would be wiser, for to-night, to concentrate on trying to disarm the hostility that was latent in him, not only for herself but towards all humanity, so as to prepare the way for further diplomacy on some later occasion on behalf of Averil and the children.

Her present task was easier than she feared at first, for now compassion was mingled with her mistrust of Randolph, who spared no pains to be a pleasant companion, and wisely refrained from any endearments, even when, presently, they danced. Dancing was followed by a short but excellent cabaret. After, they danced again. Earlier in the evening the restaurant had been rather empty, but presently supper parties crowded in after going to the theatre or seeing a film.

Sharlie, intent on building up friendly relations between herself and Randolph for the sake of George and Gay, did not notice the man who, sitting with a party of four at the next table, recognised her, but failed to catch her eye. Towards midnight she told Randolph she would like to leave. She had been rather dreading the homeward drive, afraid that he might stop the car somewhere along the road and want to have what she had heard Nicola call "a petting party." So when he said, "Not in a hurry, are you? How about stopping for a bit?" her heart missed a beat. She was relieved when he responded to her answer, that she was sleepy and would rather get back as soon as possible, by saying, "Well, it's up to you. To-morrow is another day!"

About the same time that she arrived back in her room, Copper Kendall entered the anteroom of the officers' mess at Rockdown Camp. There he found Major Heronshaw and Captain Brounlie, who had been working late together over a training scheme, and now were having a nightcap before turning in.

"Good film?" Ronald Brounlie asked him presently.

"Not at all bad."

"What sort of a dive is the Green Lizard?—You did say you were going on there, didn't you?"

"Not at all bad. Quite a pleasant crowd there, too.— Oh, by the way, do you remember that girl who played such a smashing game of tennis the other Sunday? She was there, with Heighbrook, at the next table. Both of them far too busy to see me, though!"

"H'm. Pity. I thought he was a nasty piece of work," said Ronald.

Richard said abruptly, "Well, good night, you two!" and went away.

Ronald said, "Oh, lord! Do you suppose I dropped a brick? I had forgotten he took us there."

"Lord, no! I don't think he knows Heighbrook any better than you and I do . . . Y'know, I think he's been a bit off colour, this last day or two. Wants a spot of leave, probably."

"It's only about six weeks since he came back from leave."

Copper grinned. "Six weeks is eternity where leave's concerned!"

Nicola and Randolph went to Bournemouth, returning late, on the Saturday, and on Sunday had a tennis party. Some of the guests stayed on for supper, Richard among them, as Sharlie learned from Mary.

"That Major Heronshaw is here again. Stayed on for supper, too. Ever such a nice gentleman, Jackson says, not like most of the crowd Mrs. Freemantle goes with. I wonder if he fancies her? I'm sorry for him if he does. He wouldn't, if he'd seen the temper she was in this morning when I said I hadn't time to iron out her frock!"

If only I could feel she'd make him happy, Sharlie thought, I wouldn't mind so much. Not quite so much. But she'll take everything he has to give, and offer nothing in return . . . Oh, *why* are men so blind?

Since he was so occupied, she saw no more of Randolph until she went with him on Monday morning to the station so as to bring back the car. He asked her if she would go out with him again next week-end, and she said she thought it might be possible, but would make no promise. She had got to keep his interest for the present, and the surest way of losing it would be to let him be certain of her. He was that not uncommon type of man to whom the chase was everything, but who would be off upon another trail the moment it had ended. Between now and next week-end she would have time to think out the best way of trying to win his confidence so as to influence him for the children's benefit, and Averil's. But it wasn't going to be easy. Confidence was a quality that would be hard to cultivate in that volatile nature.

She would be having extra work to deal with during the next few days, and she was glad of it, for rainy weather had set in so that it was impossible to garden, and the more work she had on hand, the less time was available for her battle to keep Richard out of her thoughts. Mr. Ramswell had been ill during the week-end with a sharp chill. The doctor had decreed that he must stay at home during the week instead of returning as usual to his business in the Midlands, though he might deal with urgent matters by telephone and letter if he liked. His wife suggested sending for his secretary, but she was in the middle of her yearly holiday, and he did not like the idea of having her substitute, borrowed from a departmental manager who had gone to Sweden for a week or two, to stay here. She was efficient, but she didn't know his ways. Miss Raven could deal with the small amount of correspondence that was urgent.

Every morning, therefore, for an hour or so Sharlie went to his room to put through telephone calls and take down letters. At first she did so with reluctance, having a very definite impression that Mr. Ramswell was a thoroughly unpleasant character, overbearing, domineering, and tyrannical, his only standards material ones, and above all snobbish to the point of being ludicrous. But when she had seen more of him she found herself according him a reluctant liking. She discovered that his faults were based not upon arrogance, but on humility, which was, surprisingly, the keystone of his character. Always in the back of his mind lurked the memory of his humble origin, the poverty of his boyhood, and instead of feeling pride and satisfaction in all he had achieved, his admiration and envy were for one thing that never could be his: the heritage of an ancient lineage. Sharlie could sense that beneath his bumptious, pompous manner was hidden a state of naive astonishment that by his own efforts he had acquired Swanswick and its superb contents, and that he felt himself something of an intruder in the rooms that he had caused to be so magnificently furnished—as though, thought Sharlie, he were a ragged urchin venturing, awe-stricken, into a place of hitherto undreamed of luxury and wealth. Although his attitude was foolish and exasperating, she could see in it a pathos that was touching. Poor little rich man who, having so much, had missed so much he might have had!

She thought that he was like the dog in Aesop's Fables. Though he would never drop the bone in his possession, he could not fully savour it because of hankering for the one he looked upon as being more desirable.

One morning as she was taking down a letter the door-handle rattled, then turned slowly; the door opened a crack and George squeezed through.

"Hullo!" He said confidingly, "I've run away from Nannie." Burrowing in the pocket of his corduroy shorts he produced two fruit drops to which a good deal of fluff adhered. He held one out to his grandfather and the other to Sharlie. "Have one!" he offered.

Gravely they thanked him.

"Aren't you going to eat them *now*?"

His grandfather cleared his throat; Sharlie explained that she would keep hers till later, "so as not to spoil my lunch."

"That goes for me, too," said Mr. Ramswell.

"Goodness! I shouldn't've thought one fruit drop would take up all that amount of room," said George, gazing pensively at his grandparent's portly figure. He leaned against Mr. Ramswell's knee, fingering a seal that dangled from his gold watch chain. "Can I have this when you're dead?" he asked, but without waiting for an answer went on: "Why do I have to go out always with Nannie when the children at the lodge play by theirselves all day?—Listen—is that her calling?"

A sharp voice floated along the passage. "George! *George*! Where are you?"

"Maybe I'd better go," said George. His head came round the door again a moment later. "But acourse I'd *rather* have you living, Grandfather, than that dangly thing for mine!" He disappeared again.

"He's a caution, that lad!" said his grandfather proudly. "Lucky, too. There's nothing that he lacks. He'll never have to struggle up the ladder. With a start like he's got he should reach the very top." He sighed. "If I'd had his advantages, Miss Raven, there's no knowing where I would have got by now! As like as not I might be Lord Lieutenant of the county!"

Sharlie, greatly daring, asked, "What advantages has George that you lacked?"—then felt herself flush scarlet, feeling that she had been impertinent and merited a snub.

But no snub came. "A background. The best education money can buy. And a long line of blue blood reaching far behind him."

"I should have thought that to be brought up by one's own mother in the littlest, humblest home was worth all the blue blood in the world," said Sharlie, egged on by the thought of Nannie's hard face and Averil's unhappiness to tread on dangerous ground.

"You're young, and young folk nowadays have a lot of half-baked notions about all men being equal and all that. Take it from me, my girl, that isn't so. You'll never make a silk purse from a sow's ear."

"Nobody wants a silk purse nowadays. They're out of date. For hard wear and good value give me a pigskin purse, every time!"

She had said enough. Too much, perhaps? "We'll have to finish this letter if it's to catch the midday post. I'd got as far as 'in consideration of the long delay entailed—' "

When she had finished taking down the letter and taken it away to type, Mr. Ramswell stood a long time with his thumbs thrust in the armholes of his waistcoat, staring unseeing from his window.

"A real nice lassie, that," he said at last aloud. "Wrongheaded—but life will teach her sense, come time. A pigskin purse, indeed!" He smiled indulgently.

As usual, Nicola made some excuse when Friday came for evading going to Bath to meet her brother. Sharlie meant to do the week-end shopping and have tea before going to the station, but the shopping took longer than she had expected, and there was no time for tea when she had finished, so she went straight to the station. Having some time to wait before the train was due, she went on to the platform to try to buy a magazine she wanted at the bookstall.

As she passed through the ticket barrier she dropped her magazine and dived to pick it up. Someone who was coming from the other direction bent with the same intention, and their heads narrowly escaped collision. Laughing, they straightened up, each holding a corner of the magazine, and looked at one another.

"*You!*" exclaimed Sharlie and Richard simultaneously.

CHAPTER NINE

FOR one brief moment Sharlie could have sworn that Richard's eyes held tenderness, and desperate longing, and delight at seeing her. Instinct cried out in her triumphantly, *I was right! He loves you!* and for that golden instant happiness was hers again.

Then reason came once more into its own: she told herself her wish had been the father to the thought, for now he looked no more than pleasantly surprised to see a friend.

In some indefinable way he had changed, even in the few days since she had seen him. His face seemed thinner, harder, more inscrutable. Perhaps, she thought forlornly, Nicola was proving difficult, temperamental and capricious. Some girls might have felt it was his just reward for being fickle, but Sharlie's heart cried out, *Oh, Richard! Darling Richard! I would have been kind to you, given you love and understanding without stint, done everything I could to make you happy. . .*

She said, "I've come to meet the London train."

Richard said simultaneously, "I've come to meet the train from London."

They laughed. Sharlie turned back with him on to the platform, and by mutual, unspoken consent they paced slowly side by side along its length.

Silence between them had formerly been a happy state, tranquilly content. There had been no need, then, of words between them. They had been in tune. But now all that was changed. Silence hung heavily, tense and uncomfortable. If only, Sharlie thought, it had been possible to clear the air by explanations! Yet how could one have spoken of the ending of a relationship that had been undefined, as delicate as gossamer? Besides, on her side there was nothing to tell: her feelings were unchanged: and no man would be likely to explain. "I thought I loved you, but when I met Nicola that evening at the Regency I knew I'd been mistaken."

She felt a desperate need for words to cover the constraint between them, and suddenly found herself chattering in a way utterly foreign to her, of inconsequential trivialities. It was as though a part of her looked on, detached and helpless to prevent her lips from filling the precious moments with empty prattle, scarcely waiting for an answer to a question, in her anxiety to camouflage the situation.

Had Richard read the latest novel that everyone was talking about? . . . She thought it the best book she had read for years. They said that it was going to be filmed . . . Had he had time yet to explore the interesting bits of Bath—the Roman baths, Jane Austen's house, the Abbey? . . . It was odd, wasn't it, how when one was passing through a place one took such trouble to see the sights, but if one lived there, as a rule one never bothered. When she had been at York she hadn't spent more than five minutes in the Minster until the week that she was leaving—yet when she'd been motoring through Durham she had spent an hour in the cathedral . . . Durham was lovely, wasn't it? Norwich, too, and Salisbury, though it was disappointing inside . . .

Richard strode beside her, looking at her now and then, listening attentively to all she said, answering "Yes," and "No," and "Isn't it?" at fitting moments. His expression gave no clue to his thoughts; inscrutability dominated his thin tanned face.

It seemed to her no time at all, and yet as though eternity had passed, when the London train was signalled. Sharlie said, "We'd better go along beyond the bookstall—at least, I'd better, Randolph usually comes in the part that pulls up just a little farther on." She must have given Richard the impression that she usually met Randolph at his carriage door, instead of waiting by the barrier or in the car. Not that it mattered . . .

The train was coming. "Here it is. I—"

Richard interrupted her. "Sharlie, tell me—are you happy?"

The engine slid alongside, and they stood there facing one another. Briefly each saw misery in the other's eyes, only to conclude a moment later that what they saw was a reflection, not reality, as Sharlie forced her trembling lips to smile, and Richard, though unsmiling, schooled his face to blankness.

138

Sick with humiliation Sharlie thought, "So, in spite of all my efforts to hide my feelings, it's been obvious to him that losing him has hurt me badly. Well—he shan't think so any more!"

Pride whipped the colour to her cheeks, helped her to say, wide-eyed and smiling as though puzzled and amused, "Happy? Why, of course I am! Why in the world should you imagine that I'm not?"

"I just—wondered." He looked at her a moment longer, searchingly. "Good. I'm glad. Nice to have seen you!"

He saluted, then turned away to meet a khaki figure covered in gold braid and scarlet tabs and medal ribbons.

Sharlie stood surrounded by hurrying figures and buffeted by their packages, unaware of curious glances, wondering what had prompted Richard's question. Was his conscience pricking him concerning her? Did he still like her well enough to care that she might be unhappy? And if she had answered "No—I'm utterly miserable," what would he have said or done?

Well—speculation would profit her not at all. Probably she would never know the answers . . .

Randolph's puzzled voice said at her elbow, "Hullo! Day-dreaming? You looked as though you were a medium in a trance!"

Sharlie switched her mind from her own problems to those of Averil.

A snatch of talk she overheard between two women standing on the pavement as the car waited at a crossing for the traffic lights to change set her thinking along new lines. One said to the other, "Well, what can you expect? That's human nature!"

It struck Sharlie that if only one expected more of human nature, instead of using the term in a derogatory sense, one might be well rewarded. Why was it that "human nature" was so often used to cover greed and coward-ice and deceit, as though its finer qualities, such as courage and self sacrifice and unselfishness, had no existence? Was this the blunder she had made in reckoning how best to tackle Randolph over the question of letting Averil have the children? Had she, because he had shown her only selfishness and flippancy and callous indifference to other people's happiness, taken it too much for granted that he lacked better qualities? Would it be wiser to change her tactics, and instead of taking the line that for his own sake he must want freedom, appeal to all the best in him?

She felt a strange sense of compulsion to do it now, without delay, as though a second opportunity would never come. She told herself it was absurd: already he had said, "Well, how about another party? Are you game to have a meal and dance to-morrow?" and she had hedged, not giving him a definite answer. To-morrow evening, even to-night, if she arranged it so, the chance was hers. It was ridiculous to be impatient. . .

Randolph said curiously, with a sidelong glance, "What's happened to that golden voice? You don't seem to be using it this evening!"

Still that strange instinct urged her on to seize the opportunity at hand instead of waiting. Impulse had its way. She said, "I want to talk to you. Now. How about drawing in on to the verge? The road is wide here."

If Randolph felt surprise he gave no sign of it, merely suggesting that to turn in along a little-used side track might be a better idea. It was the one where Averil had told Sharlie the story of her marriage . . .

"No. What I've got to say will only take a minute or two."

"No petting parties? Aren't you a hard-hearted Hannah!"

But he did as she had asked without an argument. When he had lit a cigarette she said:

"I'm worried about George and Gay. What happens to them now is going to affect them all their lives. Childhood's impressions are never quite outgrown. At their age they need their mother. As it is, they haven't even got a father—I'm sorry to be so blunt, but you hardly ever see them, do you?—only a nurse who knows all about calories and hygiene and that sort of thing, but nothing about loving them. *You* don't want them. Won't you be generous and let their mother have them?"

Randolph exhaled smoke through flared nostrils. "So that's what you were after when you told me how much happier I would be if I were free of shackles and all that, the other evening!"

"Yes. Though I hated doing it, I persuaded myself that the end justified the means. I've realised since that it doesn't. So instead of using guile—or trying to!—I'm being frank with you."

"Their grandmother dotes on them. So, for that matter, does the old man. You can't make out they're starved of all affection!"

"Oh, I know—Mrs. Ramswell adores them! But the nurse only lets her be with them at stated times, and scarcely ever alone. And if she doesn't get it all her own way in the nursery she goes to Mr. Ramswell and threatens to leave. And because she asked a bigger wage than any other nurse who applied for the post, and looked after a duke's grandchildren before she came to Swanswick, he's horrified at the merest hint of losing her and says that she's to have it all her own way. So she does. But I don't think it's a good way for George and Gay."

"You're asking me to give up a lot more than you realise. Why d'you suppose I cling to my parental rights?"

"Oh, I have no illusions about that! 'Parental rights' are worth a lot in your case. Luxurious week-ends. A more or less permanent home for your sister. Goodness only knows how much in hard cash from your father-in-law because of his obsession with your family title and 'blue blood' and all that sort of thing. To sacrifice so much would be a very generous thing to do."

He laughed, and there was no amusement in the sound. "Generosity isn't much in my line, I assure you!"

"It could be, if you'd let it . . . You've told me that your childhood was unhappy. It would be wonderful if you would sacrifice yourself to let your children have all that you lacked at their age!"

Common sense told her that for any normal person there would be nothing "wonderful" about it: it would be merely natural. But Randolph wasn't normal. He was warped and twisted. One must make allowances.

She went on, "You would lose a lot by it, I know. But you would gain the lasting satisfaction of knowing you had done something to be proud of, lived up to the best in yourself."

Randolph laughed shortly. " 'Best in me!' " His voice was scoffing.

"I mean it. There's too much good in you to let you know real peace of mind if you build up your own prosperity by treating your children shabbily, hurting them as you were hurt."

Randolph sat staring moodily through the windscreen. Then he turned his head to look at her. Steadily her candid eyes met his cold ones, with their strange flecked pupils. He sighed. "Sharlie, you're very sweet . . . If I had known you soon enough, things might have been—well, different. It's too late now."

She cried, "It's never too late! The past is dead. The only thing that matters is the future. You can shape that as you please."

Sombrely he said, "The past can overtake you, poison all the future."

"Ye-es . . . The past can sometimes change the happenings of the future. But it can't touch *you*, yourself, your personality, unless you let it. And that's what matters most of all . . . You'll think it over, won't you? About the children?"

Randolph started up the engine. A touch of his old flippancy returned as he said, "I'll think about it, yes. No harm in that!" Driving along the avenue he asked her, "I suppose you'll feel you've brought off something pretty big if I do what you want."

"*I*? I shan't have done anything at all. I'll feel that *you've* done something pretty big."

She spoke the truth. For another man it would have been the natural thing to put his children's welfare first. For Randolph, to put anyone on earth before himself was something of a miracle.

He drove the car straight to the garage, saving her the trouble of putting it away after leaving him at the house. She didn't realise how unusual was such thoughtfulness on his part.

Her bicycle still leaned against the wall; she had forgotten to put it in the laundry with Mary's earlier in the day after an expedition to the post. She would put it away later in the evening, but to do so now would involve discussion of the reason, which might prove embarrassing if, as she suspected, it had been Randolph who was in the habit of taking it!

142

Randolph took his suitcase and they walked together to the house. Nicola, unknown to either of them, watched for their coming at the window of the writing-room from which, unseen, she had listened, once, to Sharlie and Richard as they said a lingering good night.

She was waiting in the passage as they entered the side door.

"Will you come in here, both of you?"

Surprised, and wondering what it was all about, they followed her.

The writing-room was furnished with the studied perfection of the rest of the house. Behind the glass doors of an old French escritoire gleamed the soft colours of a Rockingham dessert service. Curtains and chair covers were of heavy hand-printed linen suited to the informal purpose of the room; curtains as fresh as though no hand had ever drawn them, covers as creaseless as though no weary body had ever weighed them down. Georgian silver inkpot, matching pen tray filled with a variety of pens, and crocodile blotter lay ready for use on a Queen Anne bureau. A Lely portrait looked down aloofly from the cream panelled walls, and a carved gilt Chippendale mirror reflected all that happened there.

Nicola swung round to face them. Sharlie shrank back behind Randolph from the look of venomous triumph on her face.

"And so, Miss Prunes and Prisms, I've found you out! This afternoon I happened to be at the front door when the postman came. I took the letters. *And* I found one that was addressed to you, in Averil's writing!" She turned to Randolph. "I opened it, of course—"

Sharlie gave a startled exclamation, but Randolph's face was stony.

"—and it appears that this poisonous snake in the grass has been corresponding secretly with Averil practically ever since she came here! See for yourself!"

She thrust the letter in his hands. He took it. Sharlie made no move to take it from him. She stood there motionless and speechless, hands hanging at her sides, frozen with horror at the look of naked hate on Nicola's face, incredulous that anything she could have done could bring such loathing on herself. She herself had felt dislike, aversion, but never anything that approached this bitter hatred.

She had not reckoned with jealousy, the ruling passion in Nicola's frigid and self-centred nature; nor was it in her own generous heart to realise how her success at tennis, followed by Richard's refusal to dine at Swanswick and subsequent departure, taking her with him in his car, had rankled. Nor had Nicola bargained, when she arranged with Randolph that he should make it seem as though a mutual attraction existed secretly between Sharlie and himself, for that attraction to become reality on his part.

Such love as was in Nicola to give was given wholly to her brother. They were kindred spirits, cast in the same mould, and drawn still more together by the common deprivations and frustrations of their childhood. He was the only human being to whom she could say shamelessly all that crossed her mind. Yet, strange to say, she had never until now known jealousy where Randolph was concerned. Even of Averil she had felt none: Randolph's wife was a means to an end, a highly desirable end in which Nicola still shared. Always she had known of his infatuation, he had never shown the least reluctance to discuss them with his sister, often ribaldly, for loyalty, except perhaps to one another, was not in the Heighbrooks' scheme of things.

But this affair with Sharlie—this was different. He didn't care to talk of her, and had snubbed Nicola when she had asked, the morning after he had taken Sharlie to the Green Lizard, "Well? Have a nice petting party last night?" She had been sickeningly afraid it might be going to be a tiresome complication until most fortunately fate, in the shape of the postman, had played obligingly into her hands.

It felt to both the girls as though a spell had snapped when suddenly, with a vicious movement, Randolph crushed the letter in a ball and tossed it on the floor at Sharlie's feet.

They had been standing in a triangle. Now Randolph stood by Nicola, the pair of them confronting Sharlie, ruthless and implacable.

"You little—!" said Randolph softly, eyes narrowed, mouth a twisted slit. "You thought you'd have me for a sucker, did you? Lord! To think that I was fool enough to fall for it, and all the time it was a put-up job between you and Averil!"

Sharlie's lips were dry. Her throat felt tight and parched. She tried to speak; her voice was a hoarse thread of sound. She swallowed and tried again, keeping her eyes on Randolph, as though they were alone together. Nicola didn't matter, but for the children's sake, for Averil's sake, for his own sake, she must win Randolph back to his belief in her.

"You must believe that every word I said to you to-day about the children came from my heart. I meant it, every syllable! Averil had no idea that I was going to mention them—"

"Fools rush in," Nicola taunted. "I suppose you'll tell us next you'd never heard of Averil before you came here!"

"I hadn't! Then one day I found her waiting for me at the gate. She'd heard of me from someone in the neighbourhood. She told me who she was, and that she'd come to ask if I would help her to see the children now and then. I would have liked to, but I felt I couldn't without disloyalty to—to my employers. So I refused. But I did promise to write to her and give her news of them. There seemed no harm in that."

"We've no proof that she didn't arrange for Averil to be with the children. Nurse was away the other week-end and Sharlie took them out. She may have taken them to Averil, for all we know!" Nicola said to her brother.

"I wrote to her about the children. I did no more than that on her account."

" 'Account' is good! I wonder who was going to foot the bill, and how much Sharlie was going to get out of it. Averil's boy friend would have stumped up, I suppose," said Nicola.

Sharlie went on as though she had not spoken. "Then I realised that George and Gay were in the care of—of a sort of robot. She isn't actually unkind to them, as far as I know, but she never likes them to enjoy any of the little things that mean so much to children. If Mrs. Ramswell suggests making toffee, or roasting chestnuts, she says it would upset them. If they want to take their socks off and go barefoot, on the very hottest day she says they would

145

get chills. They mustn't stay up half an hour later for a birthday treat, because she likes to get them off to bed and out of her way as soon as she can. She said their usual routine would be upset if Mrs. Ramswell took them for a picnic on her birthday, because she would have had to come, too, and she hates picnics. She won't let their grandmother have them on her own, because she's got a dog-in-the-manager possessiveness about them. She even stopped Mrs. Ramswell kissing them good night when they were tucked up in bed because she said it would excite them and put them off their sleep . . . So I felt for their sake I'd *got* to try to help, no matter how interfering it might seem. And so, that evening when you took me out, I tried to influence you to let Averil have them by playing on your own selfish point of view. . . After, I decided that was a rotten line to take. I don't believe the end can ever justify the means. That's why, this evening, I was straightforward about it, asked you to let Averil have them simply because I knew it was the right and decent thing to do . . . Do believe me when I tell you there was no conspiracy between me and Averil! She had no idea that I was doing anything beyond letting her have news of them, although, of course, she would have liked me to. Honestly, there's no question of a 'put up job.' You *must* believe that!"

Randolph said scornfully, "Oh, yeah? Then how do you account for this?" He picked up Averil's letter, smoothing out the crumpled paper, gave it to Sharlie, pointing at one sentence near the end. The words stared up at her.

"I know you'll help me to find evidence for a divorce . . . "

She looked up at the two confronting her, like snakes about to strike. "But that's not evidence that I was going to help her!" she protested. "Those words are only a request. They prove exactly nothing!"

Nicola spoke for both of them. "They prove enough for us. Oh, you've been cunning! That ingenuous, unsophisticated pose of yours—you did it well. But it's transparent now. That letter has spilt the beans. You'll never pick them up, no matter how you try!"

Sharlie said desperately to Randolph, "This is what happened. Averil did suggest, in her last letter, that I might

146

help her to get evidence to divorce you. I hated the idea, but felt it wasn't fair to say at once I wouldn't do it. So I didn't mention the matter when I next wrote to her. I thought it only right to think it over before I answered one way or the other. And I did think it over, and had decided that I couldn't have anything to do with it."

"And you have proof of that, no doubt?" said Nicola mockingly.

Sharlie said to Randolph, "I have no proof of anything but my own word. You've seen enough of me to know by now that you can trust me, that I wouldn't lie to you!"

But in Randolph's world, and Nicola's, everybody lied when it was convenient: everybody, that is, who was not too stupid. And Sharlie was by no means stupid.

"I was fool enough to think so, half an hour ago. You'd got me twisted round your little finger. I'd have cleared out of here. I'd have let Averil have the brats. I'd even have given up—" He broke off abruptly. To Nicola he said, "Remind me of this little episode, Nick, if ever I look like getting another bout of softening of the brain!—Not that you're likely to let me forget it in a hurry!"

Nicola's answer was a glance of mingled mockery and something as nearly approaching sympathy as those cold eyes of hers could express.

She said to Sharlie, "You're going to find it pretty difficult to get another job, with the reference you'll be given after this! If I were you I'd pack and go without good-byes. You wouldn't find a farewell interview with either of the Ramswells much to your liking now!"

Randolph said, "Wait a bit. Before we tell the Ramswells anything about this little episode let's sleep on it. We've got Sharlie where we want her. That's the main thing." He spoke as though they were alone together, ignoring Sharlie as though she were not there.

"That's that. I'm heading for a drink," he said, and left the room without another glance at her.

Nicola stood her ground a moment, staring at Sharlie, who looked steadily back into her scornful eyes.

"Well? Feeling pretty sorry for yourself?"

"No. But I'm sorry about—oh, everything. And most of all for you."

Nicola laughed. "Sorry for me? Don't waste your pity! Keep it for yourself."

She sauntered from the room, moving with her studied, mannequin gait, and followed Randolph to his room. She found him taking bottles and glasses from a cupboard. In silence he mixed drinks and gave her one. Silently they drank. Randolph said at last:

"That was a proper facer. Good thing you met the postman."

"M'm. We ought to get that girl out of here, you know. She'll only brew more trouble."

"We shan't be able to hang on here much longer, anyway. And it may come in useful having that little—here, now we have a hold on her. I'm all for postponing the next move in that direction."

Reluctantly Nicola agreed that probably he was right. To neither of them did it occur that Sharlie might make the next move on her own.

Sharlie, alone in the writing-room, sank on a chair because her legs were trembling too much to carry her upstairs to her own quarters, and dropped her swimming head in her hands.

Presently she picked up Averil's letter from the floor, where it had fallen, and smoothed it out. It was a short letter, without a formal beginning.

Thank you a thousand times for all the help you've given me. It's such a comfort to know you're on the spot and that you'd let me know at once if anything fresh develops. I feel utterly desperate about everything, time drags on and I seem no nearer a solution of my troubles, and I can't go on like this much longer, I simply can't. I know you'll help me to find evidence for divorce if there's a chance of that at your end. David agrees that it's the only way for me to get the children.

> *Yours very gratefully,*
> *Averil Heighbrook.*

Yes: the letter did make it look as though Sharlie had done far more than merely sending Averil news of her children's welfare. To expect Nicola and Randolph, with their cynical outlook, to believe her explanation was too much to have hoped for.

What was she to do now? She longed to go away from here at once, to leave the grand house that was so unhomelike, where everything seemed twisted out of its true perspective, and natural instincts were distorted into ugly shapes, so that instead of being trustful one became suspicious. She longed to escape into the world that was familiar to her, where family relationships were normal and happy, and people didn't scheme and plan for their material ends, but went through life with kindly motives.

To leave would be quite easy. To-morrow morning she could give Mrs. Ramswell a week's notice, saying that the place was too lonely for her, or that she would prefer a job in a town, or that the work here wasn't quite what she had wanted. Yes: that was what she would do. She would break away from this place where her expectancy of happiness had been frustrated, and where she had unwillingly become entangled in the ugly chaos of the Heighbrooks' affairs. To make a new beginning was her only hope of forgetting Richard, and forget him she must, if ever she were to know peace of mind again.

It seemed incredible that only a few hours had passed since she had walked beside him up and down the platform, chattering of trivialities when her heart ached with the passionate longing to be back on their former terms of understanding that was too deeply rooted to have need of words. If she could only ring him up, tell him she needed his advice, arrange a meeting, then pour out all the complicated story of the Heighbrooks, and of how she had become involved in them! To speak of it to him would clear her mind, and set things in their true perspective. The mountain would become a mole-hill, seen through Richard's eyes. If only—!

Sharlie pressed her lips tightly together to stop their trembling. "If" was a word to be cut out of her vocabulary. Vain regrets helped no one. Henceforth she must take a leaf from Mrs. Ramswell's book, bury her head, ostrich-like, in the sand of little things, so as to blind herself to the loss of the one thing she had wanted above everything in life.

At last she rose to go to her own room. She stood a moment in the passage, listening, fearful of meeting anyone in her present distraught frame of mind. No sound of life nor movement reached her, and she went quietly up the little staircase, thinking how thankful she would be to leave this house that seemed to her so far from being a home.

Soon after midnight Sharlie, hearing faint movements near her door and then outside, knew that Randolph must be going out. She wondered how long it would be before these nocturnal expeditions of his were found out, and how his father-in-law would react to the discovery. Even if their object were discreditable—and why, if not, should he go out so stealthily?—it was quite possible that the old man's snobbery would make him judge his son-in-law indulgently, as though the sowing of wild oats were a highly creditable pastime when indulged in by the aristocracy, though reprehensible were his butler or his office boy concerned.

She fell asleep determined that in the morning she would tell Mrs. Ramswell she must leave a week hence. Yet when morning came she felt she couldn't do it after all, couldn't forsake the children if there were the smallest chance that she might help to reunite them with their mother, couldn't leave Mrs. Ramswell before the crisis broke—the crisis she was sure was coming, as one senses the apporach of storm.

Now that she was going to stay, for her own peace of mind she must tell Mrs. Ramswell all that had happened regarding meeting Averil and corresponding with her, otherwise she would be constantly on tenterhooks for fear that Nicola would tell her: Nicola would be sure to do it so as to make her behaviour sound disloyal. She went as usual to deal with the day's letters, determined first of all to broach the subject of Averil.

"Before we do the letters, I—there's something I must tell you—"

Sharlie was interrupted by the ringing of the telephone. She answered it. "Maples would like to speak to you about those mattresses."

While Mrs. Ramswell took the call, Sharlie waited, looking about her with the appreciation that never lessened at the simple, charming room that was a lonely woman's refuge from the formal, studied luxury elsewhere in the house. Here the storm would break if Mr. Ramswell should discover that his wife had known her secretary was in correspondence with the daughter to whom he had forbidden any dealings here until she should return to live again as Randolph's wife . . . Sharlie, surveying the situation from this angle, began to wonder if, after all, to tell the story of her dealings with Averil might not result in selfish easing of her own conscience at the expense of Mrs. Ramswell's peace of mind, and possibly involving her in serious trouble later.

Better, she reluctantly decided, to reconsider it at leisure before she burnt her boats. So when, her telephoning finished, Mrs. Ramswell asked her, "You wanted to tell me something?" Sharlie answered, "Only about the new kitchenmaid. Mrs. Tollworthy thinks she'll never be the slightest use at cooking, but she's excellent at housework, so perhaps she could take Lucy's place when Lucy leaves next week?"

In the ensuing discussion of domestic matters and the morning's work she pushed her personal problems to the back of her mind. The morning passed without a visitation from Nicola, whom she had half expected to appear, on mischief-making bent.

Mary, bringing her lunch, remarked, "That Major Heronshaw's for ever here! He and another gentleman he's bringing with him are expected again to tennis this afternoon. We all hope it's the tennis he's after—not Mrs. Freemantle! It would be ever such a pity if she was to catch him, and him such a pleasant gentleman, Jackson says."

Sharlie made some non-committal answer. Mary went on chattily.

"There's been another burglary, at Corby Court, the butcher's vanman told Mrs. Tollworthy. Some lady staying there had all her jewels taken from her dressing-table and nearly died of fright, having a weak heart, when she woke and saw the man. She fainted dead away and lay unconscious, nobody can say for how long, till she came round and gave the alarm, but by that time it was too late. You'd wonder the police have never caught the man nor got a clue!"

"They may have lots of clues, for all we know. What does surprise me is that people are so careless with their jewellery when everybody knows about the burglaries!"

Mary explained that Corby Court had been shut up for some time, and the owners, only recently returned there, might not have heard of the masked burglar whose escapades had been the talk of all the countryside for weeks.

Sharlie had to go to Bath that afternoon to fetch some fish that had not been delivered, as arranged, by bus. "Take the car, and go to a film, if you would care to," Mrs. Ramswell had suggested. It was a glorious afternoon, and she had no particular desire to spend it in a stuffy cinema, but still less did she like the thought of being here knowing that Richard was with Nicola, perhaps seeing him, hearing them talk together as they came in for tea. Far better to go out, and stay out until all chance of encountering him was over.

At the garage she noticed with annoyance that her bicycle still stood there. Last night she had been too upset by the unpleasant scene with Nicola and Randolph to remember her intention of putting it away. Wondering if Randolph had borrowed it again, and if so, whether it had suffered any damage, she went closer, to inspect it.

Something was hanging from the handlebars, as though it had been caught and left there unawares when the last cyclist had dismounted: something long and limp and black.

Sharlie unhooked it from the bell, where it was held by a piece of black tape. She smoothed it out, examining it curiously.

She gasped incredulously, "Oh!" And then, in horror, "*Oh—!*"

The object lying in her hands was a black velvet mask, such as a highwayman might have worn in olden days— *such as a burglar might have worn last night.*

CHAPTER TEN

SHARLIE stood in the garage, staring with mingled fascination and repugnance at the mask she held, limp as a black snake. It was like the key-piece of a jigsaw puzzle, linking the others into a connected picture. She marvelled that until now she had not realised the meaning of Randolph's stealthy expeditions in the night, his interest in any thing one had to tell him of the burglaries, his frequently expressed admiration for the burglar's daring.

A broken sentence flashed across her sharpened perceptions:

"I'd have even given up—"

She had wondered what it was he would have given up for her if Nicola had not effectively destroyed his faith in her integrity. She knew now that it was a career of crime.

The sound of distant footsteps made her start, her nerves on edge, afraid it might be Randolph himself, who, having missed the mask, might be on his way to see if he had dropped it here. She couldn't face him: couldn't face anyone with composure until she had recovered from the shock of her discovery and decided what to do. The footsteps were approaching rapidly. Cramming the mask in her pocket, Sharlie sprang into the car and pressed the self-starter, praying that the engine would start up at once. Her first attempt met with no success. She tried again. This time the car sprang into life. She backed it out of the garage. The running of the engine deadened other sounds, and she had no idea where the footsteps might have taken their owner until Randolph's face looked in, only a few inches from her own. His eyes stared into hers. Sharlie stared back, seeing a new world of desperate ruthlessness in their agate irises, so strangely flecked with amber.

She must go. She'd got to get away. She'd got to think! If she reversed a few more yards the avenue, and escape, would lie ahead. Her foot touched the accelerator and the car slid slowly backwards.

Randolph cried, "Stop a minute! We've got to have this out—"

"When I get back. I'm late—"

He seized the handle of the door beside her, as though by force he could hold back the car. His eyes were frightening. Their dilated pupils held her gaze, as though by force of hypnotism.

"To tell with that! You'll stop," he told her harshly.

She had reversed far enough. The avenue lay clear ahead of her. She forced her eyes away from his compelling stare and pressed on the accelerator. The car shot forward, wrenching Randolph's hand from the door. Sharlie could see his figure in the mirror, diminished to pigmy size, impotent yet menacing, as she sped away along the tunnel roofed by leaves and branches.

Afraid that he might take the car he shared with Nicola and follow her, she did not take the road to Bath, but having reached the gates turned in the other direction. Beyond the village she took a narrow side road and pursued a swift though tortuous course along lanes and byways, until it seemed safe to assume that she had shaken off pursuit, if he had followed. She slowed down, looking for a halting-place, and presently drew up on a strip of rough grassland beside a pond. Farm buildings lay on the other side of the road; a barn, with sulphur lichen staining its red tiles, cartsheds, byres, a solid old farmhouse with a pear tree growing against it and in front a garden with fruit bushes and vegetables bordered by flowers. A tortoiseshell cat lay playing with her kittens by the door; a girl in a blue overall came out to shake her duster; seven fat white ducks waddled across the road to join their fellows in the pond.

Gradually the happy scene had its effect on Sharlie, and the wild beating of her heart slowed to its normal rhythm. Here, in the world of every day, the situation she had left behind at Swanswick seemed fantastic and unreal. If only she need never return there! The idea flashed through her mind that she might drive to Bath and have the car returned to Swanswick by a garage, then go by train to London—back to York—anywhere, so long as she might escape from her unhappiness, and the ugliness in which she had become embroiled. She had enough money with

154

her for the journey to York. Mary would send all her belongings after her. It would be easy!

Yet in her heart she knew that there was no escape for her. One couldn't run away from things that must be faced. One couldn't leave unhappiness. No matter where she went, she would find no cure for the aching loss of Richard.

Now she must face the problem of her discovery that Randolph was the burglar. The obvious course was to go to the police in Bath and tell them all she knew. And yet she couldn't bring herself to do it without first considering whether she could find some other way out, some way that would not bring disgrace upon his wife and children. To carry out her obvious duty would involve betrayal of innocent people . . .

If only she could tell the whole story to someone sane and sensible who could look at it from a detached point of view and therefore see it clearly! If only she could discuss it all with Richard.

She sat for a long time, watching the ducks, and struggling with herself.

Randolph stared after the car with narrowed eyes. He had not missed the mask, and had no reason for suspecting anything was amiss, yet all the morning he had been restless and uneasy, and so irritable that Nicola had snapped that he was no fit company for anyone, and flung away to her own room.

After lunch some vague, indefinable intuition had drawn him to the garage, and at once the look in Sharlie's eyes, the current of shock vibrating in the air, had warned him that she had discovered something. He stood there, hands thrust deep in his pockets, rocking gently from toes to heels and back again, considering what he ought to do. If she had somehow stumbled on real evidence of the truth, she might be on her way to the police. If, on the other hand, she had been merely putting two and two together, she would probably hold her hand until she had something definite to tell them. The question was whether he should make a get-away at once, or take a chance and leave here in the usual way to-morrow, get in touch with a man with whom he'd been involved in several black-market deals, who had a friend who had a plane, and fix it somehow to leave the country in the next few days. His absence would be unsuspected until next week-end when he was due back here. In Ireland he had contacts. Belgium, too. Later, he could get in touch with Nicola. They might join forces. . .

Footsteps made him start. His brows twisted irritably. Nerves not as good as they had been: another straw that showed the way the wind was blowing.

An under-gardener came round the corner, wheeling a woman's bicycle. A week ago Randolph would have given him no greeting, but to-day silence fretted him. " 'Afternoon!" he said.

Cullen said, "Good afternoon, sir." He had no love for Mr. Heighbrook, and his face was blank. The bicycle was Mary's; she had lent it to his wife, and in return he meant to do a job that needed seeing to for her before returning it to the old laundry. Leaning it against the wall, he brought some tools from the garage and set to work.

As Randolph turned away his eye fell on a ladder lying in a corner of the yard. A year ago he wouldn't have noticed it, but in the last few months ladders had played a part of some importance in his doings. He said, "Bit careless, surely, leaving a ladder lying around like that?"

"What, with the burglaries, you mean, sir?"

"Yeah."

"Och, they'll not come here," the Scotchman answered confidently. "It's not as though we had big week-end parties here, and ladies staying with a lot of trinkets and the like."

Randolph shrugged. "Maybe you're right."

When he had gone the gardener looked about and listened. Then he crossed the yard and stooped, hands on bent knees, to look at the old ladder he had fixed to look like new, with a quick dash of paint, one rainy afternoon. He saw with satisfaction that the recent rain had done no damage to the careful work he had put in, camouflaging the places where he had sawn two rungs nearly through, so that if a man's weight rested on them they would snap.

Whistling, he turned back to Mary's bicycle. Lurking still within him was the Davie Cullen who had been for ever playing tricks on people as a laddie, putting soda in his mother's sugar bags, and pepper among his sister's face powder, and highly inappropriate picture post cards between the pages of the schoolmaster's text-books so that they would fall out at inconvenient moments. It would be a fine piece of luck, he told himself, supposing that the burglar did come here, and looked about, the way they said he must, and found the ladder, and it was the means of catching him. Not risky, either, for nobody save Cullen himself came to the garage except Miss Raven and Mrs. Freemantle, and now and then Mr. Heighbrook, to get out one or other of the cars. And you didn't need a ladder to get out a car. . .

To reach his own room Randolph had to pass Nicola's. Her door was open, and she called to him.

"Rando? It's too maddening—they've telephoned from Rockdown to say Richard can't come after all."

Randolph had forgotten about tennis. "What's up?" he asked indifferently.

"I don't know. Sounded as if he might have had to go off unexpectedly. I told Ronald Brounlie to bring someone else instead."

Randolph, without comment, went to change. Nicola stared with brooding eyes at her reflection, thinking that she couldn't make head or tail of Richard. Constantly though he came here, she seemed no further on in that direction than when first she met him. Always he was charming and polite, yet something in him seemed withdrawn. As a rule, she knew at once whether a man found her intensely fascinating or was utterly indifferent to her: there was no middle course for men where Nicola was concerned. But Richard was different. Richard's feelings were a mystery. He must be attracted by her: otherwise why should he seek her out whenever he was free? If time were on her side and she took care to play her cards well, she might have him in the landing-net before the summer's end, thought Nicola, mixing metaphors superbly. But if this telephone message meant he had been summoned suddenly to a new appointment . . .

Nicola snatched up a shoe and flung it viciously across the room.

Sharlie came at last to a decision. She drove to Bath, and having got the fish and done some other shopping, had some tea and then drove back to Swanswick. Half-way along the avenue she stopped the car. Richard was bound to come this way from playing tennis. She would leave the car and hail him so that he must stop. Then she would tell him all the story, for her need was greater than her pride, and this was something too involved to handle by herself. She would take care to tell it quite impersonally.

It seemed to her far longer than the half-hour she had waited, when she heard a car leaving the house. Her pulses quickened, and she gazed eagerly down the long avenue, only to see with sickening disappointment that the car approaching was not Richard's, but an open two-seater that she recognised as Ronald Brounlie's. She had forgotten Ronald would be there; he must have driven Richard here. What should she do? To say she wanted to talk privately with Richard would be embarrassing for both of them. She was relieved of any need for making a decision when the car came nearer and she saw a head of fiery red beside Ronald's, in place of the dark one she had expected. She bent her head above her bag as though in search of an imaginary cigarette, looking up as they passed to return the adjutant's friendly wave.

So Richard hadn't come. She would have been immeasurably glad to know he had not spent the afternoon with Nicola, if only her own need of seeing him had been less urgent: so urgent that she must make another effort to get in touch with him.

Leaving the car in the avenue, she walked back to the village to the telephone box outside the post office, and rang up the mess to ask if she might speak to Major Heronshaw. A cheerful Cockney voice informed her that the major had gone away this afternoon.

She asked how long he was expected to be away? The Cockney voice made answer that it couldn't say, but letters would be forwarded, if she cared to write?

"Thank you so much," said Sharlie, and rang off. Outside the box a girl was waiting. Sharlie handed over to her, and stood undecidedly in the road, desperate in her disappointment. She had so counted on the reassuring sound of Richard's voice, on having him to share the burden of decision that after all she must continue carrying alone. Richard would have known no hesitation. For him there would have been one course and one course only. Once she had told him, everything would have looked simple and straightforward. The world would have seemed safe and sane again if only she had been able to get in touch with him.

Ought she to telephone the police at once, and tell them all she knew? That was her obvious duty . . . Or was it? She owed loyalty to Mrs. Ramswell. It would be a poor return for all her kindness to involve her and her family in a hideous scandal. Wasn't there some other way of handling it?

Head bent, she paced the road outside the call box, looking for a solution. The other girl finished her call and passed her, looking at her curiously. Slowly Sharlie entered the box, closed the door, and searched for coppers in her bag. She found three pennies, and she needed four to telephone to Bath: better to contact the police there than to do it through the village constable. She thrust her hand deep in the pocket of her coat, hoping to find another penny. Smooth and round and warm, she found one: found something else as well: a battered tin soldier George had given her that morning, minus an arm.

"He has to go to hospital, but Nannie won't be bothered with him and Gay's not big enough to nurse him properly. So could you be the Red Cross nurse and bandage him?"

Sharlie had said she would. She'd meant to put a bandage where his missing arm should have been fastened, and to make a bed for him from a small cardboard box, and sheets from an old handkerchief. George would have been enchanted. But she had forgotten: she must do it when she got back. She pictured George's eager face, the silken bubbles of Gay's hair, the innocent nursery smell of ironing, and milk, and talcum powder . . .

She dropped the coppers back in her bag.

There was no family life at Swanswick. The Ramswells saw little of Nicola and Randolph except at meals; the visitors kept to their own quarters, making it clear that they preferred their own company and that of the contemporaries they invited here, to that of older people.

After dinner Mrs. Ramswell went as usual to her own sitting-room, where she had taken up a book on bird migration when her husband joined her, smoking a cigar, prowling about the room, taking up a book, putting it down. She knew that he was thinking, as he often did, of Averil.

"Tom—won't you give in? The children need their mother. Averil needs her babies and her parents and the backing of her own home. You and I want her here. I will arrange it all, if you will only let me."

His only answer was an inarticulate sound. He stood with face averted, staring at an old coloured print of game birds. She went on persuasively, "Human relationships are the most important thing in life. The only thing of any consequence. *Please,* Tom!"

She thought his silence was a sign of weakening, and held her breath, waiting for him to speak; hopeful, yet afraid to hope too much. When at last he did speak, disappointment hit her like a blow.

"If you had married any other man but me, my dear, I doubt you would be living in a two-roomed bungalow. You must be practical if you're to get the best of life in this world. People think nothing of you till you've made your way and got a place among the nobs. If we leave Averil to herself she'll come to see sense and find out which side her bread is buttered. To be Lady Frostenden is surely worth ignoring a crop of wild oats such as any young fellow in Randolph's walk of life might sow, or a few hasty words."

There was no more that she could say.

Nicola and Randolph left the dining-room and wandered to the hall door, staring down the valley with unappreciative eyes. They did not see the opal haze veiling the distance, nor how the low sun stained grey Cotswold stone with rose and gold. They did not smell the blend of new-mown grass, and lime blossom, and white jasmine. They did not hear a willow warbler singing, late in season, in the woods. To them the country was a place that one occasionally had to tolerate, when the luxury one might chance to find there compensated for the boredom living there involved.

160

Nicola blew a chain of smoke rings. "Amazing, isn't it, how anyone can settle of their own free will in an isolated dump like this?"

"M'm. Beyond one's comprehension." He lit a cigarette. His lighter caught his sister's eye. It was a gold one, with his monogram inlaid in platinum.

"Good-looking lighter, that. New cuff-links, too—onyx and diamond, no less! Been going it, haven't you?"

"The best," her brother said, "is good enough for me."

"The best costs quite a lot of money. Where d'you raise it all?" she asked him curiously.

"You don't suppose I toil five days a week in the City for nothing, do you?" he answered her evasively, and she said no more, but thought he must have done well lately on currency deals, or something of the sort. He gave it out that he was working in some unspecified capacity with a firm known jokingly in their circle as Morecambe and Wise, but when she had asked him for their telephone number he had been evasive.

Behind them, Mary said, "A note for you, sir."

Randolph ripped it open; read it, frowning; folded it deliberately in long, slim fingers, put in in his pocket. Nicola, knowing his love of secrecy, was piqued, but not surprised, when he told her nothing of its contents, saying only, "Better get along indoors."

He did not follow her upstairs; she thought he must have gone to telephone.

Randolph stood in the hall, listening until he heard her footsteps die away along the passage to her room. Then, moving lithe and lightly as a cat, he went to the writing-room in response to Sharlie's summons.

He found her waiting there, outwardly composed, inwardly feeling small and lonely and afraid. She had been standing, but as he came in she sat on the arm of a big chair because her legs felt suddenly as though some unseen agency had filleted them.

He shut the door and leaned against it, folding his arms, narrowing his eyes to glittering slits.

"Well? What have you got to say?"

"I found this. Hanging on my bicycle." She held "this" out to him: a scrap of limp black tape and velvet. Randolph took it, scarcely looking at it, thrust it in his pocket with her note, all the while keeping his eyes fixed on her face. So that was what had given him away. He'd known that she was on to something . . .

"So what?" he said.

Her lips felt stiff and dry. She swallowed; it was an effort to speak, but she looked him in the eye and said her say.

"So I have sent for you to strike a bargain." She felt better after that. The dictatorial arrogance had done her good. Words came more easily. "I'm going to let you get away, but only on my own conditions. You may leave as usual on Monday morning—but this time, it will be for good. You must arrange without delay for Averil to divorce you, so that the children are entirely hers. When you have done that, you must leave this country. For always."

"Baby, you sure spilt a bibful!" Randolph drawled. The cheap slang sounded out of keeping with his patrician features. "And if I don't fall into line, what then?"

"Then I shall have to ring up the police and tell them what I know."

He tried a spot of bluff. "You have no evidence."

"Haven't I? Conway knows, and Mary, too, that someone used to take a bicycle if it were left overnight in the garage. And twice you left a lot of finger-prints behind. And when I'd put them on the track they'd soon find all the evidence they needed."

He stood so long in silence, staring at her with those glittering, hypnotic eyes, that when at last he spoke she jumped as though to hear his voice again was the last thing she had expected.

"I give you best. Have it your own way."

She had expected denials, arguments, recriminations, possibly appeals. The swiftness of her victory left her speechless for a moment.

She thought of something else. "The things you took last night from Corby Court—I want you to return them."

It had been a disappointing haul; there had been little of any value. Not worth sticking out for that. "Righti-ho!"

"That's settled, then." And yet she didn't feel that anything was settled. The mockery on his face robbed her of any triumph she might have felt. "If I don't hear from

162

Averil within a week that you're arranging matters with her lawyers. I shall get in touch with the police. If you leave any traces here of what you have been doing, it won't be my fault.—Does Nicola know what you've been up to?"

"Hasn't a notion."

She believed him, liar though he was. "If you keep your part of the bargain, I'll keep mine. But if you don't, I'll have no mercy. Now I'm going. Open the door, please."

He made no move. There was such menace in his eyes that Sharlie felt a sickening fear of what was in his mind. No one was within ear-shot . . . Then he stepped aside, opening the door, bowing in mock deference as she passed out.

Next day Sharlie felt utterly spent. She tried to read, but could not concentrate; went for a short walk, but was too tired to go far; spent a few minutes in the nursery, but felt vague and far away, so that George presently said, reproachfully, "You're not listening like you usually do!"

She said remorsefully that she was sorry; it wasn't that she wasn't interested in the brick fort he was building for his soldiers, but she was feeling tired and stupid.

"Stupid? How can you be, and you a grown-up-lady?" George demanded, round-eyed.

"I don't feel very grown-up, sometimes," Sharlie told him.

Anxiously he studied her. "You won't start getting a bone in your leg, will you, the way Nannie does when me and Gay wants to do a thing she doesn't?"

Sharlie assured him that she would acquire no extra bones.

Soon after tea she went to bed, telling Mary she would want no more to eat to-day. The sympathetic housemaid, coming quietly to her room during the evening, found her asleep, and crept away, leaving a glass of milk beside her bed.

Afterwards, Sharlie was to wonder why she had awakened so abruptly in the small hours, since there had been no movement on the staircase by her door: to wonder whether it had been some sixth sense, warning her that something was amiss, that made her sit up, listening intently.

Moonlight lay in bars of silver light across her room. Although her straining ears could hear no sound, it was impossible to settle again to sleep. She slipped a coat over her nightdress, then went down quietly to the side door, moving as stealthily as Randolph must have moved on that same staircase many a time.

The door was locked and bolted. Shuddering, she leaned her head against it, weak from the intensity of her relief. Why she should have been so certain something was wrong she could not tell, yet she had been positive that the unbolted door would stand in evidence that Randolph had gone out. Thankful and reassured, she turned to go back up the little staircase.

Something made her pause. She had not made it a condition of their bargain that Randolph should go out no more with criminal intent from Swanswick, never dreaming he would have the effrontery to do so, knowing what she knew. Yet as she stood there shivering, intuition strengthened to conviction that, despite the evidence of the locked door, he had gone . . .

And now that sixth sense took possession of her, stronger than reason, urging her to action, making her shaking hands slide back the bolt and turn the key.

She stepped outside and listened, head lifted, and for a moment forgot her errand, thinking only of the world of ivory and jet surrounding her, the fathomless star-scattered sky, the cool night air, sweet and mysterious after the indoor odours of a well-kept house. Then, hugging her coat about her, she turned in the direction of the garage, skirting the house, then following the dark path through the shrubbery, her light feet in their bedroom slippers making no noise.

The yard lay blank and empty in the moonlight. Sharlie took the garage key from where it hung behind a gutter pipe, and with a pounding heart and shaking knees thrust it in the keyhole. A moment later she was stepping through the wicket door into warm darkness that was stuffy with the smell of oil and petrol.

She fumbled for the light switch, did not immediately find it, could have wept in her impatience as her hand groped over the rough wall. When at last her fingers found projecting smoothness she drew a sobbing breath in her relief. Drowned in light, dazzled and blinded, at first she peered in vain for what she sought.

And then the bicycle took shape. Her bicycle, standing exactly as she had left it yesterday. . .

Reason had told her she would find it here, since Randolph had not left the house by the side door. Later, she was to wonder why intuition had refused to be appeased: why, having locked the door and hung the key away, she should have stood tense and listening, waiting for disaster. . .

Randolph had no intention of keeping to the bargain he had made with Sharlie. Nor did he suppose that she would keep her side of it, once he had given Averil her freedom and the children. After that, she'd talk. You couldn't trust a woman. You couldn't, in his experience, trust anyone.

To-morrow morning he would leave as usual, and then, at once, make contact with that fellow in the currency racket. They said he could fix anything for anyone who made it worth his while. A plane, maybe a fishing boat— somehow he'd get to Belgium or Denmark. He'd feel safer that way, even though Sharlie, being bats about the children, might be bluffing and might keep her mouth shut for their sakes if he risked staying in this country. He'd got a hunch it would be better to get out.

As for doing anything about divorce, he'd be a proper fool to lose the only hold he had on Averil, and through her, on old Ramswell's cheque-book! Some day it might be worth a lot to him.

Jackson, coming to lay out his dinner-jacket on Sunday evening, was surprised to find him packing articles he usually left here.

"Won't you be coming down next week-end, sir?"

"No. I'll be going to friends in Sussex."

That would give him something of a start, if he were not expected here. Later, he might write to tell them he had got a job abroad. That must depend on whether Sharlie held her tongue, or not. He'd have to keep a close eye on the English papers.

He'd be a fool if he returned the things he'd taken from Corby Court! They'd bring in a few pounds. He put them in the toes of a pair of shoes: a jewelled watch, a string of pearls that might be cultured, a nice pair of paste clips, and packed them in a small case with his toilet articles and pyjamas. Might have to travel light, but that weighed no more than a pound or two.

He couldn't sleep that night. At last he put the light on and lay smoking, planning, cursing himself for having driven a poor bargain with the fence in Soho. If he'd had any sense he'd have stuck out for twice the money.

Bit paradoxical to lie here in this house crammed with treasures worth a fortune, worrying about money. Pity the old girl didn't care for jewellery . . .

Suddenly he started up, propping himself on one elbow. Until now he'd only taken jewellery, since that was easiest to get rid of. But once he'd got abroad, it might be different. He'd heard of fences who got hold of stuff for rich collectors. One or two small canvases, flat in the bottom of a suitcase—!

But they'd be missed at once. Sharlie would realise what he was up to. She might talk.

Then he remembered that the parlourmaid had gone yesterday to hospital for an emergency appendix operation. It was she who kept the library, which was seldom entered by any other member of the household. He had seen Mary going there to dust this morning, in her place; it was on the cards that she might leave it untouched for a day or two, as it was extra to her own work, and was practically never used. Worth gambling on—?

Two small Van Dycks hung there, and a Meisonier. Cut from their frames and sold abroad, they'd keep him in the lap of luxury for months. . .

He'd have to make it look like a job from the outside. Well—that should prove easy enough!

He slipped on trousers, a dark pullover, and gym shoes; took a strong sharp knife, a sheet of thick brown paper, a small pot of glue, and put a pair of cotton gloves in his pocket. He did not take his usual route by the side staircase, for fear of being heard by Sharlie in her room, but instead went stealthily along the corridor from his room to the main stairs. He switched on no lights, but used a

166

torch. It sent a shaft of light ahead of him across the dark hall, where a Gainsborough lady looked at him down her elegant nose, and a sardonic gentleman by Lawrence watched him to the door. Swanswick was well run to the smallest detail. The key turned smoothly in the lock, the bolt slid back without a sound. Randolph stepped out into the night.

Oblivious to the beauty all about him, he headed for the garage. On his way he passed along the terrace under the window of the library, then made a detour so as not to walk beneath the windows of the servants' rooms. The ladder lay in the yard, where he had seen it yesterday. He grinned remembering the gardener's confident "Och, they'll not come here!" in answer to his own suggestion that it might come in handy for the burglar, should he visit Swanswick.

Putting on the gloves, so as to leave no finger-prints, he took it up. It was well balanced, and he carried it without difficulty, moving soundlessly in his light shoes: Sharlie, entering the yard only a moment after he had left it, heard no sound but the chirp and flutter of a dreaming bird.

Beneath the window of the library he put the ladder in position. Then he smeared the paper he had brought thickly and carefully with glue. Stuck firmly on the window-pane nearest the hasp, it would hold the glass when he had broken it with a skilful crack, so that it did not fall tinkling to the floor.

At the last moment he put on the mask: it was unlikely that anyone would hear him, but he would run no risk he could avoid. Carefully he adjusted the position of the ladder, saw that it was steady, and began to mount.

He was no more than seven feet from the ground when the step Cullen had sawn through gave way beneath his feet. His leg shot through, behind the ladder. Randolph clutched a creeper, ripped it from the wall, lost his balance and fell outwards, backwards, dragging the ladder on top of him . . . He knew the stone balustrade edging the terrace was rushing up to meet him, and his last despairing cry of terror tore the night like rending silk.

Sharlie, hearing it, knew it was for this she had been waiting. She ran in the direction of the sound.

CHAPTER ELEVEN

SHARLIE, perched aloft on a step-ladder, straightened the picture she had been hanging, then looked about her at the long, low room whose windows looked out on a medium-sized walled garden, whose old-fashioned borders sloped down to a beck that tumbled down a Yorkshire dale. Beyond it, fields and woods climbed up to meet the heather. One might have thought, looking at such a view, that Farrabeck Lodge was buried in the country, yet, its Georgian doorway opened on the market-place of a small country town.

Averil, crouched on the floor beside a bookcase, sat back on her heels, looking about her, too. "Odd, isn't it, to see furniture and pictures one has known elsewhere, in such a different setting!"

"Just what I was thinking. But your mother's things look more at home here than they ever did at Swanswick."

"Yes. This is her kind of house, and Swanswick wasn't."

For Swanswick had been sold. The Ramswell family had left the neighbourhood where they had never been particularly happy and had eventually met with such disaster, and returned to the north country where they came from.

"This time you'll choose a house to suit yourself," Tom Ramswell had told Eleanor, "and furnish it as you've a mind, and please yourself about the way you run it." He had lost much of his assurance and assertiveness since the discovery that the son-in-law he had so respected and admired had been a thief, and worse. Instead of laying down the law he would consult his wife and daughter over matters in which formerly they had had no say: his faith in his infallibility had been badly shaken. Sharlie, though she pitied him, hoped he would never regain the old cocksure confidence that had raised up a barrier between himself and his wife.

Eleanor had spent hours closeted with house agents, and visited innumerable houses of all sorts and sizes, and had finally chosen Farrabeck, a medium-sized house of the

Georgian period she loved. It was in a countryside well known to both herself and Tom; they would be able to pick up old threads here, and renew old friendships.

Then the exertion of house-hunting, combined with delayed reaction from the shock of Randolph's death and its attendant circumstances, and the long strain preceding it, had laid her low. She had spent a fortnight in a nursing home while her husband and daughter, helped by Sharlie, dealt with the initial stages of the move. A few days ago Mr. Ramswell had taken her to spend her convalescence in a country house hotel in the Border country. George and Gay were with them—no longer in the cramping charge of the prim nurse Sharlie had so disliked, but happy in the care of their old kindly nannie, who had been reinstated by Averil without a word of protest from her father.

Many of the contents of Swanswick had been sold. There was not room for all of them in Farrabeck, and besides, many of them, lovely though they were, would have been out of place, too sumptuous for the homely atmosphere that was Eleanor's natural setting. Most of the staff were staying on with Lady Bartlesham, who had bought the house, but May, the kitchenmaid, had come to Farrabeck as cook, and Mary, who was going to be married in a week or two, had come as well, to help them to move in. The furniture and luggage had arrived here yesterday in vans; Sharlie and Averil by car. They had spent last night at the local inn; to-day, all of them had been hard at work, helped by the gardener and his wife and daughter, and to-night they would be able to sleep here.

All afternoon Averil and Sharlie had been busy in the room that would be Mrs. Ramswell's sitting-room, arranging furniture and books and hanging pictures, so that at least one corner of the house would be a comfortable haven where they might retreat after their labours elsewhere.

Mary looked in. "My word! This room looks different from yesterday, and no mistake! I'll bring your supper in here, shall I? You could have it on that little table by the fire. There's a grand lot of kindling in the shed by the back door, and logs as well. I'll get it going while you have your baths. The water's nice and hot—May likes the boiler, it's a kind she's used to."

"Oh, Mary—*lovely!*" they cried, and presently, agreeing that they had done enough work for one day, went up the echoing, uncarpeted stairs to two adjoining bedrooms where the beds had been made and bare essentials were in place, while ornaments and pictures were stacked ready for arrangement later.

"Doesn't it look *grim!*" Averil exclaimed ruefully, standing in the doorway of the room that would be Sharlie's.

"It won't be, when I've scattered things about a bit." And certainly it did look less bleak and formal when her toilet things lay on the dressing-table and her nightdress on the bed.

There were two bathrooms. Water was running in the one beyond Averil's room, so Sharlie took the more distant one farther along the passage, whose windows kept a vigil up the dale towards the distant Cleveland hills. While the bath filled she leaned on the window ledge, looking out into the blue dusk that was aromatic with the bittersweet of autumn: chrysanthemums and rotting leaves, bonfires and new-made ploughland, wood smoke, and full stackyards. Lights in farm windows up the valley hung like bright flowers in the meshes of the dusk.

Sharlie had been thankful, during the past weeks, for all the work and responsibilities she had had to shoulder, filling her time and thoughts, preventing her from dwelling on past horrors that were best forgotten. Yet when she was very tired, as now, those horrors had a way of thrusting through the safe and sane affairs of every day, forcing themselves on her reluctant consciousness. As she let her tired body relax in the warm lapping water, she knew that if for once she faced her memories, instead of trying to evade them, she might rout them and so finally escape.

Deliberately she turned her mind back to the ghastly moment when she had found Randolph lying in the moonlight, with his masked face upturned towards the sky, and his hands outstretched as though in mute appeal for pity, and had known that he would never move again.

Deliberately she dwelt on the kaleidoscopic happenings that had followed: interviews with the police, and yet more interviews . . . Averil's arrival with David Sherren,

170

who had driven her from London and remained at Swanswick during the next few nightmare days, a tower of strength and kindly common sense . . . The inquest, and the peering, curious faces . . . Headlines in the local papers—*"Peer's Heir Leads Double Life"*—*"Jekyll and Hyde Existence of Well-Known Playboy"* and the like . . . Voices in the village when she passed, whispering, "it was her that found him!" . . . Mr Ramswell, grey-faced and looking shrunken, as she rose to leave him after taking down some letters on the day following the inquest, and he stopped her for a moment so that he might say to her:

"You were in the right of it, about a pigskin purse being the best value every time—and I don't mind admitting it." . . . Nicola's first frenzied grief, and the hysterical accusations she directed chiefly against Averil, though they were levelled against all and sundry . . . Her departure immediately after the funeral, without a farewell word to anyone, sullen and arrogant, driving the car she had shared with Randolph. Sharlie had wondered at the time whether a quiet wedding would be arranged between her and Richard during the next week or two, and had studied the marriage announcements in *The Times* with sickening dread that she might see their names there.

Three weeks later, glimpsing the name Freemantle, she had braced herself to face the agony of reading of their wedding. But the name coupled with Nicola's had been strange to her.

"On Sept. 1st, in London, Juan Sebastian Roderigo da Parandez, of Lisbon, to Nicola Freemantle."

Averil knew something of the bridegroom. He was a wealthy business man, it seemed, with vast financial interests in South America. Nicola had certainly feathered her nest well, although her husband must be fully thirty years older than herself. Had she, Sharlie wondered, thrown Richard over for a richer man? Or was it he who had chosen to go no further with their association? Speculation would avail her not at all: it was improbable that she would ever know the ending of the story that had brought her so much pain.

Back in her bedroom, brushing out her hair, she wondered whether her path in life and Richard's would ever meet again, and had to face the bitter fact that it was most unlikely. Brief encounter, and for her the happiest she would ever know, had been their lot . . . Where he was now she had no idea. She had not heard of him since, meeting Ronald Brounlie in a Bath bookseller's, she had asked him casually after talk of other matters, "Is Major Heronshaw at Rockmoor still? I haven't seen him lately?"

And was told, "Oh, didn't you see it in the papers? He flew to Washington as a member of a military mission at a moment's notice—took the place of Brigadier Hartlip, who was injured in a motor smash only three days before they were due to go. Now I come to think of it, I believe he was starting off to Swanswick to play tennis when they telephoned for him to go to London right away to fix things up."

"How lovely for him! No, I didn't know. Just at that time I was rather avoiding looking at the papers."

Ronald Brounlie, looking embarrassed, had stammered sympathetically that he didn't wonder—must have been a ghastly time for all of them at Swanswick! And they had said no more of Richard.

Since then she had scanned the papers eagerly for mention of the defence mission in America, and had occasionally been rewarded by a colourless crumb of information. Ten days ago she had seen that they were on their way home. By now Richard might have returned to Rockdown, though Ronald Brounlie had hinted that it was highly probable he would be moved soon to a more important post . . .

In future all that she would know of him would be from reading of him in the papers. So she would follow his career, would learn from time to time of his successive promotions. So she would know of his engagement, then his marriage . . . later that he was the father of a son . . . She would be sure to see his photograph occasionally, taken at some military function, leaving an investiture, standing in the doorway of a church, his dark head bent to look into his bride's smiling eyes . . .

She had been wrong in trying to escape unhappy memories! Better to linger in the past than face the lonely future . . .

Sharply Sharlie checked her thoughts as Averil's door clicked open and she passed along the passage on her way downstairs. This was no time to battle with unhappiness. She'd got to turn her back on it, put on a mask of cheerfulness, join Averil by the fire. She slipped into a warm blue house-coat, for the September nights were chilly, and found Averil sitting in the firelight. Mary had put a small round table by the hearth, and presently served them a savoury casserole of young rabbit cooked with herbs and mushrooms, followed by cheese soufflé, light and crisp as foam.

When they had finished and the meal was cleared away, they sat back peacefully in their deep chairs, blinking sleepily at one another.

"Early to bed, I think, don't you?" said Averil. "It isn't going to be easy, though, to tear ourselves away from such a gorgeous fire!" She took a cigarette, and offered her case to Sharlie, who shook her head, then asked her, "Don't you ever smoke? Not even when you're tired?" Not waiting for an answer, she went on, "I didn't tell you, did I, that David will be coming to the King's Head for the week-end?"

"Is he? I'm glad. He's charming. So dependable and kind."

"He is, isn't he? He'd never let one down." Averil rested her chin on one hand and leaned forward, staring in the fire. She made a charming picture, with the leaping flames gilding her face and hands, brightening her dark hair, and deepening the amber of her house-coat. Sharlie thought how greatly she had changed since their first meeting: her mouth, that had been set in such determined lines, was gentler, softer, and in her hazel eyes serenity had replaced the former look of misery and strain.

Averil said, "He's looking for a country practice. David I mean."

Sharlie was startled. "Really? After making such a name in Harley Street?"

Averil sounded defensive as she said, "Well, country people need good doctors just as much as town ones!"

"Of course. It will be splendid for the people whereever he eventually settles." But she had been thinking of David's own ambition, rather than his patients.

Averil hesitated. Then, still looking in the fire, she said, "It's early days to talk of it—but I'd like you to be one of the first to know. I'm going to marry David in a month or two, after we've got mother well established here. It's because he thinks the children would be happier in the country that he's giving up his London practice."

"I am so glad! For both of you. The children, too. I'd hoped—oh, long ago, when I first met David, that some day this might happen."

Averil slid to the floor, her hands clasped in her lap, looking up at the sympathetic face above her. "Oh, Sharlie —I ought to be so utterly, deliriously happy! But I can't be. I'm so worried about George and Gay——" Her lips trembled, and she bent her head so that her hair fell in a dark cloud about her face.

"Worried about them? But why? David is so good with children. With him, they'll have the happiest possible upbringing."

"Oh, I know! It isn't *that*. David is everything that I'm not—patient and tolerant and 'slow to anger.' He can give them all I lack. No—it's the heritage I've given them that sends me nearly crazy when I think of it. A father who was utterly lacking in any moral sense at all, unscrupulous and cruel and callous. I know it's horrible of me to speak so of him, now he's dead, but even death can't wipe out knowledge . . . Always I'll be watching them, dreading to see his characteristics cropping up in one or other of them, making mountains out of mole-hills, exaggerating ordinary childish faults into the beginnings of their father's failings, knowing I'm doing it, yet not able to stop it. And in time they'll realise what's happening, and the atmosphere of home will become tense and warped and ugly, and—oh, Sharlie! I can never blame myself enough if George and Gay don't grow up into ordinary, decent, happy people! . . . It haunts me so, this dread for them, that I've never mentioned it before, not even to David. Only, just now, it suddenly grew too much for me. I *had* to speak of it, to save my reason . . . Don't ever say a word of it to anyone—and forgive me for such an outburst!"

Sharlie said, "There's nothing to forgive. I'm glad you told me. If you bottle up your troubles they get all out of focus. And I'm certain that you're wrong about the dangers of a bad inheritance." She paused, groping for words.

"I believe," she said, "a man is the reflection of the treatment he received in childhood—not of his forebears! A child *needs* love and sympathy, and to feel he matters terribly to someone. Lacking those, he can't develop properly. He's like a seedling with a stone on top of it. Eventually he may struggle from beneath the stone, but always he'll be warped in some way, as a plant would be."

"D'you think that's what went wrong with Randolph?"

"I'm sure of it! I know, from things that he and Nicola let fall, they felt, as children, that their parents didn't want them—"

"That's quite true. Randolph never forgave his father for it."

"No . . . I could see that. And because of it, I think he bore a grudge against the world in general. It had given him an inferiority complex, too. I believe that's why he took to burglary. I believe he saw himself as a romantic sort of Raffles, taking daring risks, and it helped to reinstate him in his own estimation . . . It must be humiliating to be an unloved child."

"He always seemed to—well, to have a pretty high opinion of himself!" said Averil dubiously.

"*I* think that very often when someone brags and boasts and throws his weight about, it's a sure sign that he's doing it to bolster up his own self-confidence. And people who are cynical and hard—yes, and even cruel—are far more to be pitied than blamed. It usually means that life has treated them so harshly in their childhood that in a pitiable idea of self-defence they've built a crust of callousness about themselves, as a protection. But George and Gay will grow up in the security of your love, and David's, and never need that armour."

Averil looked up at her with searching eyes. "Funny," she mused, "you seem to know so much more than I do, though I must have had far more experience than you! . . . I've always had a notion that I ought to bring my children up as 'tough guys,' so that life can't hurt them too much. D'you agree with that?"

Sharlie shook her head. "Life will toughen them quite soon enough. They don't need toughening from a mother. They need an anchorage. If ever I have children—" (But I shan't, she thought: the only man whom I could want as father of my children would be Richard. *Richard!*—) Steadying her voice, she went on. "If ever I had children, I should try to think of them as empty vessels, to be filled with happy thoughts, and kindly feelings, and compassion for the unfortunate, and—and the love of birds and flowers and hills and rivers and the seasons, so that there was no room in them for ugliness. I'd give them animals to look after, so that they'd learn responsibility. And above all, I'd let them know that I believed in them."

Averil was silent for a long while. "You've made me feel quite different about it all!" she said at last. "I feel as though you'd broken a malignant spell." She paused.

"Sharlie—I *hate* myself for hating Randolph!"

Sharlie thought of Nicola, and nodded thoughtfully. "Yes—I know how you must feel! Hate is a boomerang. But I believe I've found a cure for it. One must imagine all that has led up to making the hated person hateful. The frustrations that have warped him, disappointments that have been embittering, humiliations that have stung until he strikes out at the nearest person in retaliation. Hate soon turns to pity if you think along those lines."

"If only I could practise what you preach!"

"You can," Sharlie assured her. "It'll come in time, if not at once—like touching one's toes. Minds can be exercised every bit as much as bodies.—Oh, dear—I *do* seem to be laying down the law!"

"You're doing me a power of good, bless you. I feel quite sane and sensible again." Averil gave a long sigh, as though a load were lifted from her shoulders. A little longer she sat crouched beside the fire, staring in the flames. Then she stretched and rose in one lithe movement.

"I'm going to write a line to David. Then to bed." Taking a pad and pencil, she switched on a reading lamp and began to scribble on her knee.

Sharlie slid from her chair on to a footstool, clasped her hands about her knees, and for the hundredth time tried to decide how she should steer her future course. Once Mrs. Ramswell was established here with everything running smoothly, she would have no real need of Sharlie. They had discussed the matter, and the older woman had protested that she wanted Sharlie to stay on as long as she was happy here. Although her need of secretarial help would be far less in future, she could be useful in a variety of ways. But Sharlie felt the time had come for her to leave. The gardener could act as chauffeur when he was needed, and with May to help in this compact house, and the gardener's wife to lend a hand in any crisis, the Ramswells would be very comfortable; Sharlie would be no more than a spare wheel, making too little use of her capabilities, while the results of all her training rusted from disuse. Besides, apart from such considerations, it would be best for her to make a fresh start in a new life where she might more easily forget the unhappiness of the past months. Yes—she would stay here for a few weeks longer, then look for other work: work that would keep her fully occupied.

The telephone rang shrilly in the hall. Averil sprang up. "I'll go—it must be Mother or David, no one else knows this number yet. Oh, I do hope the children are all right—"

She ran out. Presently she came back. "It's for you. Long-distance call. A man. I thought it must be a wrong number, but he spelt out your name when I expressed a doubt. Hurry, or his three pips will be piling up!"

"I can't think who it can be. I don't even know the number myself!" She ran out, closing the door behind her to keep the room warm.

The telephone was in the hall. A man, Averil had said. The only man in Sharlie's world was Richard, but it was absurd to think of him, absurd to hope . . . It must be some official of the charity for which Mrs. Ramswell had done so much work, who had got her number from her employer and was ringing up to ask for information of some sort. Possibly she had omitted some vital detail from a letter, made some mistake . . .

"Sharlie Raven speaking."

"This is Richard Heronshaw."

"Oh, yes? How are you?" (*Keep calm, you idiot! He's only telephoned to ask for Nicola's address . . .*)

"Very fit, thanks.—Sharlie, I've only just heard about the tragedy at Swanswick. I've been abroad for a few weeks, and then when I got back the whole thing had blown over, so I never saw it in the papers. Then someone mentioned it this evening in the mess—I'm back at Rockdown. I'm terribly sorry. You must have thought me so—unfriendly—not to write to you."

She said politely, in a cool, impersonal voice, "Oh, not at all! Why should you?" (*Odd that he hadn't heard of it from Nicola. Surely she couldn't have been so furious when he didn't come that day to tennis that she would have no more to do with him? Even imperious Nicola couldn't be as unreasonable as all that! Or was she? Had she married her rich Portuguese in pique and anger? Or because having written to Richard in such a manner as to burn her boats so far as he was concerned, she had had to turn to the only port available when the storm broke? . . . Did Richard know that she was married? . . .*)

"Well—if I'd known, it would have been the least I could have done. Listen—I'm—" Three pips sounded. "Three minutes more, please.—I'm coming north the day after to-morrow on a new posting. How would it be if I drop in to see you, on my way?"

She'd see him, hear his voice, touch his hand, even if he only came for news of Nicola—!

"That would be very nice." (*Nice! Of all the utterly inadequate words!*)

"Right. I'll look in some time, probably latish, on Friday afternoon."

Sharlie made some pleasant rejoinder, then asked how he had discovered where she was.

"I rang up Swanswick, Jackson answered. Gave me your address and telephone number. Very simple, really!"

Three more pips. "Till Friday, then. Good night," said Richard.

"Good night . . ."

She stood for several minutes in the chilly hall among wooden cases, some with straw and other packing scattered from them, half-unpacked, and furniture dumped down in inappropriate places, staring at the black, impersonal instrument whose shrill summons had given life a different colour. She was thinking that if she had had any pride she would have told Richard she was too busy moving in to see a visitor, would have shown him that

178

since on his side the friendship that had grown between them had abruptly lessened, she had no mind that it should be renewed . . . But where love was, there could be no room for pride.

Averil looked at her over the flap of the envelope she was licking.

"You're looking very pink, my dear!" she said. For the first time since she had known Sharlie she detached her mind from her own problems to wonder about the other girl's life. Did she have a love affair? And if so was she happy in it?

Sharlie asked casually, "Am I? It's rather cold, out there.—It was Major Heronshaw, ringing up from Rockdown. He used to come to Swanswick sometimes. He had heard from Jackson that your parents had moved here, and asked if he might look in on his way north to a new appointment, some time on Friday afternoon, as he'll be passing quite near here. I thought you wouldn't mind—?"

"Of course not!" Averil was intrigued, and Sharlie knew it. To put an end to any romantic notions that might be growing in the other girl's mind, she added, "He has just come back from being in America with a military mission. Probably he wants news of Nicola—he used to see a lot of her, last summer. I wonder if he knows she's married."

Averil was disappointed. All the same, when Friday came she announced that she was going to tea with Mrs. Bland, the doctor's wife. There might be nothing between Sharlie and this man from Rockdown, but if there were, it would be just as well to leave the coast clear so that she might have him to herself.

Soon after lunch Sharlie changed into her favourite suit, a new one, of tweed checked in two shades of blue, and a blue knitted pullover that matched the lighter check. She looked at her reflection critically, wondering whether Richard would notice that she had grown thinner, wondering what had changed about her face in the last months, trying to analyse that difference, yet not realising that it lay in an awareness in her eyes that they had lacked when first she came to Swanswick, an added firmness, given by endurance to her lips. Now, if he should come early, she was ready.

She spent the afternoon with Averil, sorting linen, putting it in neat piles in the airing cupboard. sticking labels on the edges of the shelves, trying to absorb herself in what she did and yet aware in every fibre of her being of all that happened in the house: hoping when the second post came that it was Richard who had rung the bell, hoping the same thing when a new errand boy came with groceries to the wrong door, and again when someone came collecting for the Cottage Hospital. Still there was no sign of his arrival, and the time came for Averil to go out to tea. Presently Mary came, looking sympathetic, saying that she supposed she'd better put tea by the fire at once, instead of waiting any longer for the visitor? And Sharlie, trying to sound as though she had forgotten the existence of a possible visitor, had answered that there was no point in waiting, as quite possibly Major Heronshaw wouldn't come at all. (Yet surely he'd have telephoned if he had changed his plans? Could there have been an accident?)

Outwardly unperturbed, inwardly in a fever of apprehension, she went down to the table Mary had drawn up for her beside the fire, with buttered toast, and honey in the comb, and shortbread from the village baker, and a fruit cake May had found time to make.

"I've put two cups. It's not so late, the Major may still— Listen! Was that the bell?" said Mary, and was gone to answer it.

Sharlie, listening tensely, heard her cross the hall and open the door, her welcoming voice, answered by the deeper murmur of a man's. Then Richard was beside her, bringing in an atmosphere of frosty air and Harris tweeds and Turkish cigarettes—Richard, looking even taller than she had remembered him, perhaps because he looked a good deal thinner than before, smiling at her, taking her hand in his strong clasp, utterly unaware that by his presence everything was transfigured—that the fire blazed more brightly, and the tea looked more inviting, and the colours of the chairs and curtains gained in depth, while the chrysanthemums and dahlias swayed and nodded in a delirious dance of bliss that he was there.

Now they sat together by the fire. Sharlie's appetite, that had deserted her since she knew that he was coming, failed her completely, but Richard had lunched early and fared badly, so was able to do justice to the meal, and ate enough to gratify Mary's hospitable instincts when she came to clear away.

When she had gone they drew their chairs nearer the fire. The resin in the fir logs hissed and crackled, giving out delicious aromatic odours. Between the undrawn curtains the sky was pale and frosty. They talked of anything and everything but Randolph's tragic end and the unhappy circumstances connected with it: of Farrabeck and its neighbourhood, of George and Gay, of books and films, of Richard's experiences in America. On the surface they were friendly and at ease, but Sharlie, conscious of constraint, was well aware that Richard felt it, too. No link seemed left between them. Their words had failed to bridge the gulf that had so steadily widened between them since that disastrous evening at the Regency Hotel.

Time was slipping by. Any moment now, if silence fell, Richard would say that it was time for him to take the road again. Feverishly Sharlie talked on, saying anything that crossed her mind, no matter how trivial—anything to keep him here a little longer.

Suddenly she became aware that Richard was paying no attention to what she was saying, and broke off, feeling foolish, in the middle of a sentence.

Richard said, "I'm sorry. I've not been listening to a word you've said for the last five minutes. Mannerless of me. But we've talked so much, and said so little, haven't we?"

She nodded silently, wondering if he, too, were remembering that summer evening in the garden of the Plover's Rest, when they had seemed so perfectly attuned, and he had said, "You make it quite impossible to go on resisting you—" and of how successfully, ever since, he *had* resisted her. . . .

Richard leaned forward. "Sharlie—I've been wondering—"

The front door slammed. With all her being Sharlie willed that Averil should go upstairs instead of coming in here, but an instant later, animated and vivacious, glowing from the frosty air, she joined them, greeting Richard charmingly, ringing the bell for Mary to bring drinks.

Despairingly Sharlie knew that now he'd never tell her what it was he had been wondering. When he had drunk a glass of sherry he would go, and that would be the end. And anyhow, he might have wondered only if she had any word of Nicola.

Averil, in radiant spirits because this evening David would be coming, laughed and chattered, held the floor while Sharlie sipped her sherry silently. As Richard emptied his glass she took up the decanter, held it towards him. "Have some more?"

"No, thanks. I must be going." He smiled at her, held out his hand. "Good-bye!" he said, making it clear politely, that he had no wish for her to accompany him to the door. He turned to Sharlie. "Coming to speed the parting guest?"

At least it was a crumb of comfort that he wanted to say good-bye to her alone. She rose, smiling. "Indeed I am. We've got to keep an eye on the umbrellas in the hall!"

Richard followed her out. He said, as soon as they were alone, "There's something I came here to say to you. I was a fool to leave it so late, but somehow we made such a fog of talk between us—"

Sharlie said, "Come in here," and led the way into a little room by the front door. It was going to be arranged as Mr. Ramswell's special sanctum; his desk was there, and chairs, and bookcases, dark shapes looming in the twilight. The light switch clicked beneath her hand without result. "Oh—we haven't put a bulb in here yet—"

Richard said, "It doesn't matter," and closed the door behind him, shutting them in together. The curtains were undrawn, and from across the cobbled market-place lights shone in the windows of the inn, tinting the blue twilight with a rosy bloom. Sharlie leaned against the desk and waited, looking up at him.

Richard said, "Sharlie—I know it isn't any use pretending it would be—what once I hoped for. But if you'll take a chance and marry me, I promise that I'll always do my best to make you happy. Will you try with me to make the best of second-best, instead of dwelling hopelessly on what might have been?"

So he did know that Nicola was married . . .

For Sharlie it made bitter hearing to be told that she must always rank with him as second best: yet it was better that there should be no pretence between them, and infinitely better than anything she had dared to hope for.

"I'd like to, Richard——" Then to her shame and horror she felt her lips begin to quiver, and her eyes were pricked by tears.

"Poor little Sharlie——" Richard slid his arm about her shoulders, pulling her towards him, murmuring comfort. She leaned her cheek against the rough tweed of his shoulder, weeping for the moment she had longed for, that had lost its glory when at last, all unexpectedly, it came.

CHAPTER TWELVE

SHARLIE called again, "Good-bye!"—then turned to look her last through the back window of the car at Farrabeck and the friendly faces grouped about its door: at Eleanor, looking happier than Sharlie could remember seeing her since she had first known her, and her husband, who was a changed man these days, having lost his old aggressiveness and opinionated manner; at Averil, who was going to marry David in the New Year, George and Gay and Nannie, Mary and May, all waving vigorously.

Richard nosed the car through the little crowd collected in the market-place to see the bride and groom departing on their honeymoon then headed for the great north road and Scotland.

Sharlie sighed. Richard glanced at her sidelong.

"Tired?"

"No. Just feeling a trifle emotional. It always makes my eyes smart when people are particularly kind—and they did give us such a nice send-off and such a lovely wedding breakfast!"

"They did indeed. I only wish you'd done more justice to it. But I've ordered a late lunch at Barrby Moor to keep you going till we get to Gardie."

"Such a friendly little name!"

"Think so? It suits it, then. I hope you're going to like it. Anyhow you'll be able to have a real rest there, for there's nothing to do but fish, and fishing's over for the season."

"It *has* been a bit strenuous, this last month," she admitted, thinking of all the work entailed by moving in to Farrabeck, combined with making preparations for her wedding.

"The last month? Yes. And for quite a while before that, too," said Richard, then wished that he had not reminded her of those last nightmare weeks at Swanswick . . . wished still more that he had been in England then, to help her through them. Not that anyone could have helped much, he reflected . . .

Less than two hours later, having lunched on roast pheasant, apple tart, and excellent coffee at the comfortable inn of Barrby Moor, they set out on the last lap of their journey through the blue and gold October afternoon. The Border hills were clear, and blue as grapes against the frosty sky; the trees were gold and rust and amber; birds were busy in the hedges where the haws hung thick in crimson clusters and the hips shone, plumpy scarlet.

They left the main road near the Border, turning westward along quiet side roads, climbing steadily between low rough walls, past lonely farms and scattered woods of larch and pine, then across open moorland where Richard must drive cautiously to avoid the black-faced sheep that wandered on the road.

At last he told her, "Shut your eyes!" and presently, "Now you may open them."

The road ran down into a narrow valley, enclosed on either side by hills of grass and heather, stained by rusty bracken, changeful in colouring as opals by reason of the shadows of clouds that moved across them ceaselessly. Lower still were cattle grazing in small rush-grown fields, bordering the twisted silver ribbon of a river that looped the ruins of a ruined peel tower, standing on rising ground. Close to an old stone hump-backed bridge, separated from the river by grass and a flower border glowing with late chrysanthemums, lay a long low house with plumes of blue smoke spiring gently from its chimneys.

"Scotland!" Richard told her. "Gardie Valley. The river is the Gardie Water, and that grey house by the bridge is where we're bound. The Gardie Inn. D'you like the look of it?"

"Love it!" She smiled at him. "I don't know anything more peaceful than to sleep within the sound of running water."

Ten minutes later they drew up outside the inn. A rosy maid came hurrying to take their luggage and the landlady came out to welcome them. "So here you are! It's fine to see you back again!" she greeted Richard in her soft, lilting Border tongue.

"It's fine to be back," he assured her, shaking hands. "This is my wife.—Sharlie, this is Mrs. MacQueen."

Sharlie smiled into shrewd blue eyes that appraised her kindly and apparently approved of what they saw. "I've heard so much of you, and of the Gardie Inn!" she said.

"You'll have it to yourselves until the week-end, for we're very quiet, this time of the year. Not that we're ever what you might call crowded, having but the seven bedrooms. I'll just show you upstairs, then Bessie'll bring your tea to you beside the fire."

She led the way along a narrow hall whose walls were hung with monstrous stuffed trout in glass cases, up a curving stair with iron banisters, to an airy room whose windows looked out on the river. "And seeing that we've plenty room just now I've given you the next-door bedroom for your dressing-room," she said to Richard, "and the bathroom's opposite, and we have plenty coke so you'll get fine hot water. You would better take your tea before you get unpacked, you must be badly needing it."

When they had eaten hot scones and strawberry jam and queen cakes by a blazing fire of peat and logs they strolled outside. The silver of the rising moon was mingled with the fading gold of sunset, giving enough light for them to see their way. They leaned on the wide parapet of the bridge, looking down into the dark water.

"I never can resist the lure of running water!" Richard said.

"Can anyone? . . . I wonder how many people have stood here, looking for fish!"

"Seeing 'em too. This is a pool where big fish often lie on the way upstream. We'll come and have a look tomorrow, when it's light.—You're cold. How about a hot bath before dinner?"

Sharlie agreed that it would be a good idea. They went indoors, and Sharlie went upstairs, while Richard, hearing familiar voices, went off to have a word with Sandy Hogg, the keeper, and Geordie Reid, another old acquaintance.

A fire was burning merrily in the bedroom. Sharlie unpacked, and hung away the suit of cornflower blue she had worn that morning for her wedding. After her bath she hesitated, wondering what to wear for dinner, then decided on a dress of palest yellow chiffon velvet, that had been one of Mrs. Ramswell's presents. For Gardie it might be overdressing—but there was no one here to criticise, and after all, it *was* her wedding night . . .

She lingered by the fire when she was ready, trying to realise that she was Richard's wife, that she would share his future and his home, perhaps his children, wondering why her heart seemed numb and frozen and incapable of feeling. Was it because she was so haunted by the thought of Nicola?

She and Richard had seen scarcely anything of one another since that evening nearly five weeks ago when they had agreed to make the best of second-best together. He had spent that night with David Sherren at the local inn, the White Hart, where she and Averil had had dinner with them. They had agreed that there was nothing to wait for, and that they would be married on his next leave. Early next morning he had left to take up his new appointment in the south of Scotland, and they had arranged the details of their plans chiefly by telephone and letter, although twice he had managed to come to Farrabeck for a night. His leave had started yesterday. He had stayed again last night at the White Hart . . . And here they were, at the beginning of their honeymoon . . .

If only it were going to be a honeymoon in all the senses of that magic word! If only—oh, if only she had been the bride that all girls dreamed of being, beloved as well as loving . . .

Footsteps outside, a light knock on the door.

"Come in!" she called.

"Hullo! You're ready. What a lovely frock. It suits you," Richard said. He came towards her, near enough to feel the material of her sleeve: so near that Sharlie wondered if he could hear the wild beating of her heart.

"As soft and warm and yellow as the plumage of a yellow wagtail," he said, smiling down at her.

She forced herself to smile back. She was thinking that since that evening when she had wept against his shoulder for the love that he had given elsewhere, he had never touched her. Was he going now to take her in his arms?

Richard's expression changed. "Sharlie—I can't bear it when you look like that—"

"Like what?" she asked him, startled.

"I don't quite know. Strained. Frightened. Surely you're not afraid of me?"

She told him, "Not of you. Only, sometimes, of life."

"Don't be. Things that seem frightening in anticipation don't turn out so badly, as a rule, when you're face to face with them.—Mrs. MacQueen sent me to tell you dinner's ready when we are."

"We're ready now—If you are!"

They had the dining-room all to themselves. Bessie brought them game soup, followed by roast chicken and fruit salad. Mrs. MacQueen herself brought in the mushroom savoury. "There's a good fire waiting for you in the smoking-room, and logs and peat beside it, for I don't doubt you would rather keep it up yourself than have me popping in and out!" she said to Richard.

They thanked her, told her they had enjoyed her dinner, bade her good night.

Bessie brought their coffee to the smoking-room and asked if that was all they would be wanting, "for if you'll be needing anything else I'll need to bring it now. I go to sleep at home when washing up is done."

They told her they had all they wanted. "The mistress bade me ask if you would put the lights out, sir, when you go up. Good night to you! Good night, m'm!"

When she had gone, Sharlie settled at one end of the sofa that was drawn up near the fire. Richard suggested sitting in the firelight, turned off the lights, then sat beside her.

We're so near, thought Sharlie, yet such miles apart! If only I didn't know he must be wishing I were Nicola . . .

Behind the sofa shadows leaped and flickered up and down the walls. The firelight stained their hands and faces with its rosy glow, found out the gold lights in the shining bell of Sharlie's hair, deepened the colour of her yellow dress. There was no sound about them but the whisper of the flames, the little creaks and murmurings of the old house settling for the night, the quiet singing of the river.

Richard slid an arm behind her shoulders, bent his dark head. Sharlie sat tense and rigid, unresponsive to his kiss, wondering if in his thought he had transformed her into Nicola, or tried to. Poor Richard . . . She told herself she had been selfish, forgetting he must be unhappy, too.

188

He drew away from her. "Sharlie—if you feel like that, why did you marry me?" he asked quietly.

She couldn't tell him that she didn't feel like that at all, that she was only fearful of betraying all she did feel. He knew—he must know that she loved him. Why else should she have married him? But it would humiliate her too much to let him know how deep and passionate that love was, when it was all on her side, matched only by his liking.

"I'm—sorry," she said.

Richard said savagely, "For God's sake don't be sorry! —*Sorry!*" He got up and lit a cigarette, then stood on one side of the hearth, leaning his elbow on the mantelpiece, looking down at her. "I thought—I hoped that we could turn our backs upon the past and never speak of it. But silence can be dangerous. It can ultimately fill the atmosphere between two people with the most monstrous shapes. Suspicions. Jealousies. I wonder—don't you think it would be better to begin by talking over things just once? Clearing the air? Getting things straightened out between us? Even if it does hurt you at the time, it may be better for you in the end. Don't you agree?"

"I—don't know." For it was bad enough to know he was in love with Nicola, that she, his bride, must always know herself a substitute, a makeshift, without hearing it put into words.

Silence hung between them, broken when a log slipped in the fire. Richard pushed it with his foot, added another log and more peat. Then he came back to the sofa, leaning his arm along the back of it, turning towards her. "Sharlie —I hate to hurt you. Do believe me when I tell you that I only do it because I'm so afraid that if we don't talk things over now, we may be haunted always by the ghost of Randolph, coming between us and the chance we have of finding happiness together. If you could only bring yourself to tell me all about the whole affair from your own point of view, I'd know much better where I stand. What chance I have."

The ghost of *Randolph*! How extraordinary! She had thought it was of Nicola he had meant that they should speak, her jealousy of Nicola that he feared. She said, bewildered, "But I don't in the least mind talking about

189

Randolph! I thought you meant we ought to discuss your-self and—something different. I didn't realise you thought what happened at Swanswick was upsetting me still. It was a ghastly shock, of course, to find poor Randolph lying dead. A nightmare. Such a frightful nightmare that it holds the quality of a hideous dream more than of reality. I shall never forget it. But already it seems curiously un-real!"

Why did he look at her so strangely?

Sharlie said, "Is it so hard for you to understand? Does it seem so heartless? You see—how can I explain—it seems more like a film I've seen than something that has actually happened."

He looked away from her. "It is just a bit puzzling. The relationship between yourself and Randolph—does that seem unreal, too?"

" 'Relationship?' How do you mean?"

He raised his eyebrows. "Well—your feeling for one another."

Sharlie considered it. "Yes, I think it does . . . I'd better tell you something nobody else knows. Right at the end I found out that he was the burglar. I tried to stop him. *That* part of it seems quite unreal. Before then, although I never liked him, it was chiefly pity that I felt for him. He seemed so—so synthetic."

"You never *liked* him? But—you were going to marry him as soon as he was free!"

"Marry Randolph? *I*?" She stared at him, aghast. "Never! Not if he'd been the last man on earth! What in the world can have made you think so?"

"Nicola told me it was so that evening when they joined us at the Regency."

"What did she tell you?"

"Just that you and Randolph were in love with one an-other and were hoping to be married when his divorce was through."

"And you believed that?"

"Why should Nicola invent it? And you did seem rather —er—friendly with him, that evening?"

"Yes. I wanted Nicola to think I was enjoying myself so that she shouldn't know how much I minded that they'd joined us."

"So you did mind?"

Sharlie bent her head.

"If I had known! If I had only guessed . . . That evening very nearly broke my heart. But listen, Sharlie: if you weren't in love with Randolph, why did you cry, that evening when I asked you if you'd marry me, on the principle that half a loaf is better than no bread?"

She let her hair fall forward, shading her hot face from the fire. "It hurts to be only a half loaf: to know one never can be more than second-best. It hurts, to know you're wishing I were Nicola—"

"*Nicola?* What in the world has Nicola to do with you and me?"

"You said it wasn't any use pretending marrying me would be what you had hoped for. You asked if I would try with you to make the best of second-best. And it was obviously Nicola you had hoped for."

"*Nicola?*" he asked again, "but why do you say that?"

"Because when you gave up seeing me, you came so often to see Nicola, and took her out. She lied to you about me and Randolph, because she wanted you herself. And when Nicola sets her heart on anything, she has a way of persevering till she gets it. And she's so magnetic."

"I only 'gave up seeing you' because there was more pain than pleasure in being with you, after I believed you were in love with Randolph. But I was worried about you. I was pretty sure he was a nasty bit of work. So I hung around with Nicola, though I couldn't stand the sight of her, because it seemed the only way that I could keep in touch with you, in case you needed help. Then when the crash came, just when I might have been of use to you, I wasn't there.—Sharlie, did you honestly believe you were no more to me than second-best?"

"What else was I to think? You told me so yourself! You said that marrying me wasn't what you had hoped for—"

"What I had hoped for was that you would have married me for love, instead of taking me for second-best. That was the way of it."

"You were so different from before. Your letters have been the letters of a friend, not of the man who was going to marry me."

"I thought you would prefer it so, until you had got over Randolph's death."

"You never even touched me, never kissed me till this evening—"

"And when I did, you hated it."

"No."

"Then why did you give such an admirable imitation of a frozen poker?"

"Did I?"

"You know you did. So tell me why?"

She held her head on one side, turning her hand this way and that, watching the firelight playing on her wedding-ring. "I thought, in what I believed to be the circumstances, it would be better for you not to know—to know—"

"To know what?" he demanded.

"How much I was enjoying it!"

"*Sharlie—!*" He caught her in his arms, pulling her towards him. Sharlie braced her hands against his shoulders, holding him away from her. "Not yet. It's your turn now to tell me something. Richard—am I a half loaf or a whole one?"

"My sweetest love, you're all the loaves in every baker's shop in all the world. And well you know it!—Does that conclude the inquisition?"

Sharlie nodded.

"Then don't you think it's time you let me know how much you were enjoying it?"

"High time!" said Sharlie, lifting her face as Richard bent his head.

— THE END —